WATTERS · LEYH · PIETSCH · LAIHO

LUMBERJANES™

STONE COLD

BOOM! BOX™

BOOM! BOX™

LUMBERJANES Volume Eight, February 2018. Published by BOOM! Box, a division of Boom Entertainment, Inc. Lumberjanes is ™ & © 2018 Shannon Watters, Grace Ellis, Noelle Stevenson & Brooklyn Allen. Originally published in single magazine form as LUMBERJANES No. 29-32. ™ & © 2016 Shannon Watters, Grace Ellis, Noelle Stevenson & Brooklyn Allen. All rights reserved. BOOM! Box™ and the BOOM! Box logo are trademarks of Boom Entertainment, Inc., registered in various countries and categories. All characters, events, and institutions depicted herein are fictional. Any similarity between any of the names, characters, persons, events, and/or institutions in this publication to actual names, characters, and persons, whether living or dead, events, and/or institutions is unintended and purely coincidental. BOOM! Box does not read or accept unsolicited submissions of ideas, stories, or artwork. #RICH - 770710.

BOOM! Studios, 5670 Wilshire Boulevard, Suite 450, Los Angeles, CA 90036-5679. Printed in USA. First Printing.

ISBN-13: 978-1-68415-132-5 eISBN: 978-1-61398-871-8

THIS LUMBERJANES FIELD MANUAL BELONGS TO:

NAME:_____

TROOP:_____

DATE INVESTED:_____

FIELD MANUAL TABLE OF CONTENTS

LUMBERJANES FIELD MANUAL

For the Intermediate Program

Tenth Edition • August 1984

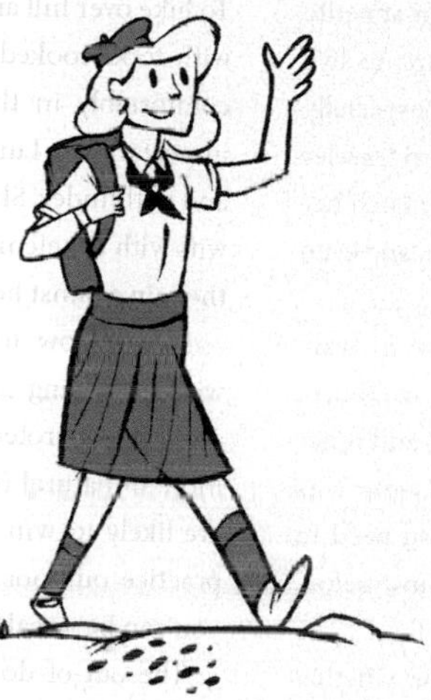

Prepared for the

Miss Qiunzella Thiskwin Penniquiqul Thistle Crumpet's

CAMP FOR [redacted] HARDCORE LADY-TYPES

"Friendship to the Max!"

A MESSAGE FROM THE LUMBERJANES HIGH COUNCIL

miss Qiunzella Thiskwin
Penniquiqul Thistle Crumpet's
Camp for
HARDCORE LADY TYPES
FRIENDSHIP to the MAX!

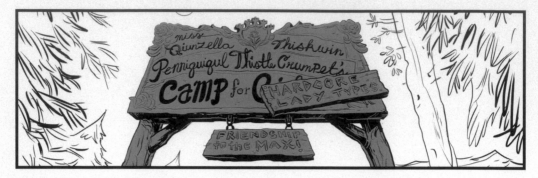

Many scouts, when they first arrive at camp, find themselves beset with homesickness. The safety and comfort of home may feel more than just miles away, and the absence of your parents may feel sharp and sudden. It is vital that you remember that your counselor is always there for you, but also that every girl who is away from home for the first time is going through this very same thing. Lean on one another in these times of uncertainty, and not only will you make it through these early pangs of loneliness, but you will discover your lifelong friends. And before you know it, your comfortable world will grow to accommodate your camp and cabin.

As you grow, your world naturally becomes larger: as a baby, you knew little beyond your parents and your nursery, but then you learned to walk and talk, and began to explore your home. Eventually, you became so skilled at walking and talking that you were sent to school, where you met children your own age, and learned and saw even more new, exciting things.

Here at camp on your own for the first time, you will meet girls who have grown up in different nurseries, homes, schools and towns… even from different countries, where they eat different foods, and speak different languages! These may not be friends who you will see everyday, but they are friends who you will always carry with you, wherever you go. And when you are home again, perhaps you will write one another long and loving letters, shipped across the continent and over the seas.

You may not realize it yet, but you have grown and changed from the homesick girls who first arrived at camp. You've survived sunburn and poison oak. You've hiked miles, and swum upstream. You've slept out under the stars, buffeted by the night-cool breeze and surrounded by people you never would have met at home. Listen to the crickets chirping, Scouts. You are here, and you are home, all at once.

THE LUMBERJANES PLEDGE

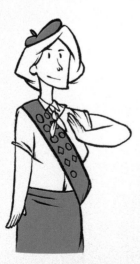

I solemnly swear to do my best
Every day, and in all that I do,
To be brave and strong,
To be truthful and compassionate,
To be interesting and interested,
To pay attention and question
The world around me,
To think of others first,
To always help and protect my friends,
[redacted]
And to make the world a better place
For Lumberjane scouts
And for everyone else.

THEN THERE'S A LINE ABOUT GOD, OR WHATEVER

STONE COLD

Written by
Shannon Watters
& Kat Leyh

Illustrated by
Carey Pietsch

Colors by
Maarta Laiho

Letters by
Aubrey Aiese

Cover by
Noelle Stevenson

Badge Design
Kelsey Dieterich

Designer
Kara Leopard

Assistant Editor
Sophie Philips-Roberts

Editors
Dafna Pleban & Whitney Leopard

Special thanks to **Kelsey Pate** *for giving the Lumberjanes their name.*

Created by **Shannon Watters, Grace Ellis, Noelle Stevenson & Brooklyn Allen**

LUMBERJANES FIELD MANUAL

CHAPTER TWENTY-NINE

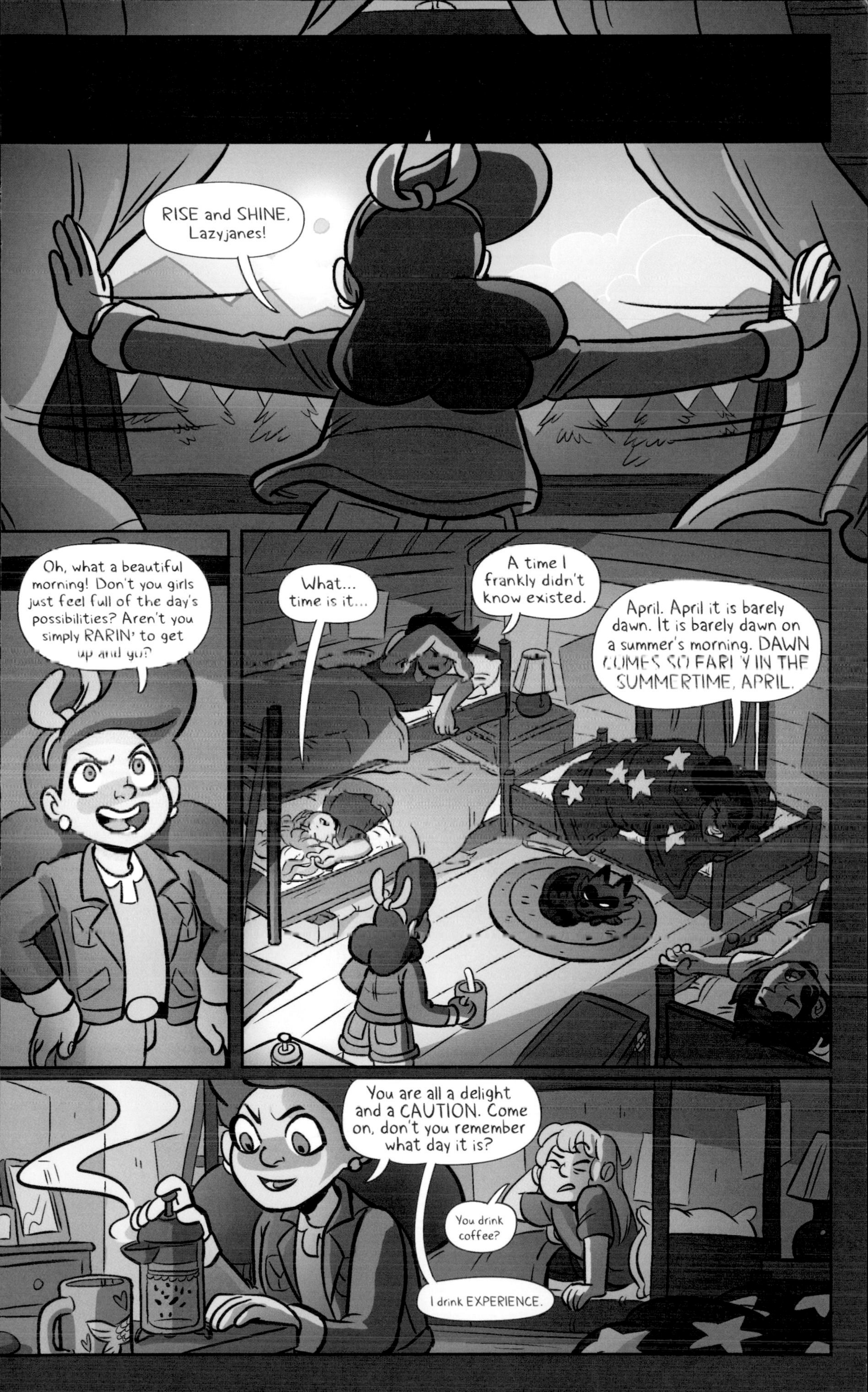
[redacted]
RISE and SHINE, Lazyjanes!
Oh, what a beautiful morning! Don't you girls just feel full of the day's possibilities? Aren't you simply RARIN' to get up and go?
What... time is it...
A time I frankly didn't know existed.
April. April it is barely dawn. It is barely dawn on a summer's morning. DAWN COMES SO EARLY IN THE SUMMERTIME, APRIL.
You are all a delight and a CAUTION. Come on, don't you remember what day it is?
You drink coffee?
I drink EXPERIENCE.

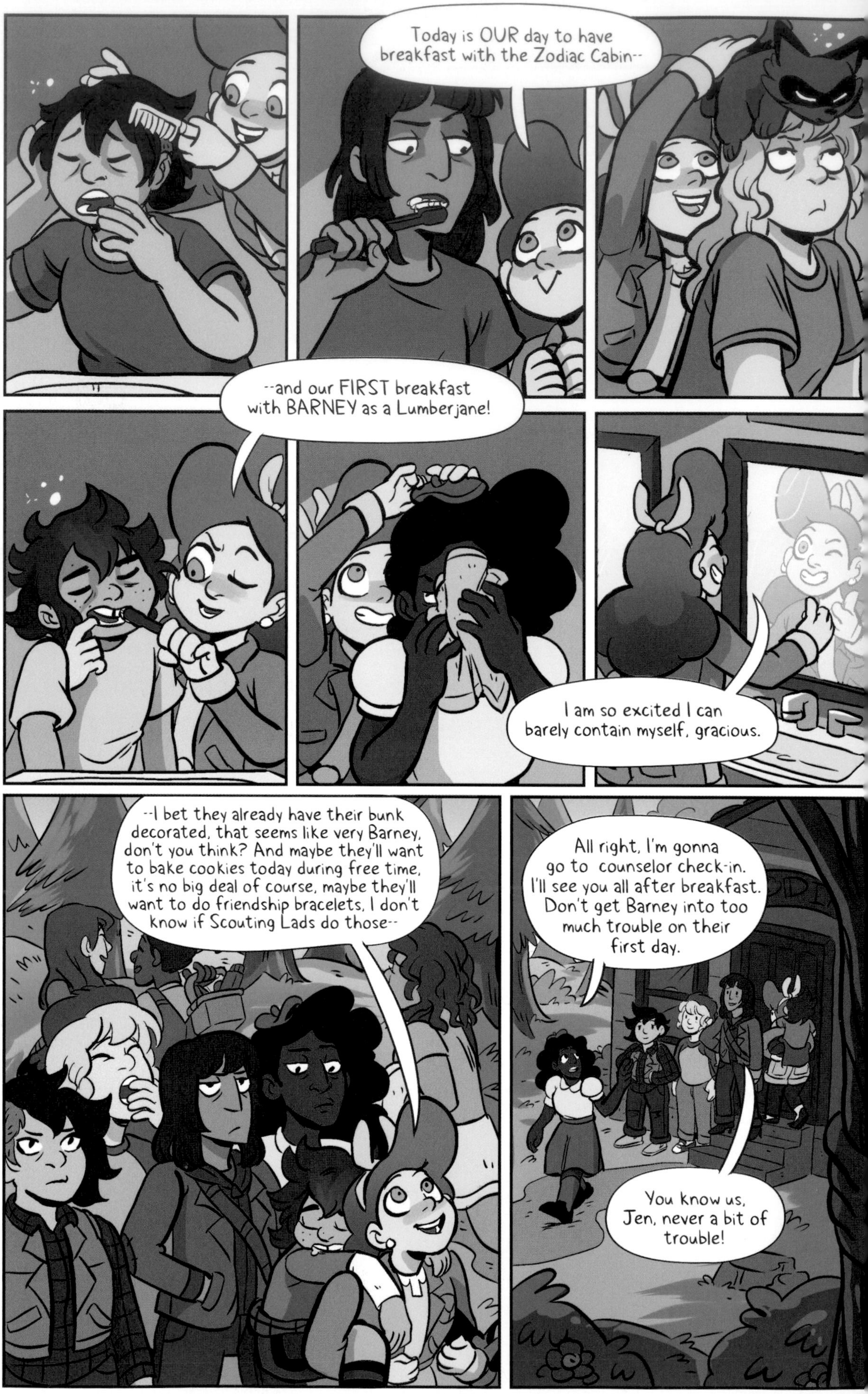
Today is OUR day to have breakfast with the Zodiac Cabin--
--and our FIRST breakfast with BARNEY as a Lumberjane!
I am so excited I can barely contain myself, gracious.
--I bet they already have their bunk decorated, that seems like very Barney, don't you think? And maybe they'll want to bake cookies today during free time, it's no big deal of course, maybe they'll want to do friendship bracelets, I don't know if Scouting Lads do those--
All right, I'm gonna go to counselor check-in. I'll see you all after breakfast. Don't get Barney into too much trouble on their first day.
You know us, Jen, never a bit of trouble!

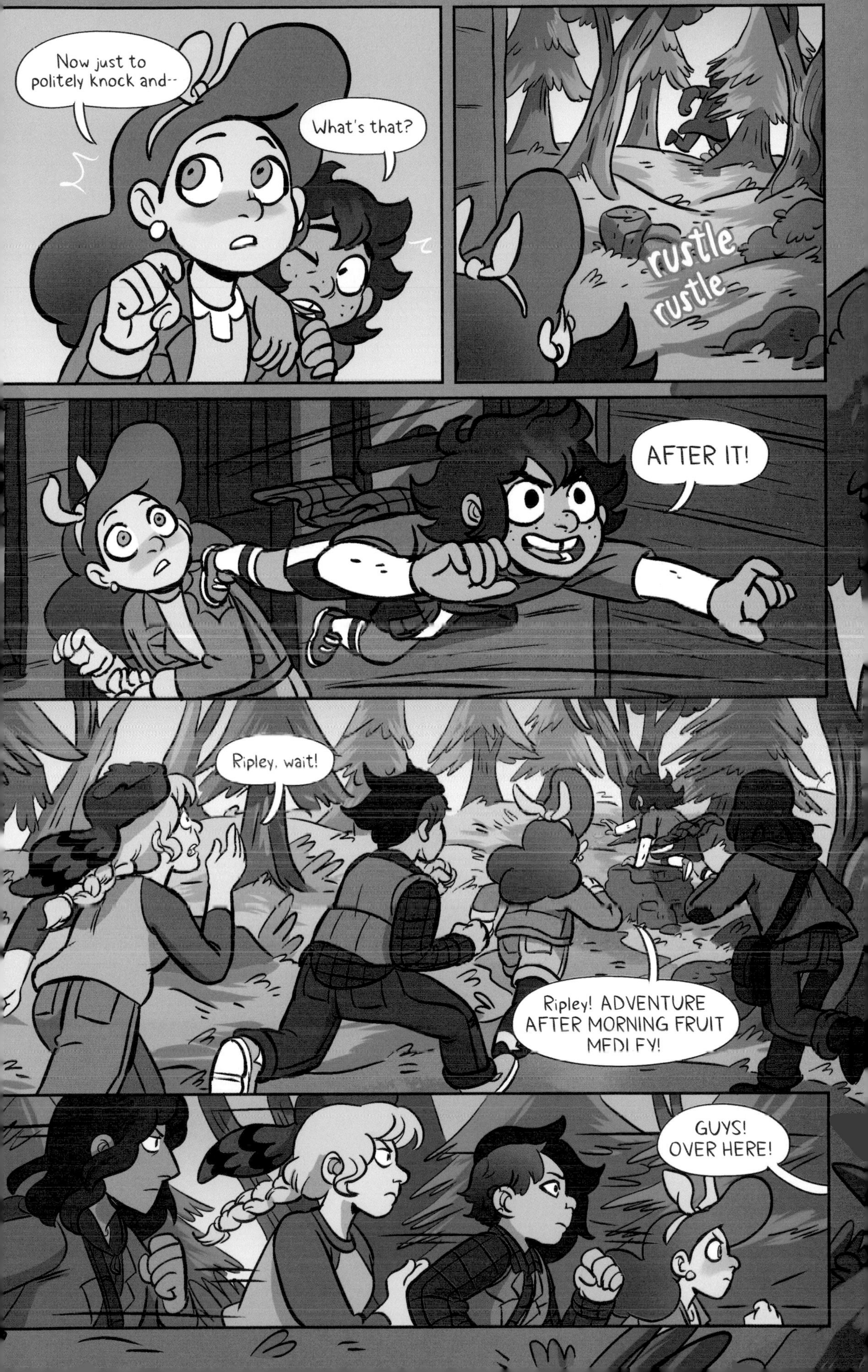
Now just to politely knock and--
What's that?
rustle rustle
AFTER IT!
Ripley, wait!
Ripley! ADVENTURE AFTER MORNING FRUIT MEDLEY!
GUYS! OVER HERE!

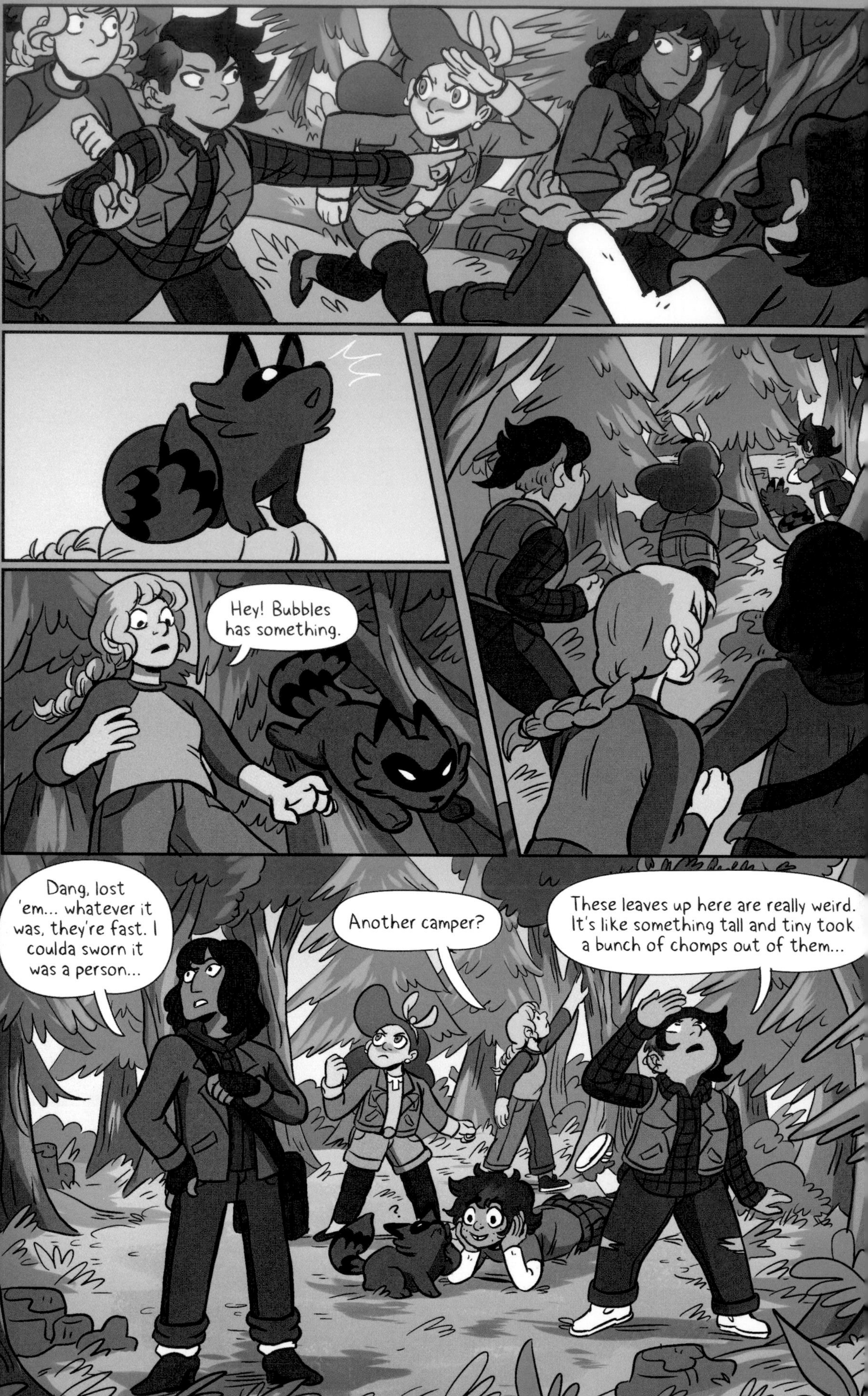
Hey! Bubbles has something.
Dang, lost 'em... whatever it was, they're fast. I coulda sworn it was a person...
Another camper?
These leaves up here are really weird. It's like something tall and tiny took a bunch of chomps out of them...

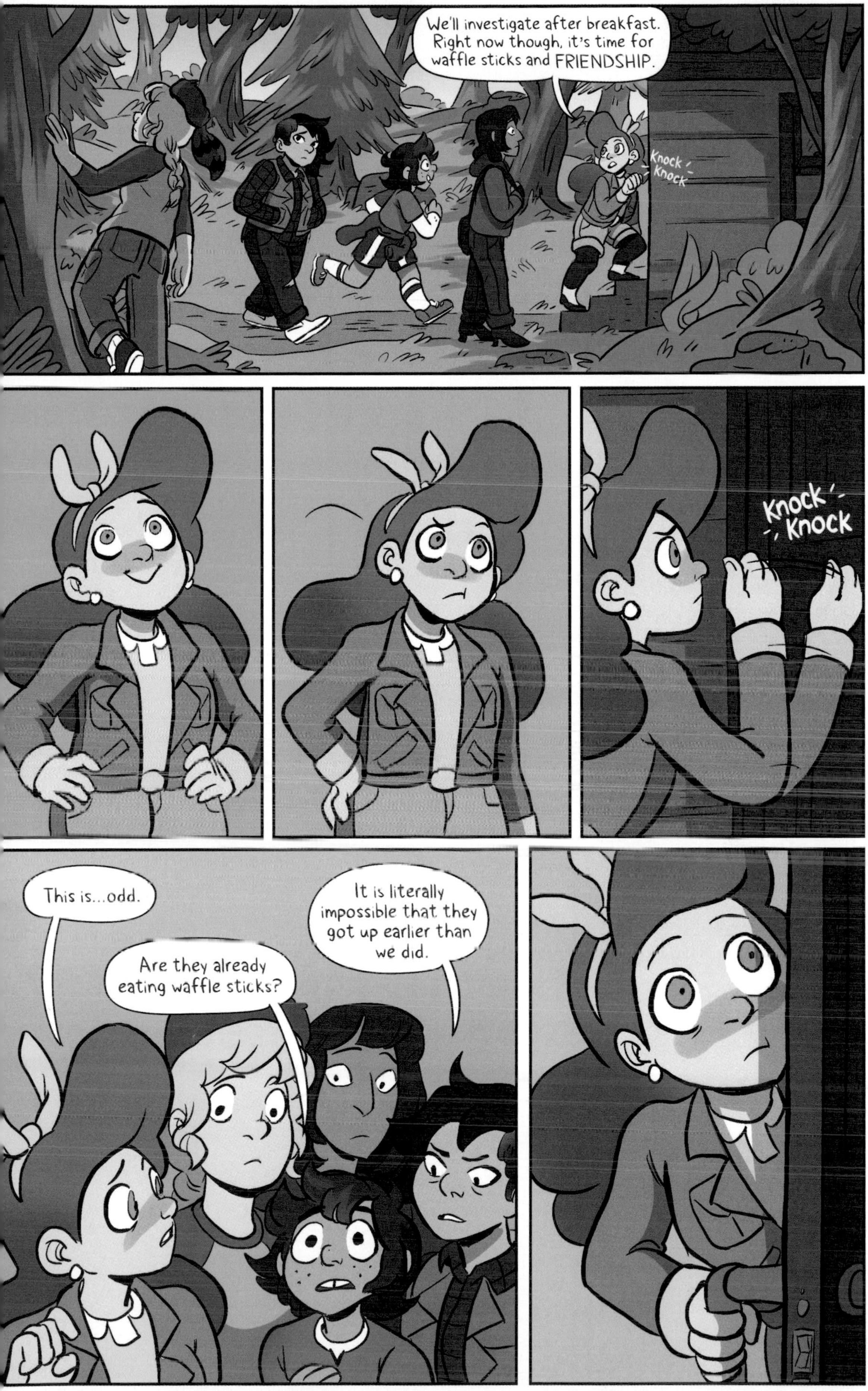
We'll investigate after breakfast. Right now though, it's time for waffle sticks and FRIENDSHIP.
Knock Knock
Knock Knock
This is...odd.
Are they already eating waffle sticks?
It is literally impossible that they got up earlier than we did.

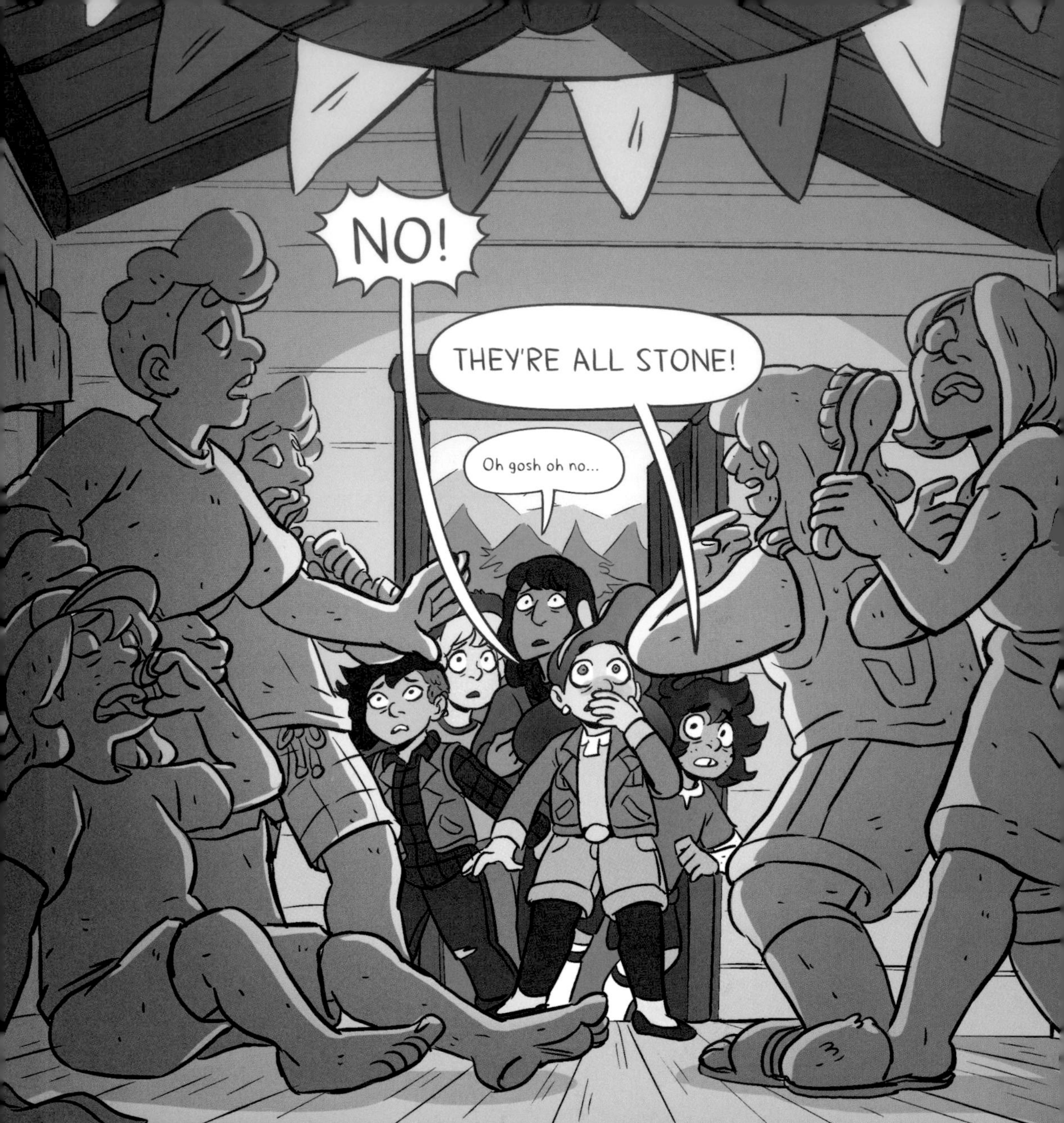
NO!
THEY'RE ALL STONE!
Oh gosh oh no...

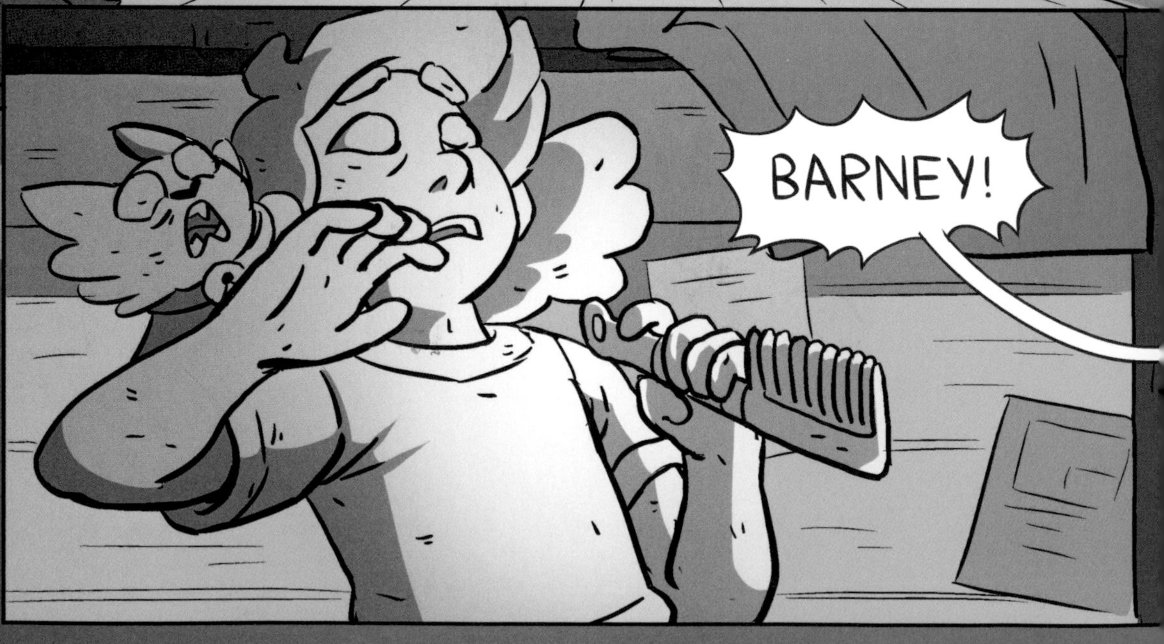
BARNEY!

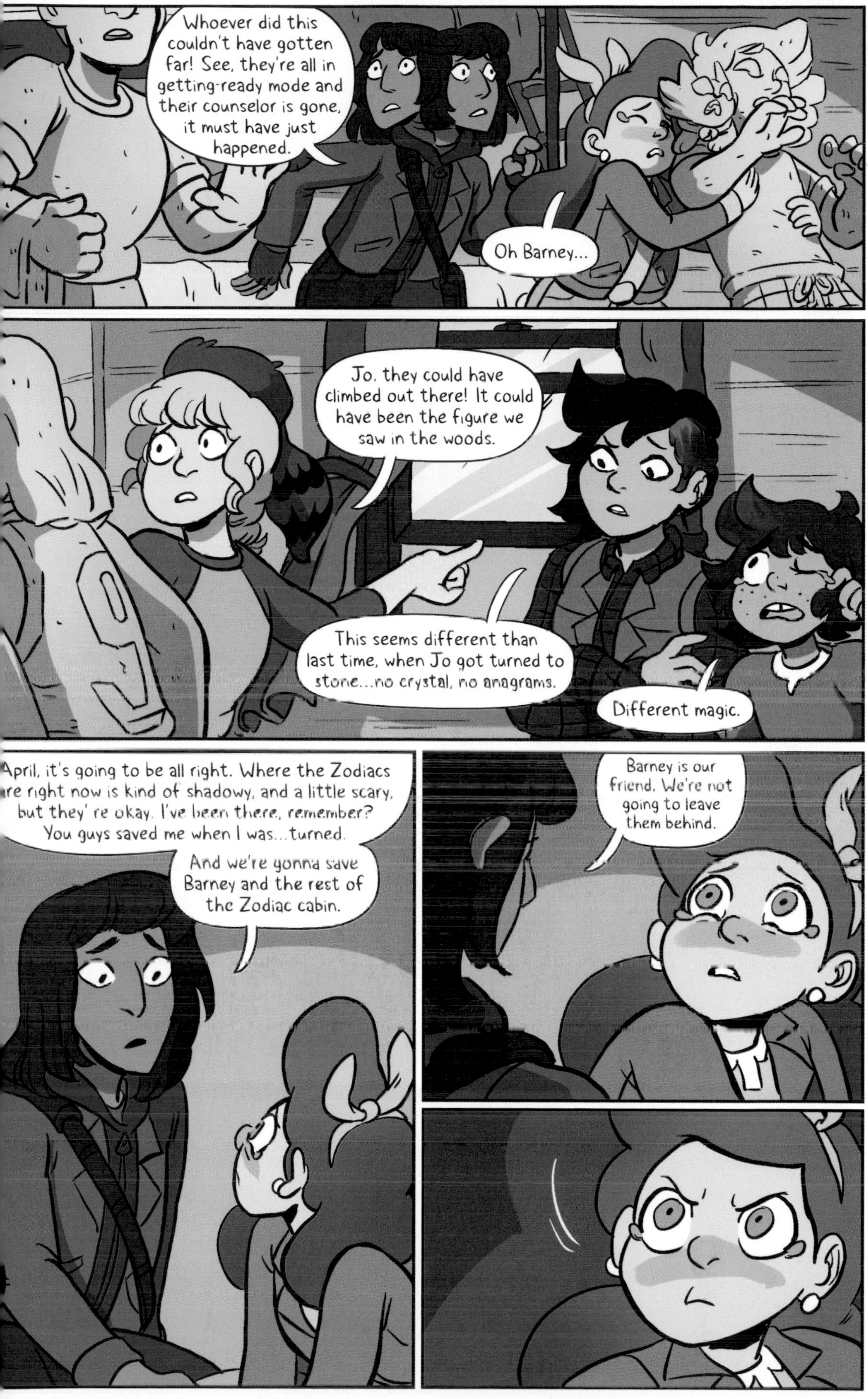
Whoever did this couldn't have gotten far! See, they're all in getting-ready mode and their counselor is gone, it must have just happened.
Oh Barney...
Jo, they could have climbed out there! It could have been the figure we saw in the woods.
This seems different than last time, when Jo got turned to stone...no crystal, no anagrams.
Different magic.
April, it's going to be all right. Where the Zodiacs are right now is kind of shadowy, and a little scary, but they're okay. I've been there, remember? You guys saved me when I was...turned.
And we're gonna save Barney and the rest of the Zodiac cabin.
Barney is our friend. We're not going to leave them behind.

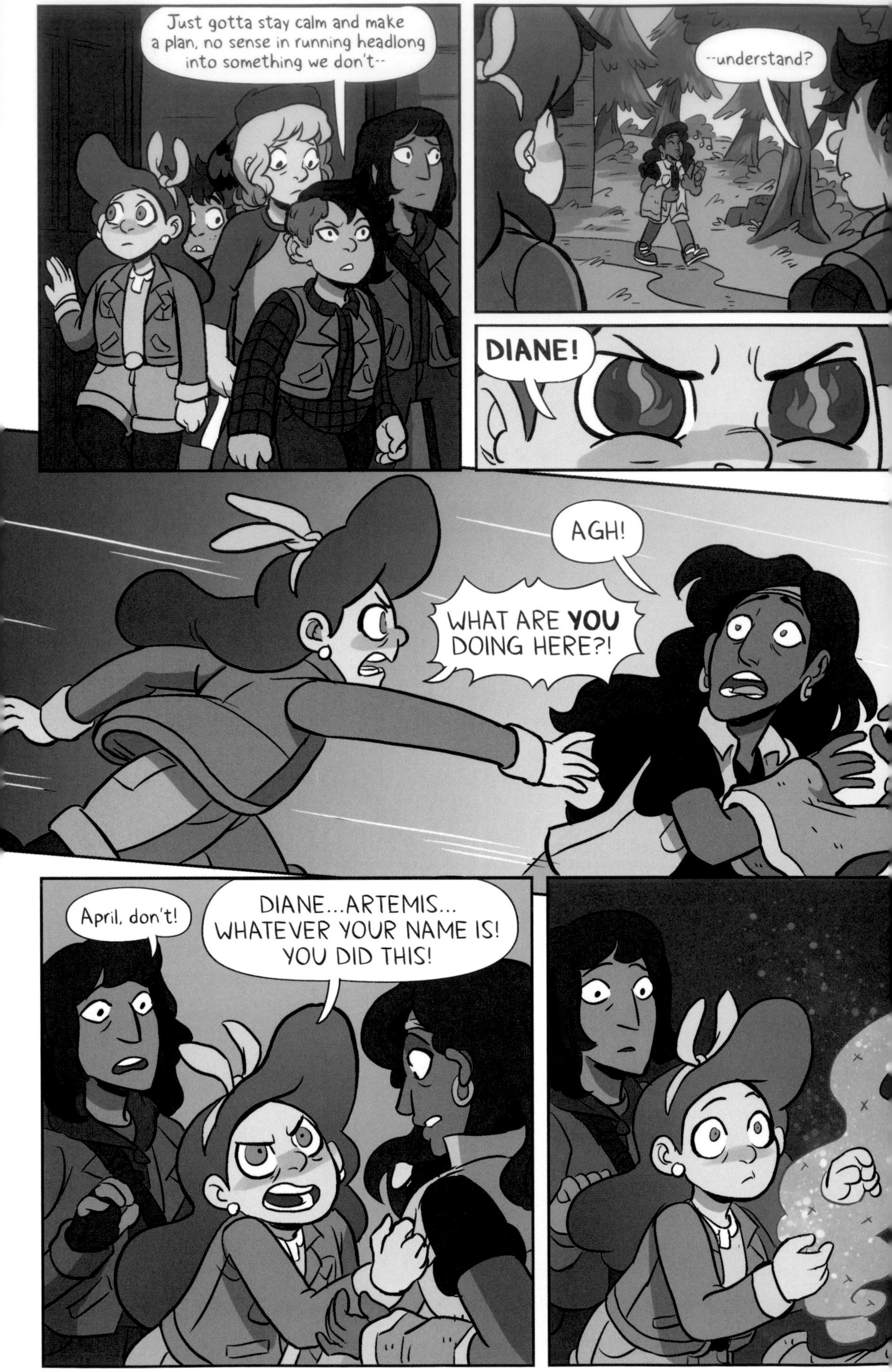
Just gotta stay calm and make a plan, no sense in running headlong into something we don't--
--understand?
DIANE!
AGH!
WHAT ARE YOU DOING HERE?!
April, don't!
DIANE...ARTEMIS... WHATEVER YOUR NAME IS! YOU DID THIS!

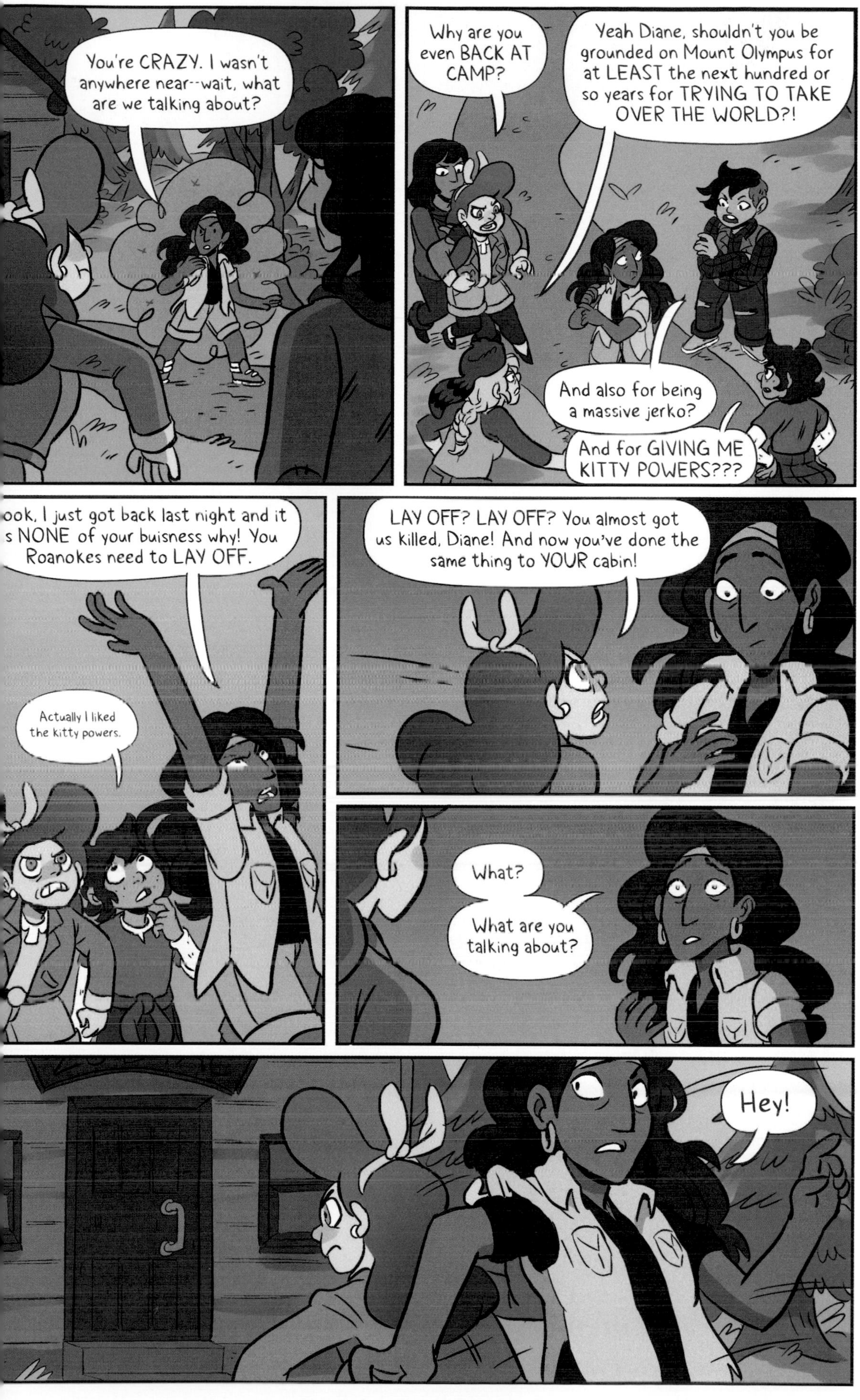
You're CRAZY. I wasn't anywhere near--wait, what are we talking about?
Why are you even BACK AT CAMP?
Yeah Diane, shouldn't you be grounded on Mount Olympus for at LEAST the next hundred or so years for TRYING TO TAKE OVER THE WORLD?!
And also for being a massive jerko?
And for GIVING ME KITTY POWERS???
ook, I just got back last night and it s NONE of your buisness why! You Roanokes need to LAY OFF.
Actually I liked the kitty powers.
LAY OFF? LAY OFF? You almost got us killed, Diane! And now you've done the same thing to YOUR cabin!
What?
What are you talking about?
Hey!

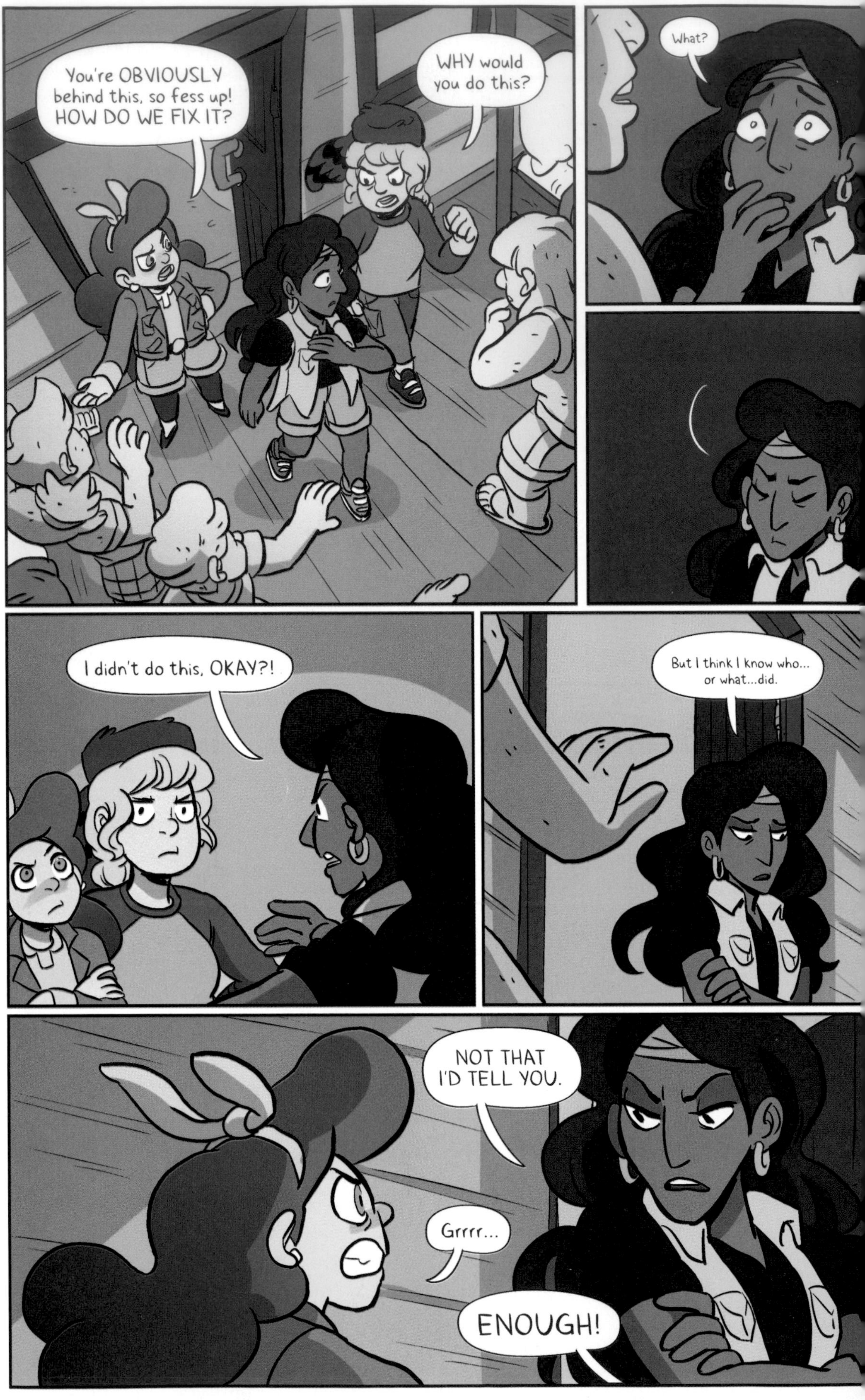
You're OBVIOUSLY behind this, so fess up! HOW DO WE FIX IT?
WHY would you do this?
What?
I didn't do this, OKAY?!
But I think I know who... or what...did.
NOT THAT I'D TELL YOU.
Grrrr...
ENOUGH!

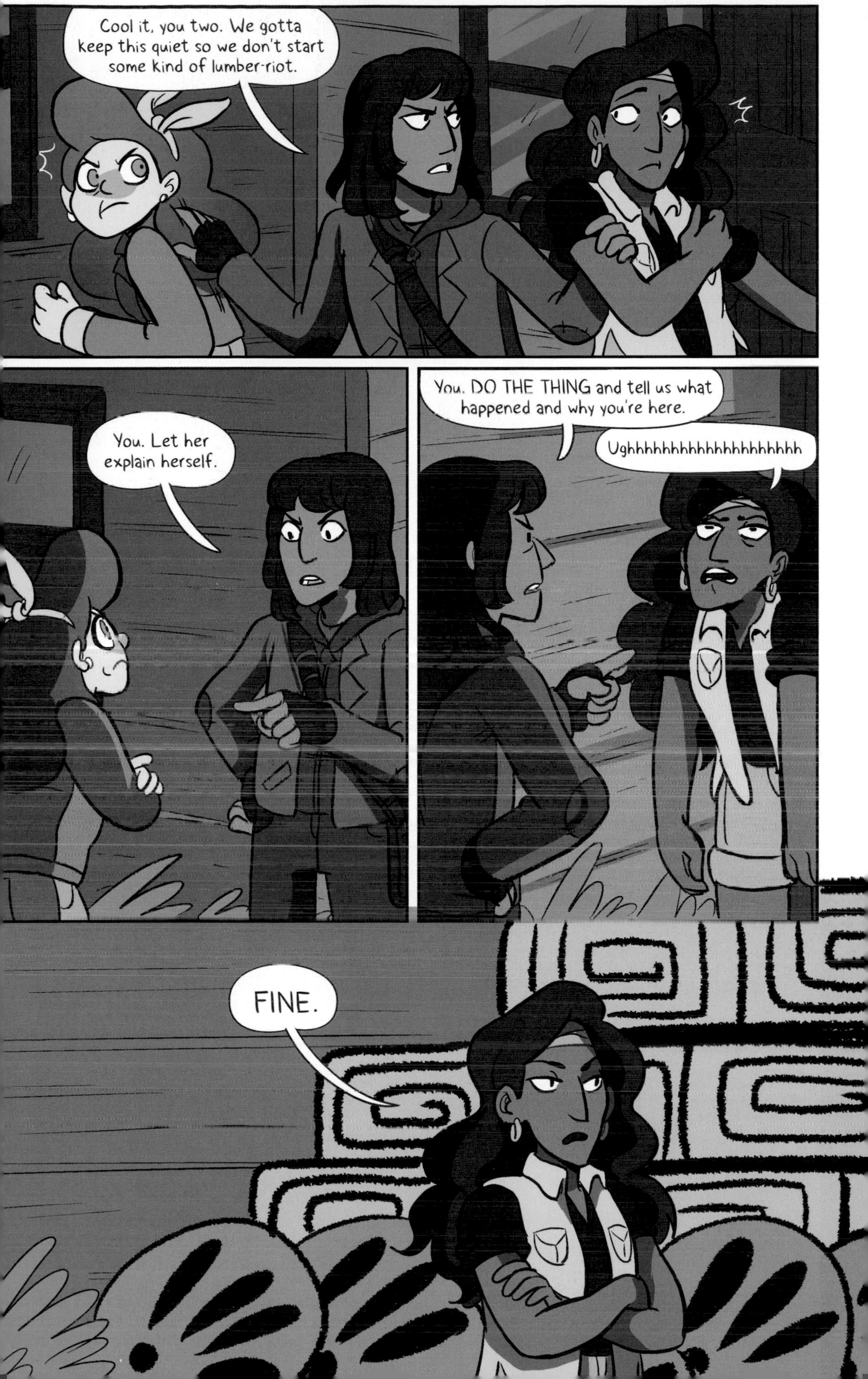

Cool it, you two. We gotta keep this quiet so we don't start some kind of lumber-riot.
You. Let her explain herself.
You. DO THE THING and tell us what happened and why you're here.
Ughhhhhhhhhhhhhhhhhhhhh
FINE.

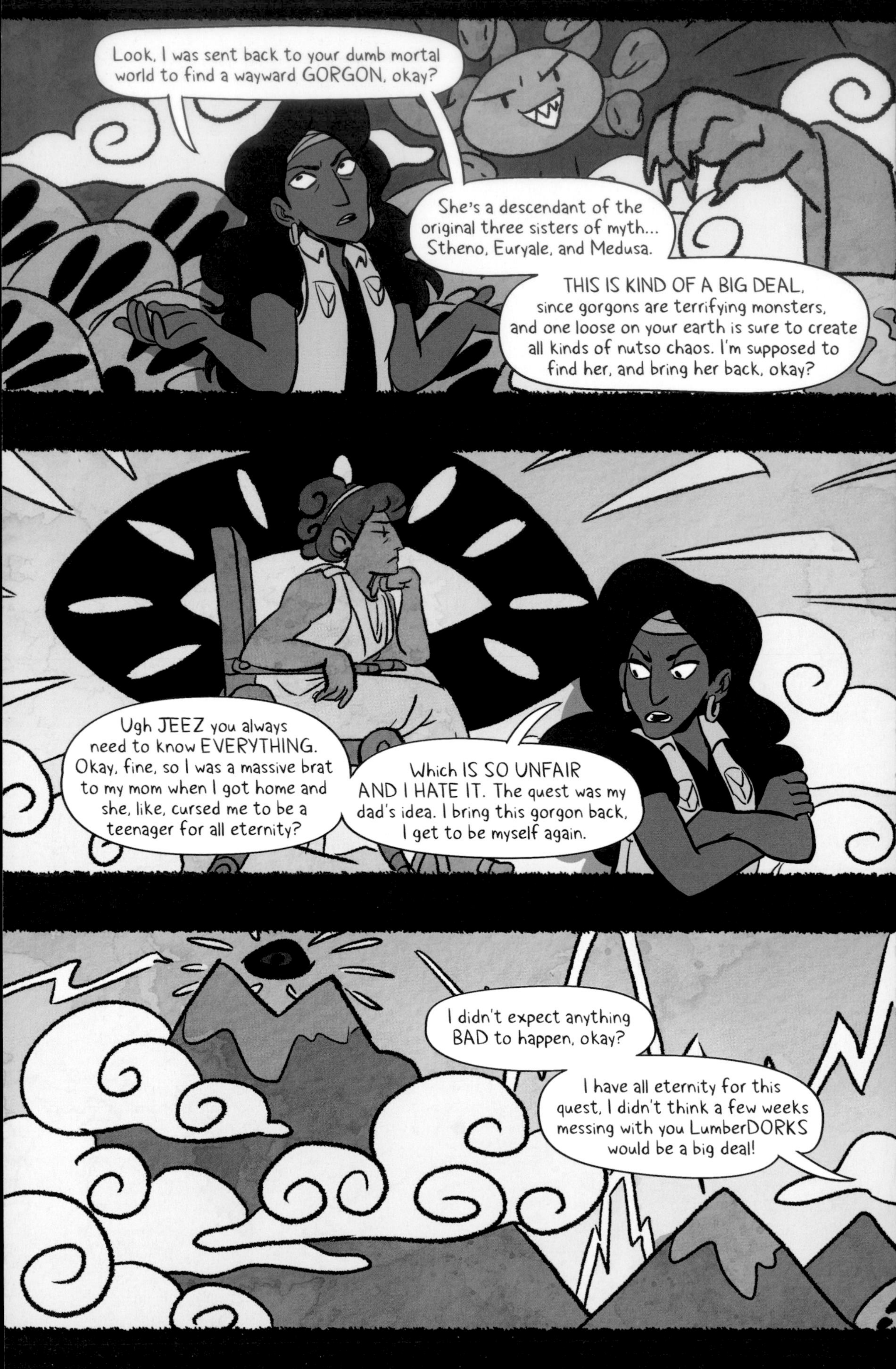
Look, I was sent back to your dumb mortal world to find a wayward GORGON, okay?
She's a descendant of the original three sisters of myth... Stheno, Euryale, and Medusa.
THIS IS KIND OF A BIG DEAL, since gorgons are terrifying monsters, and one loose on your earth is sure to create all kinds of nutso chaos. I'm supposed to find her, and bring her back, okay?
Ugh JEEZ you always need to know EVERYTHING. Okay, fine, so I was a massive brat to my mom when I got home and she, like, cursed me to be a teenager for all eternity?
Which IS SO UNFAIR AND I HATE IT. The quest was my dad's idea. I bring this gorgon back, I get to be myself again.
I didn't expect anything BAD to happen, okay?
I have all eternity for this quest, I didn't think a few weeks messing with you LumberDORKS would be a big deal!

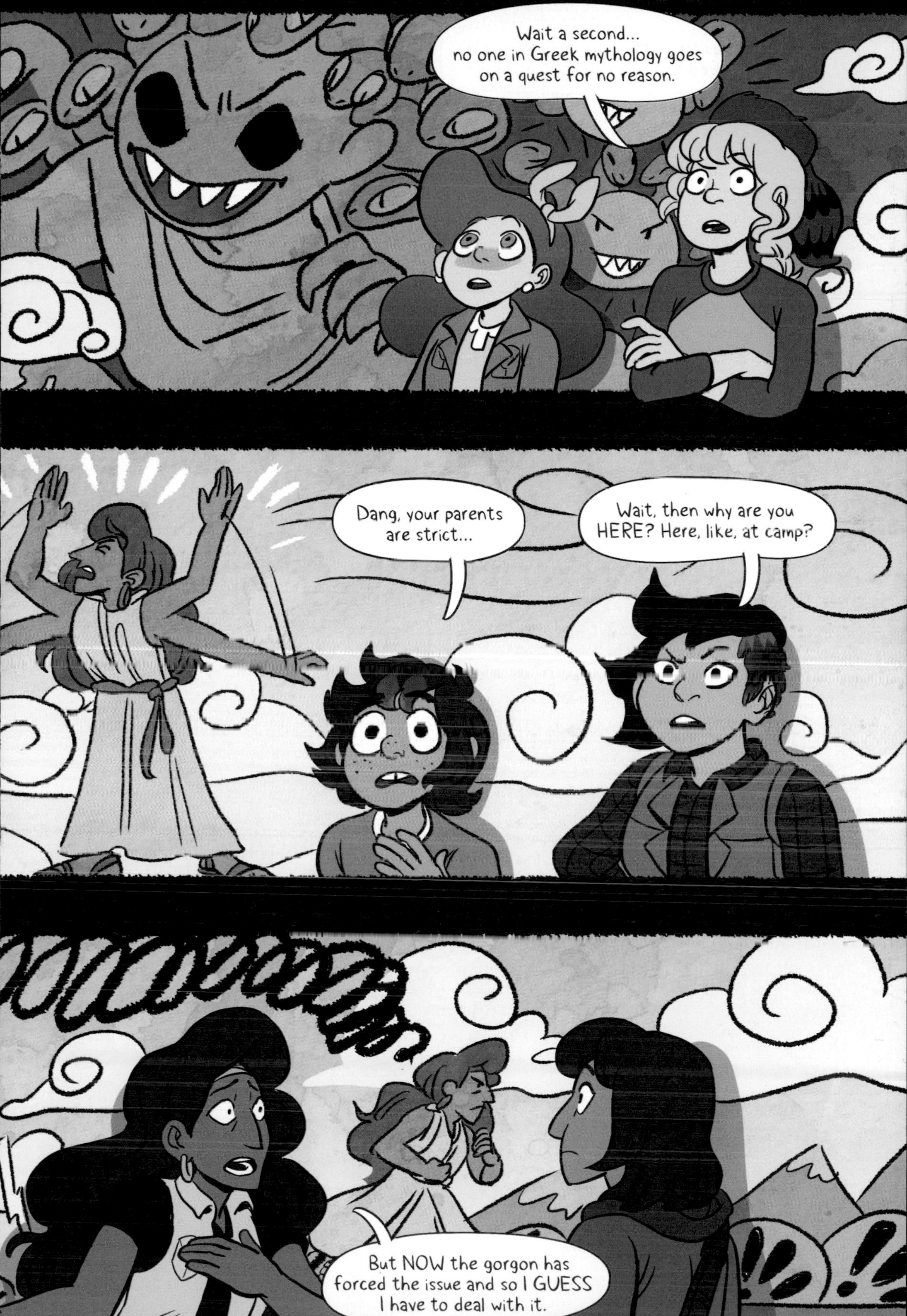
Wait a second... no one in Greek mythology goes on a quest for no reason.
Dang, your parents are strict...
Wait, then why are you HERE? Here, like, at camp?
But NOW the gorgon has forced the issue and so I GUESS I have to deal with it.

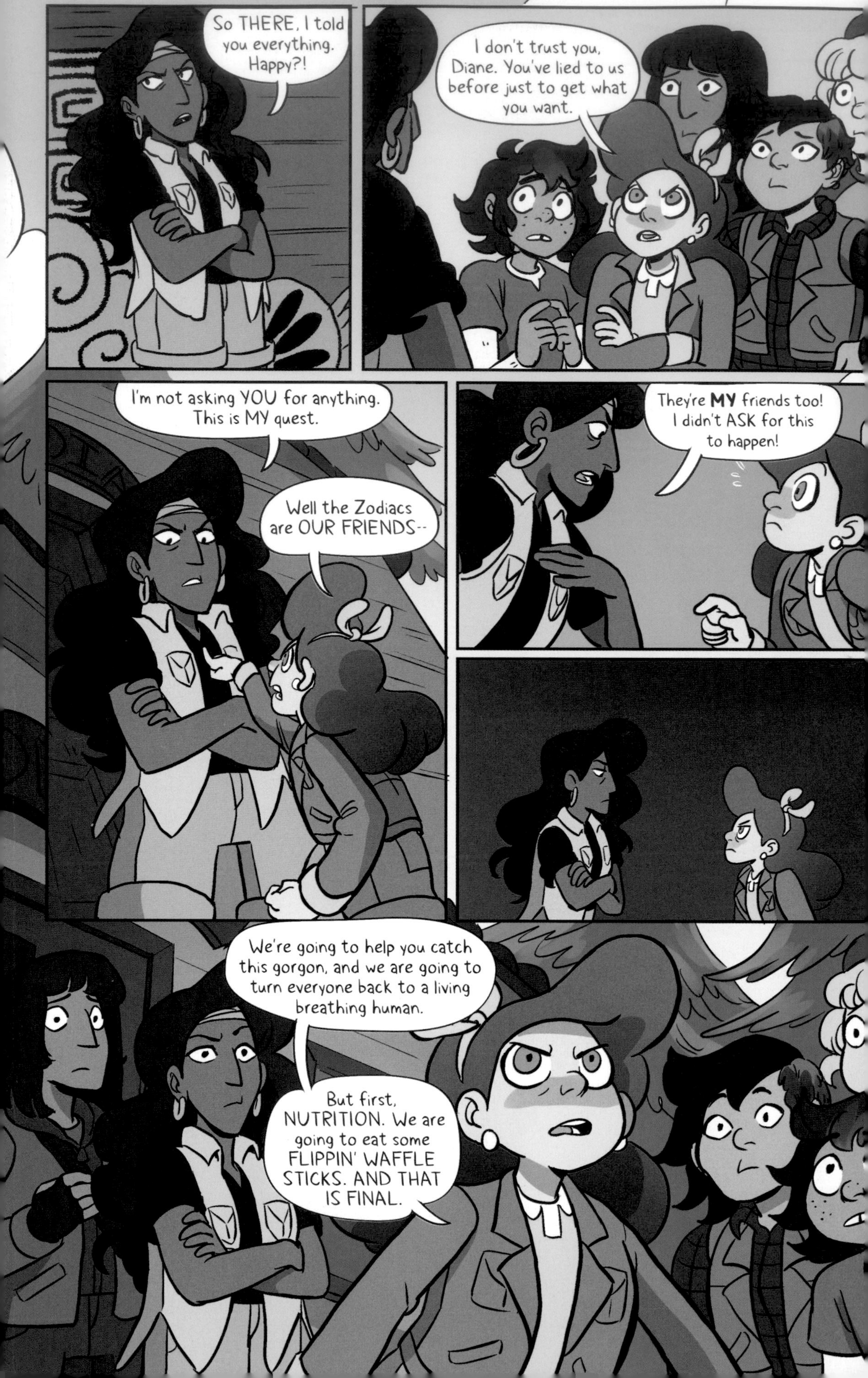
So THERE, I told you everything. Happy?!
I don't trust you, Diane. You've lied to us before just to get what you want.
I'm not asking YOU for anything. This is MY quest.
Well the Zodiacs are OUR FRIENDS--
They're MY friends too! I didn't ASK for this to happen!
We're going to help you catch this gorgon, and we are going to turn everyone back to a living breathing human.
But first, NUTRITION. We are going to eat some FLIPPIN' WAFFLE STICKS. AND THAT IS FINAL.

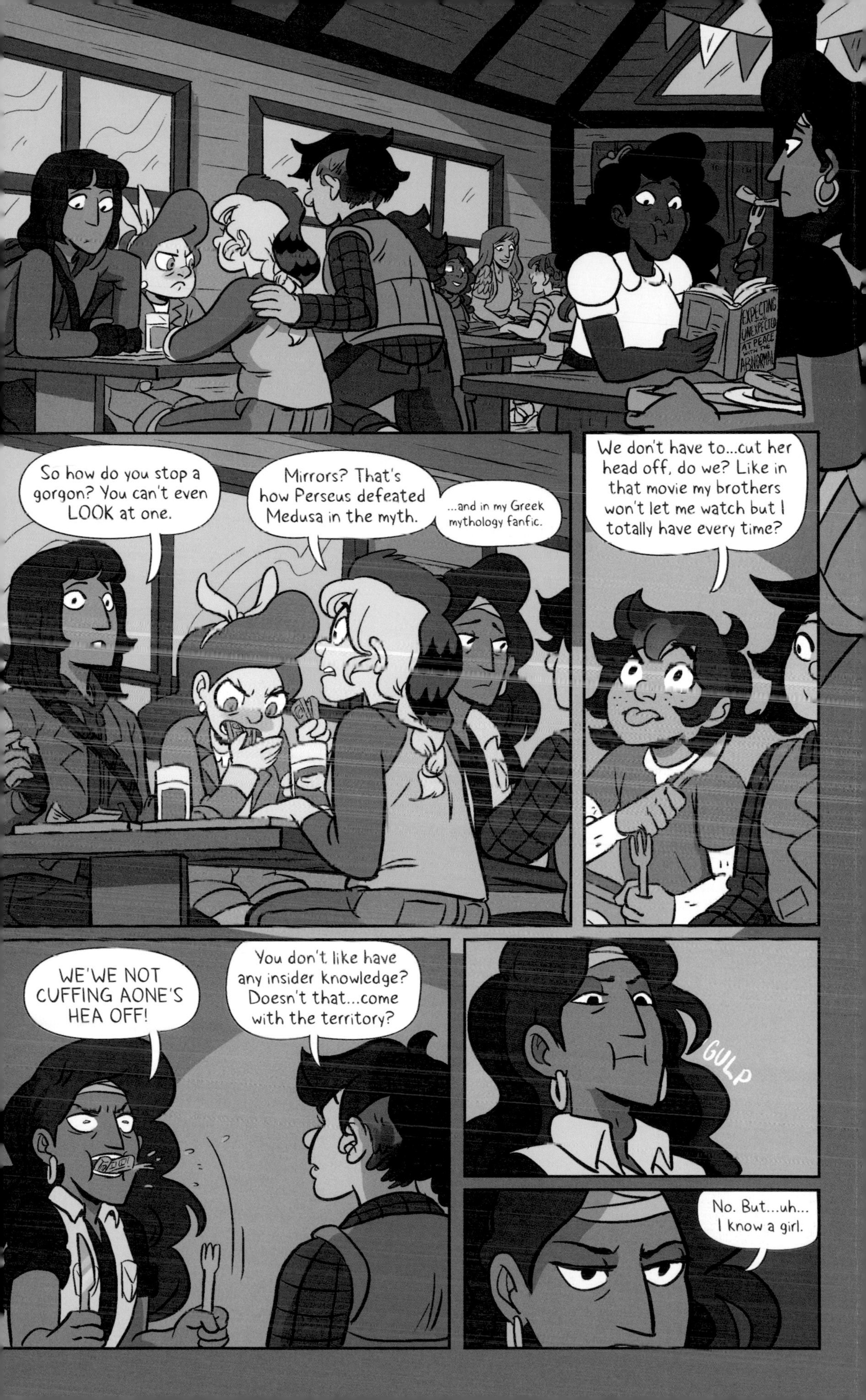
EXPECTING THE UNEXPECTED AT PEACE WITH THE ABNORMAL
So how do you stop a gorgon? You can't even LOOK at one.
Mirrors? That's how Perseus defeated Medusa in the myth.
...and in my Greek mythology fanfic.
We don't have to...cut her head off, do we? Like in that movie my brothers won't let me watch but I totally have every time?
WE'WE NOT CUFFING AONE'S HEA OFF!
You don't like have any insider knowledge? Doesn't that...come with the territory?
GULP
No. But...uh... I know a girl.

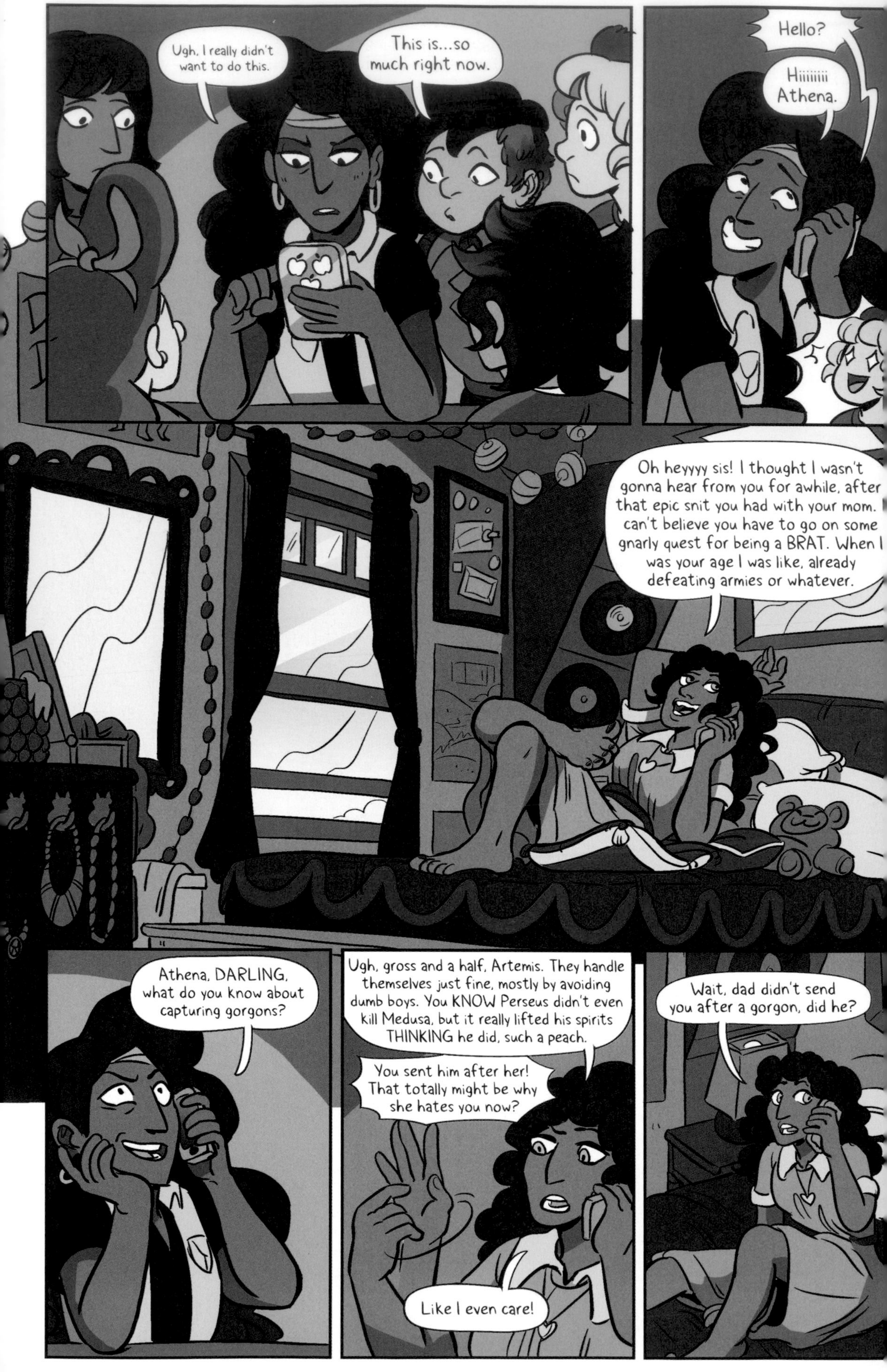
Ugh, I really didn't want to do this.
This is...so much right now.
Hello?
Hiiiiiii Athena.
Oh heyyyy sis! I thought I wasn't gonna hear from you for awhile, after that epic snit you had with your mom. can't believe you have to go on some gnarly quest for being a BRAT. When I was your age I was like, already defeating armies or whatever.
Athena, DARLING, what do you know about capturing gorgons?
Ugh, gross and a half, Artemis. They handle themselves just fine, mostly by avoiding dumb boys. You KNOW Perseus didn't even kill Medusa, but it really lifted his spirits THINKING he did, such a peach.
You sent him after her! That totally might be why she hates you now?
Like I even care!
Wait, dad didn't send you after a gorgon, did he?

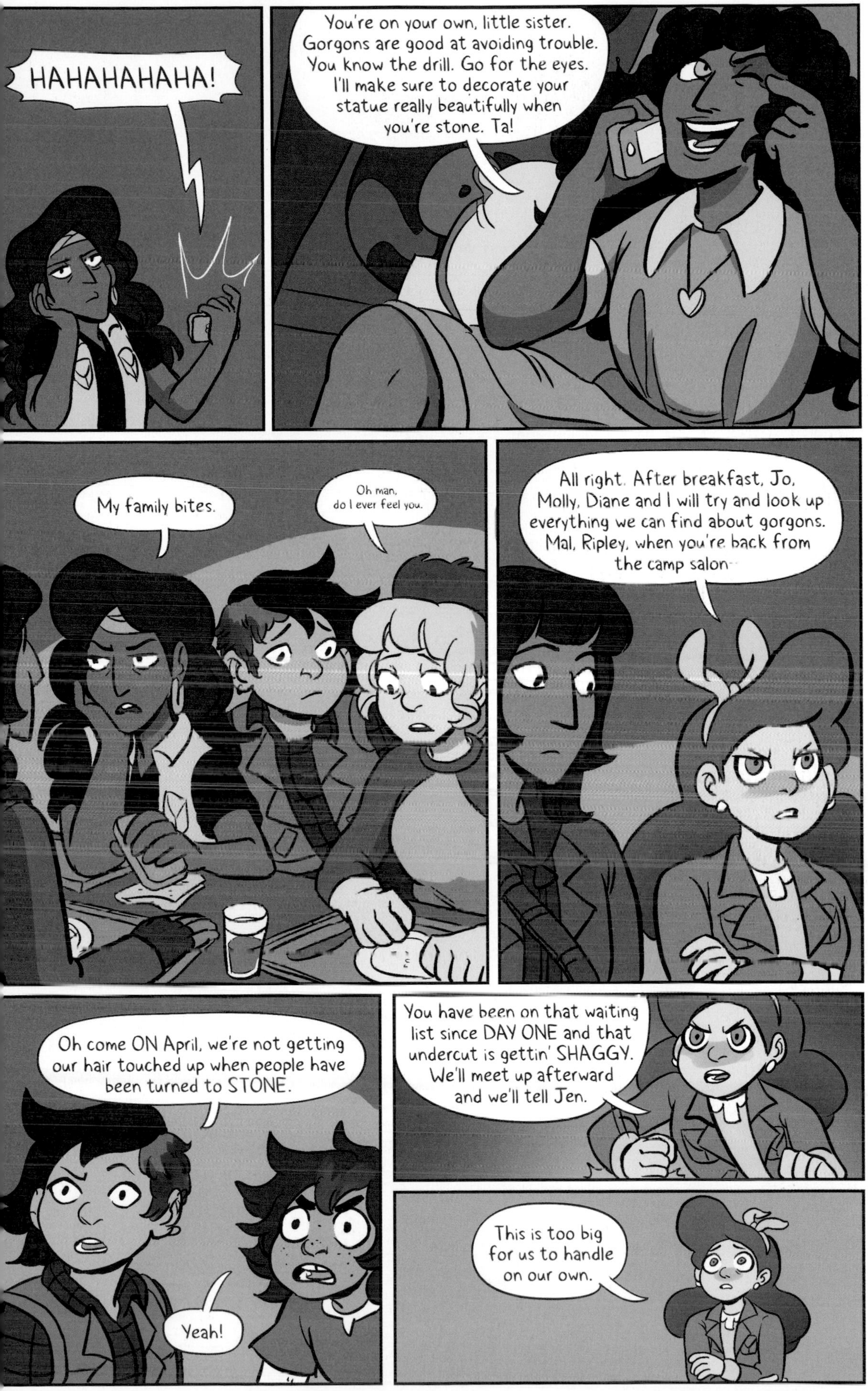
HAHAHAHAHA!
You're on your own, little sister. Gorgons are good at avoiding trouble. You know the drill. Go for the eyes. I'll make sure to decorate your statue really beautifully when you're stone. Ta!
My family bites.
Oh man, do I ever feel you.
All right. After breakfast, Jo, Molly, Diane and I will try and look up everything we can find about gorgons. Mal, Ripley, when you're back from the camp salon--
Oh come ON April, we're not getting our hair touched up when people have been turned to STONE.
Yeah!
You have been on that waiting list since DAY ONE and that undercut is gettin' SHAGGY. We'll meet up afterward and we'll tell Jen.
This is too big for us to handle on our own.

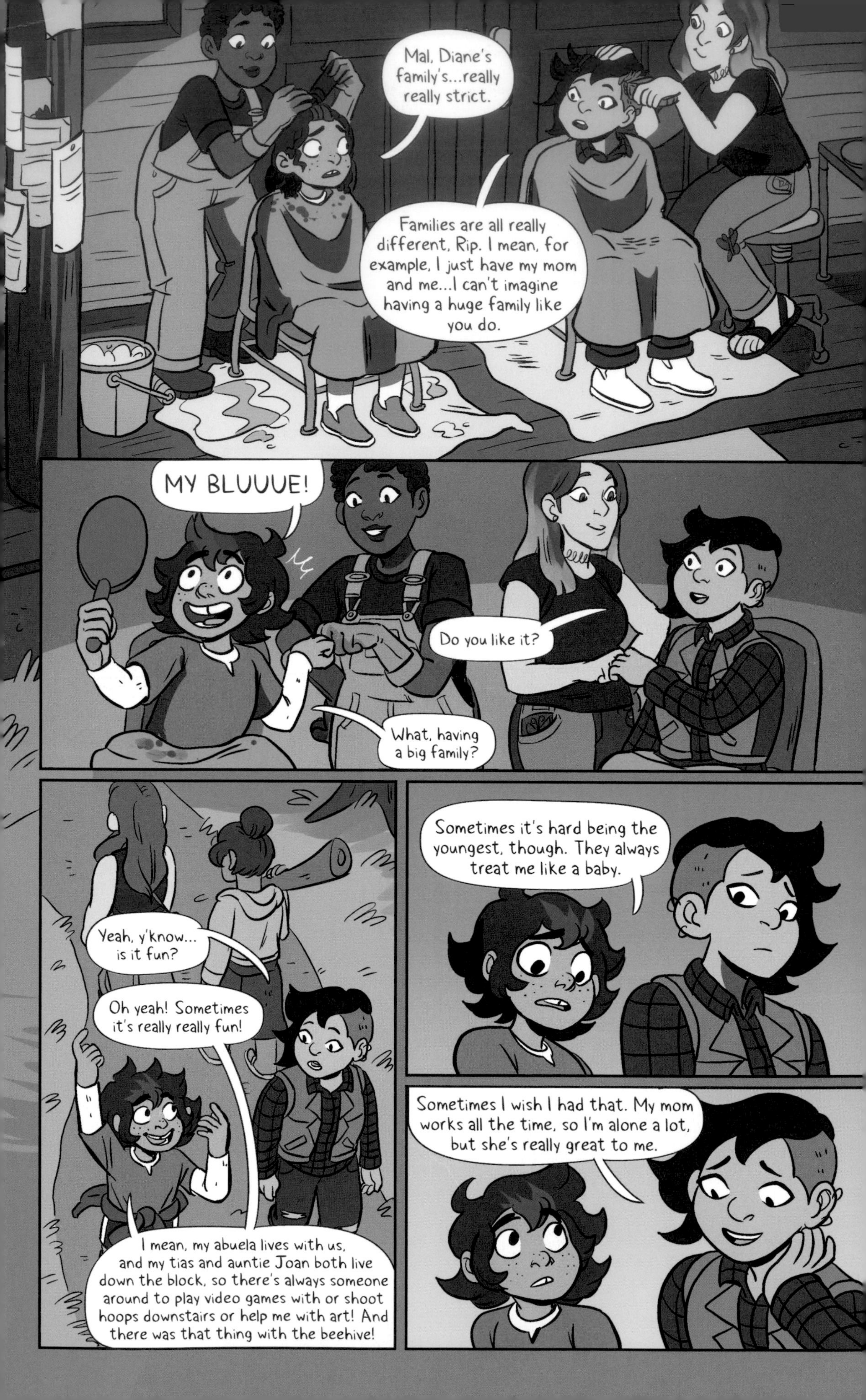
Mal, Diane's family's...really really strict.
Families are all really different, Rip. I mean, for example, I just have my mom and me...I can't imagine having a huge family like you do.
MY BLUUUE!
Do you like it?
What, having a big family?
Yeah, y'know... is it fun?
Oh yeah! Sometimes it's really really fun!
I mean, my abuela lives with us, and my tias and auntie Joan both live down the block, so there's always someone around to play video games with or shoot hoops downstairs or help me with art! And there was that thing with the beehive!
Sometimes it's hard being the youngest, though. They always treat me like a baby.
Sometimes I wish I had that. My mom works all the time, so I'm alone a lot, but she's really great to me.

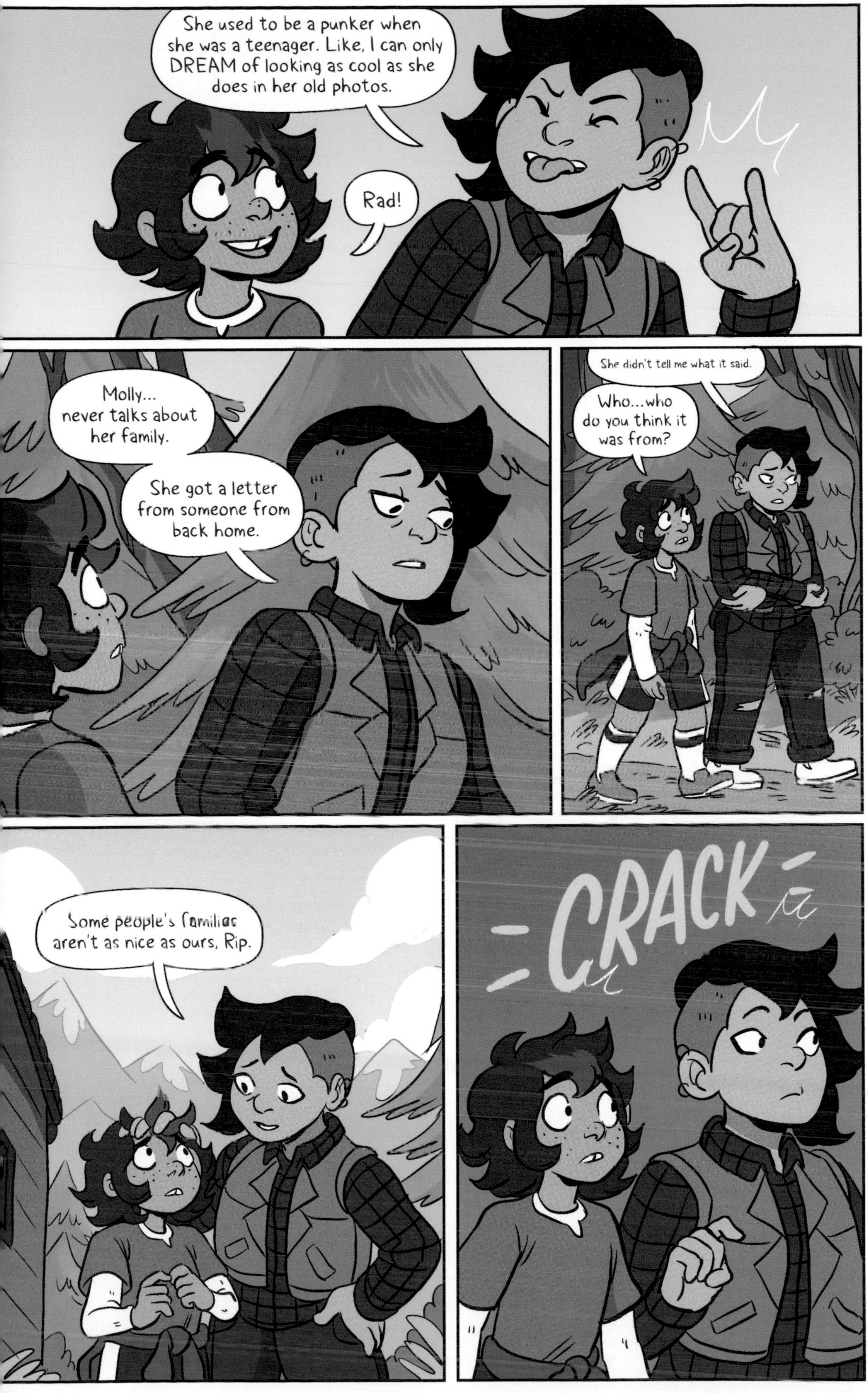
She used to be a punker when she was a teenager. Like, I can only DREAM of looking as cool as she does in her old photos.
Rad!
Molly... never talks about her family.
She got a letter from someone from back home.
She didn't tell me what it said.
Who...who do you think it was from?
Some people's families aren't as nice as ours, Rip.
CRACK

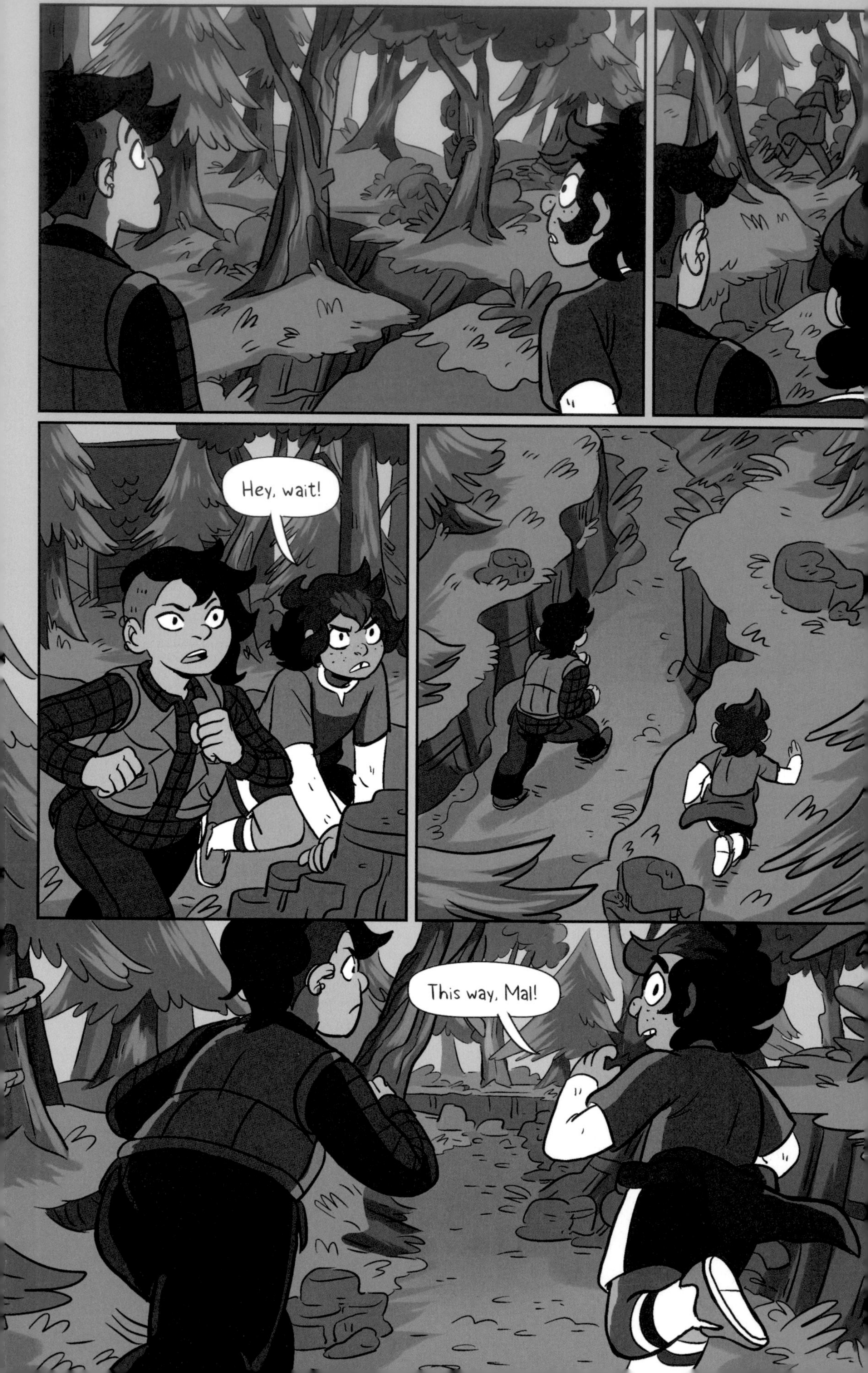
Hey, wait!
This way, Mal!

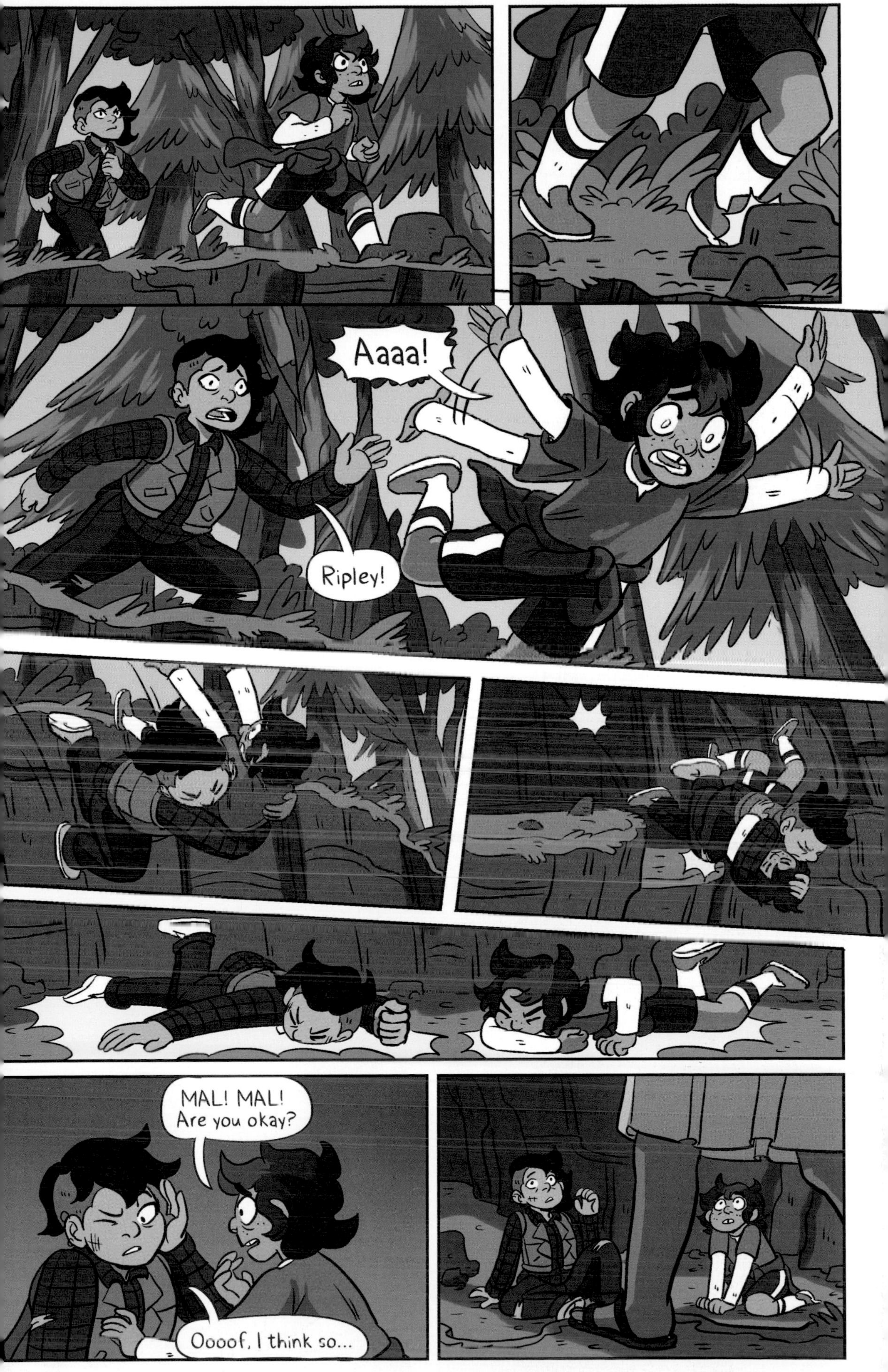
Aaaa!
Ripley!
MAL! MAL! Are you okay?
Oooof, I think so...

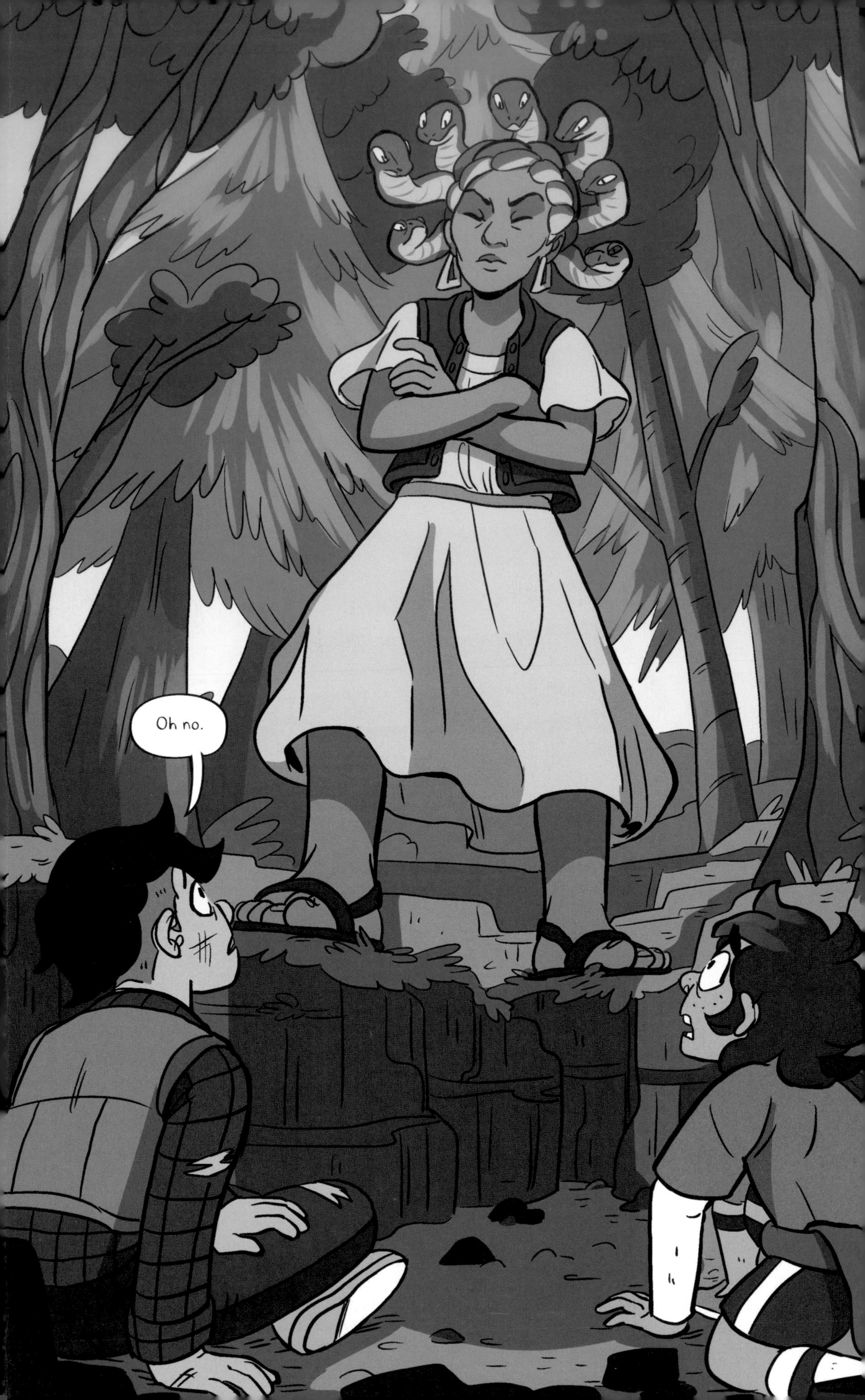
Oh no.

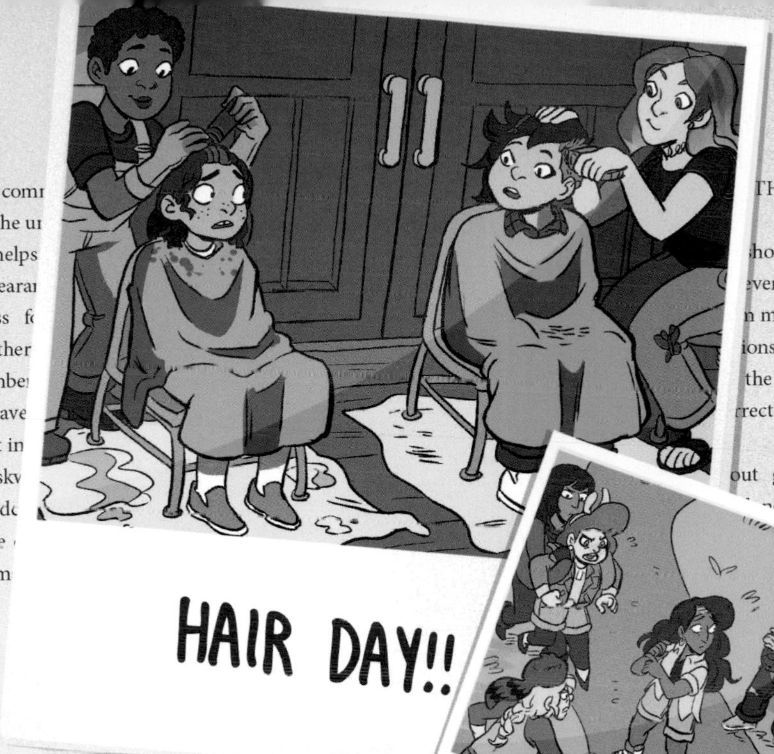
HAIR DAY!!

will comr

The ur
It helps
appearar
dress fc
Further
Lumbe
to have
part in
Thiskv
Hardc
have
them

THE UNIFORM

should be worn at camp
events when Lumberjanes
n may also be worn at other
ions. It should be worn as a
the uniform dress with
rrect shoes, and stocking or

out grows her uniform or
ng to anoter Lumberjane.
insignia she has
her
her

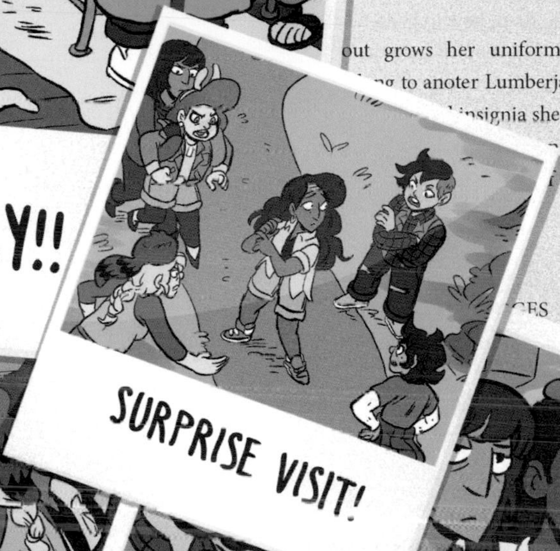
SURPRISE VISIT!

CES

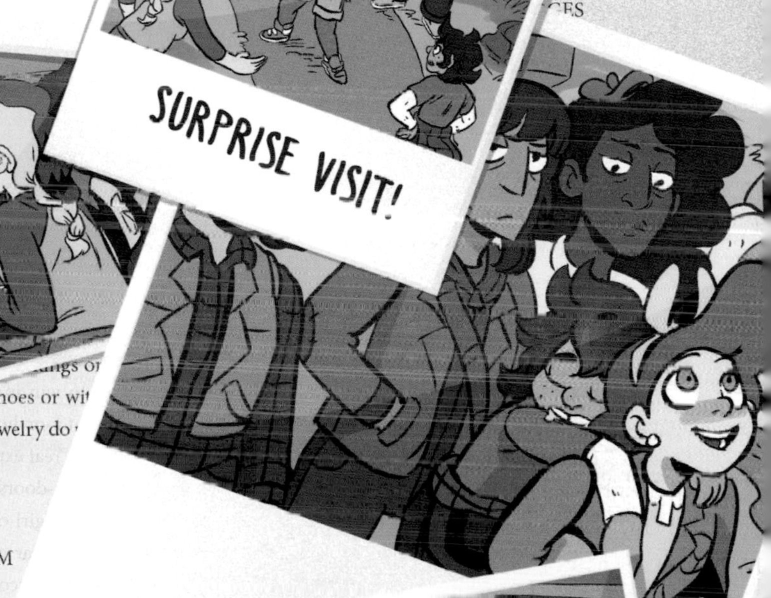

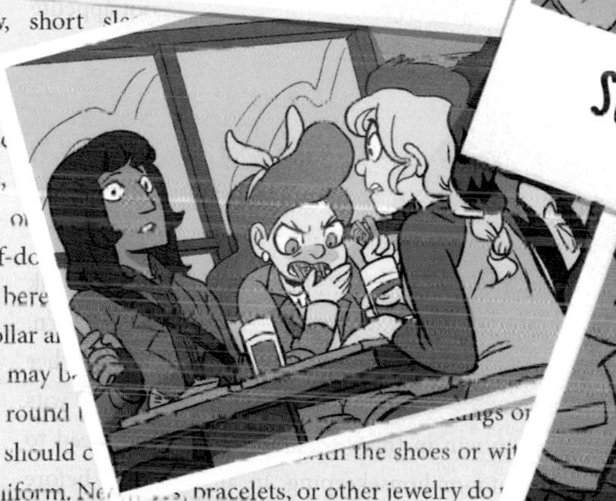

The
yellow, short sle
emb
the w
choose
slacks,
made o
out-of-do
green here
the collar a
Shoes may b
heels, round
ings or
socks should c with the shoes or wit
the uniform. Ne bracelets, or other jewelry do
belong with a Lumberjane uniform.

HOW TO WEAR THE UNIFORM

To look well in a uniform demans first of uniform be kept in good condition—clean pressed. See that the skirt is the right length for your own height and build, that the belt is adjusted to your waist, that your shoes and stockings are in keeping with the uniform, that you watch your posture and carry yourself with dignity and grace. If the beret is removed indoors, be sure that your hair is neat and kept in place with an insonspicuous clip or ribbon. When you wear a Lumberjane uniform you are identified as a member of this organization and you should be doubly careful to conduct yourself in a way that will show everyone that courtesy and thoughtfullness are part of being a Lumberjane. People are likely to judge a whole nation by the selfishness of a few individuals, to criticize a whole family because of the misconduct of one member, and to feel unkindly toward and organization because of the

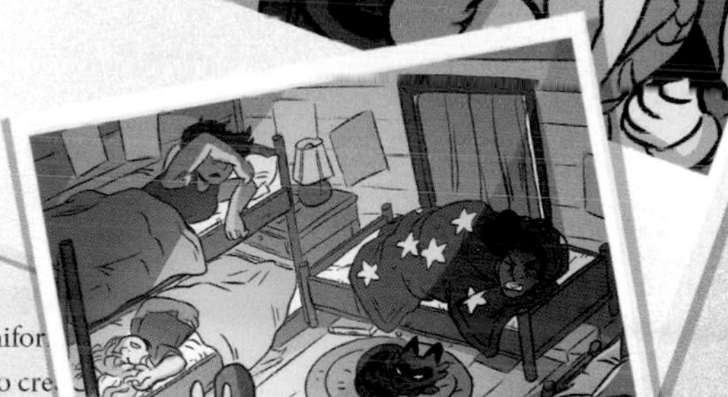
MORNING PERSON VS ...

The unifor
helps to cre
in a group.
active life th
another bond
future, and pr
in order to b
Lumberjane pr
Penniquiqul Thi ore Lady
Types, but most jnes will wish to have one. They can either buy the uniform, or make it themselves from materials available at the trading post.

LUMBERJANES FIELD MANUAL

CHAPTER
THIRTY

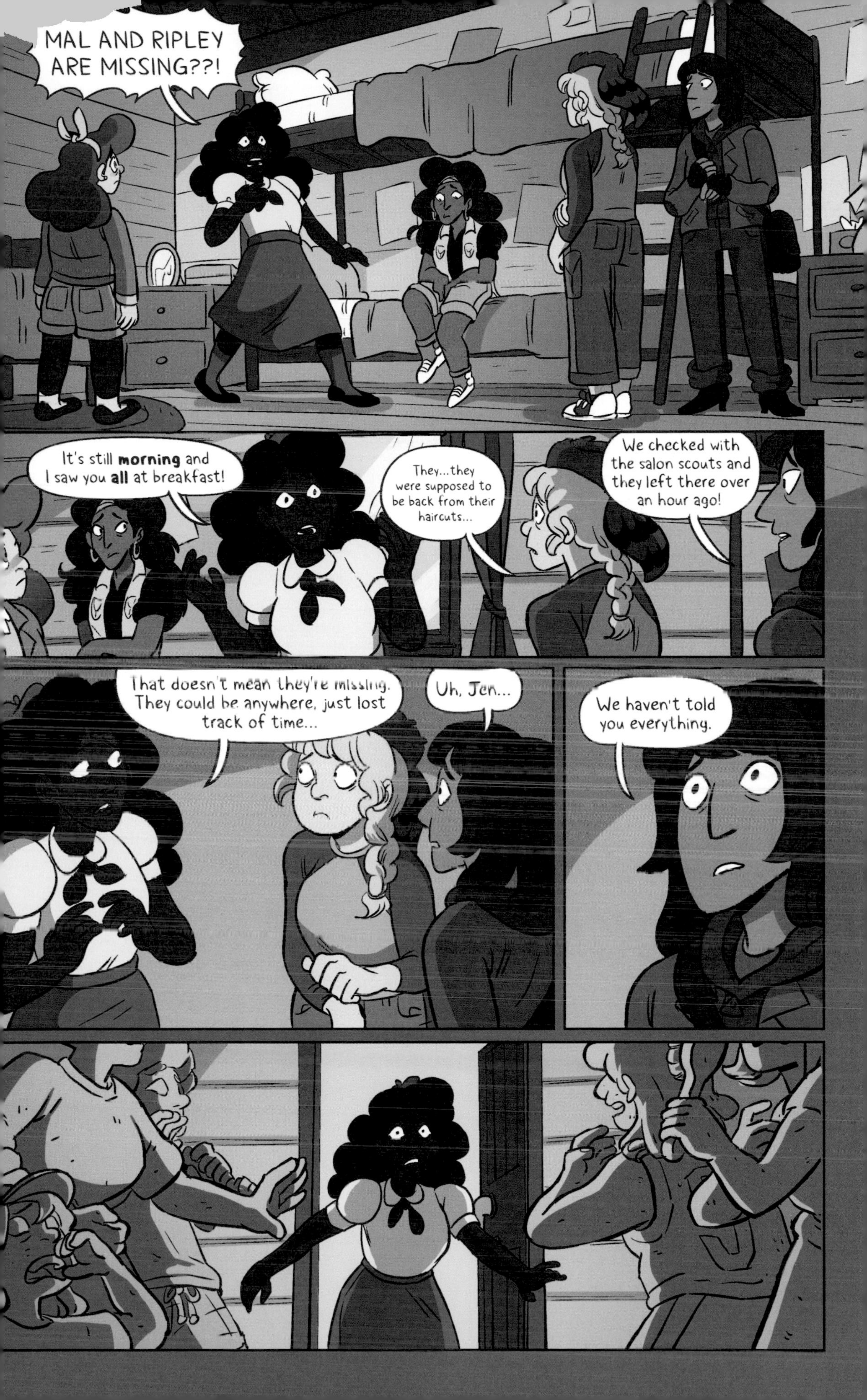
MAL AND RIPLEY ARE MISSING??!
It's still **morning** and I saw you **all** at breakfast!
They...they were supposed to be back from their haircuts...
We checked with the salon scouts and they left there over an hour ago!
That doesn't mean they're missing. They could be anywhere, just lost track of time...
Uh, Jen...
We haven't told you everything.

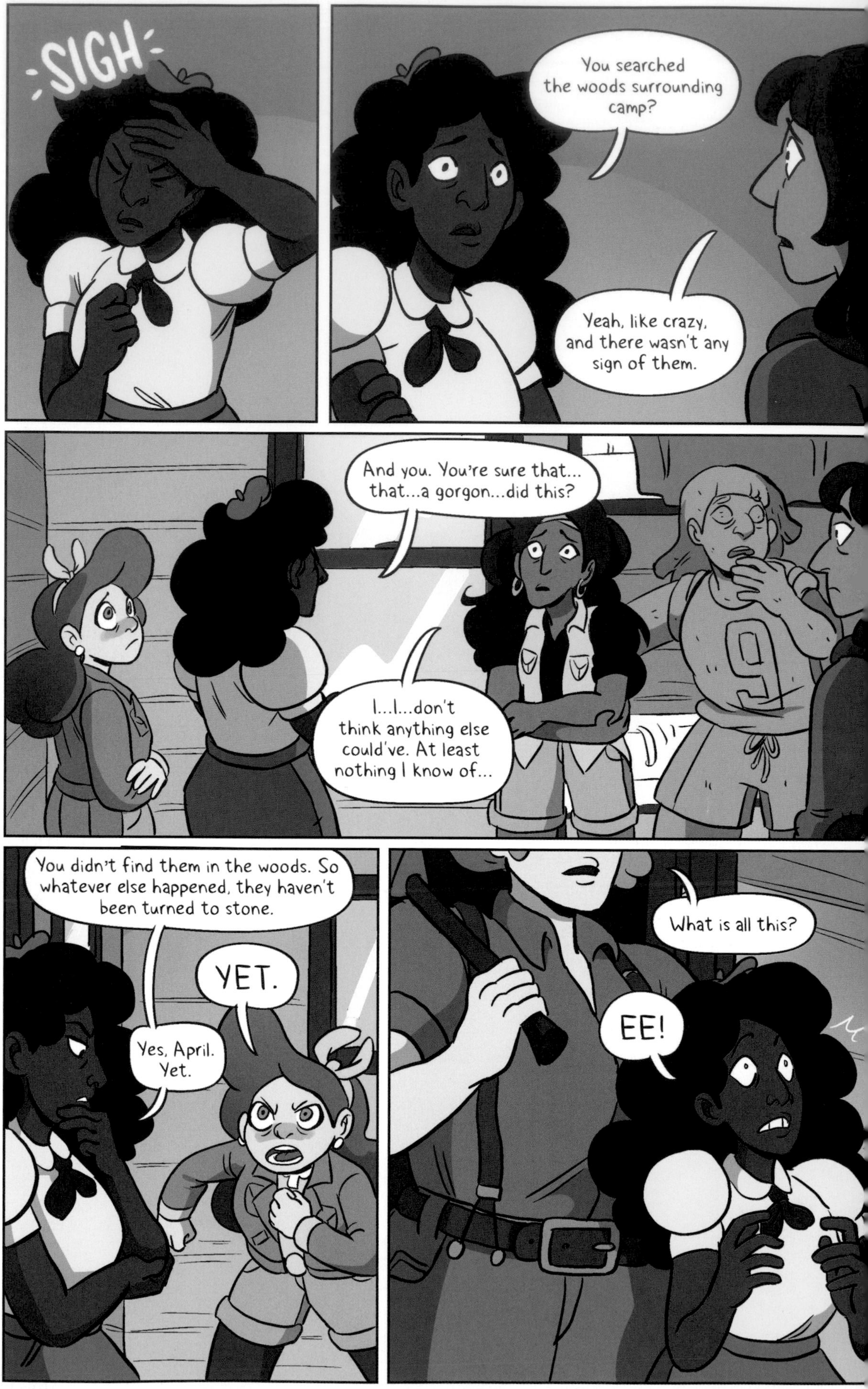
SIGH
You searched the woods surrounding camp?
Yeah, like crazy, and there wasn't any sign of them.
And you. You're sure that... that...a gorgon...did this?
I...I...don't think anything else could've. At least nothing I know of...
You didn't find them in the woods. So whatever else happened, they haven't been turned to stone.
YET.
Yes, April. Yet.
What is all this?
EE!

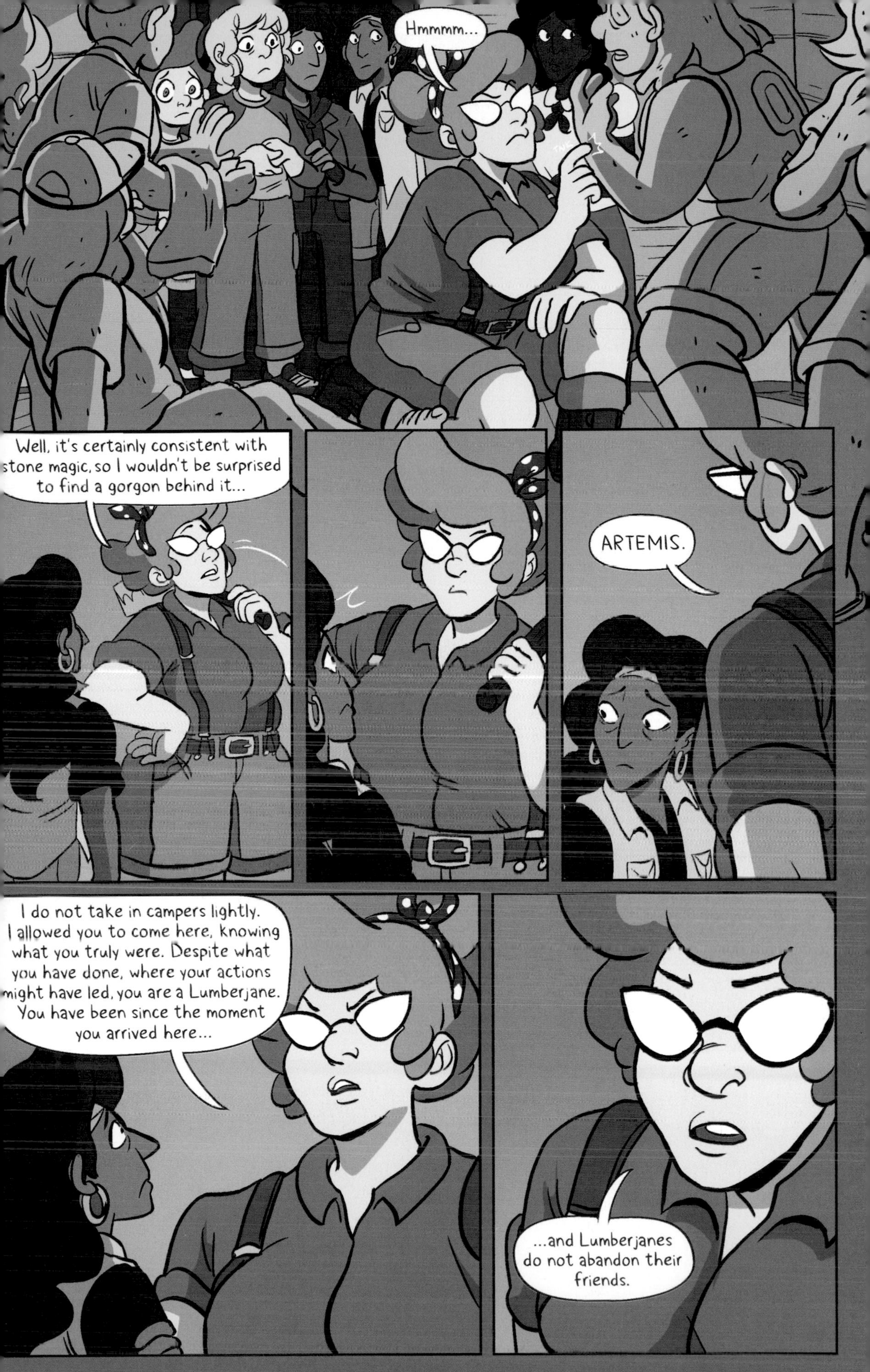
Hmmmm...
Well, it's certainly consistent with stone magic, so I wouldn't be surprised to find a gorgon behind it...
ARTEMIS.
I do not take in campers lightly. I allowed you to come here, knowing what you truly were. Despite what you have done, where your actions might have led, you are a Lumberjane. You have been since the moment you arrived here...
...and Lumberjanes do not abandon their friends.

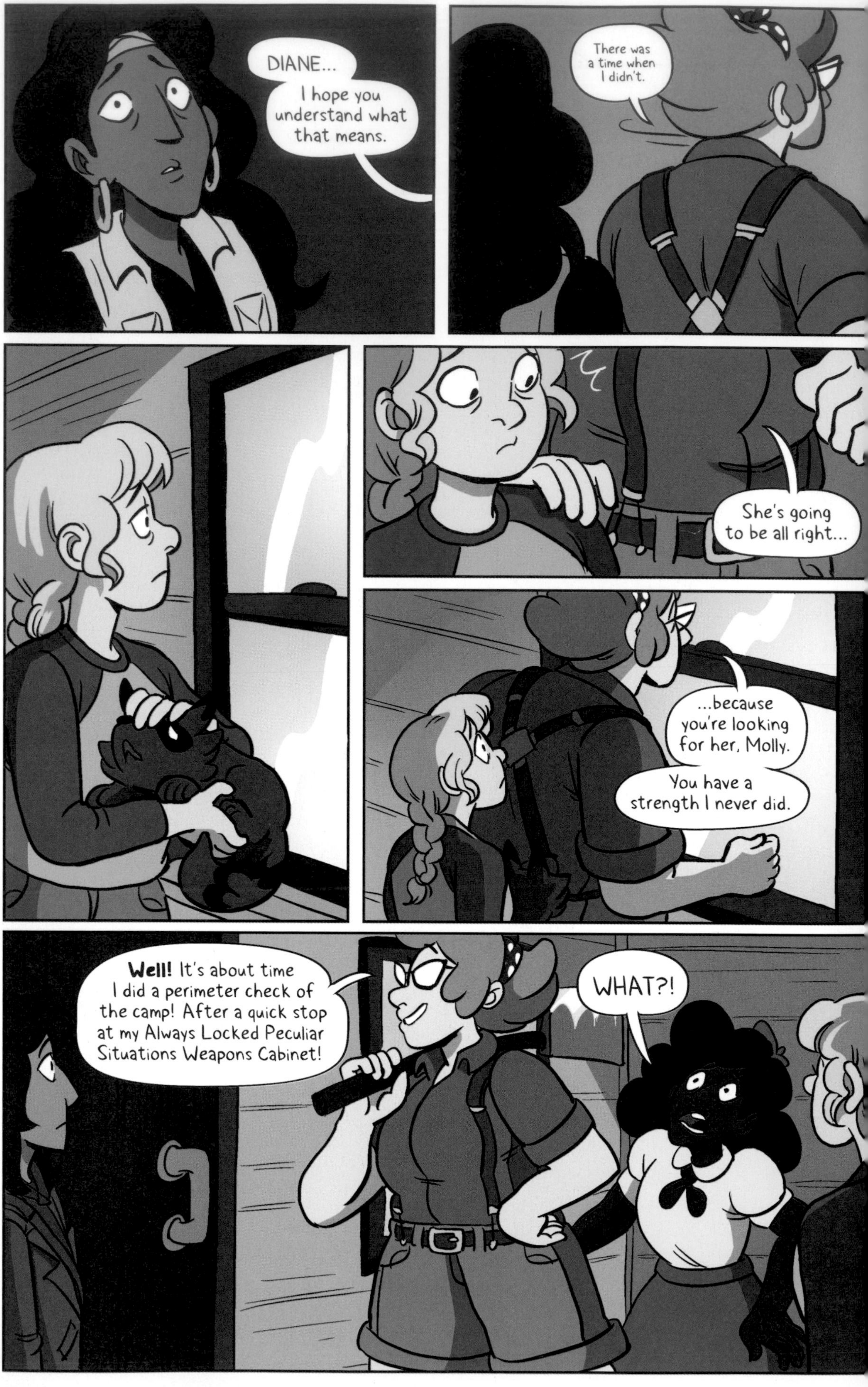
DIANE...
I hope you understand what that means.
There was a time when I didn't.
She's going to be all right...
...because you're looking for her, Molly.
You have a strength I never did.
Well! It's about time I did a perimeter check of the camp! After a quick stop at my Always Locked Peculiar Situations Weapons Cabinet!
WHAT?!

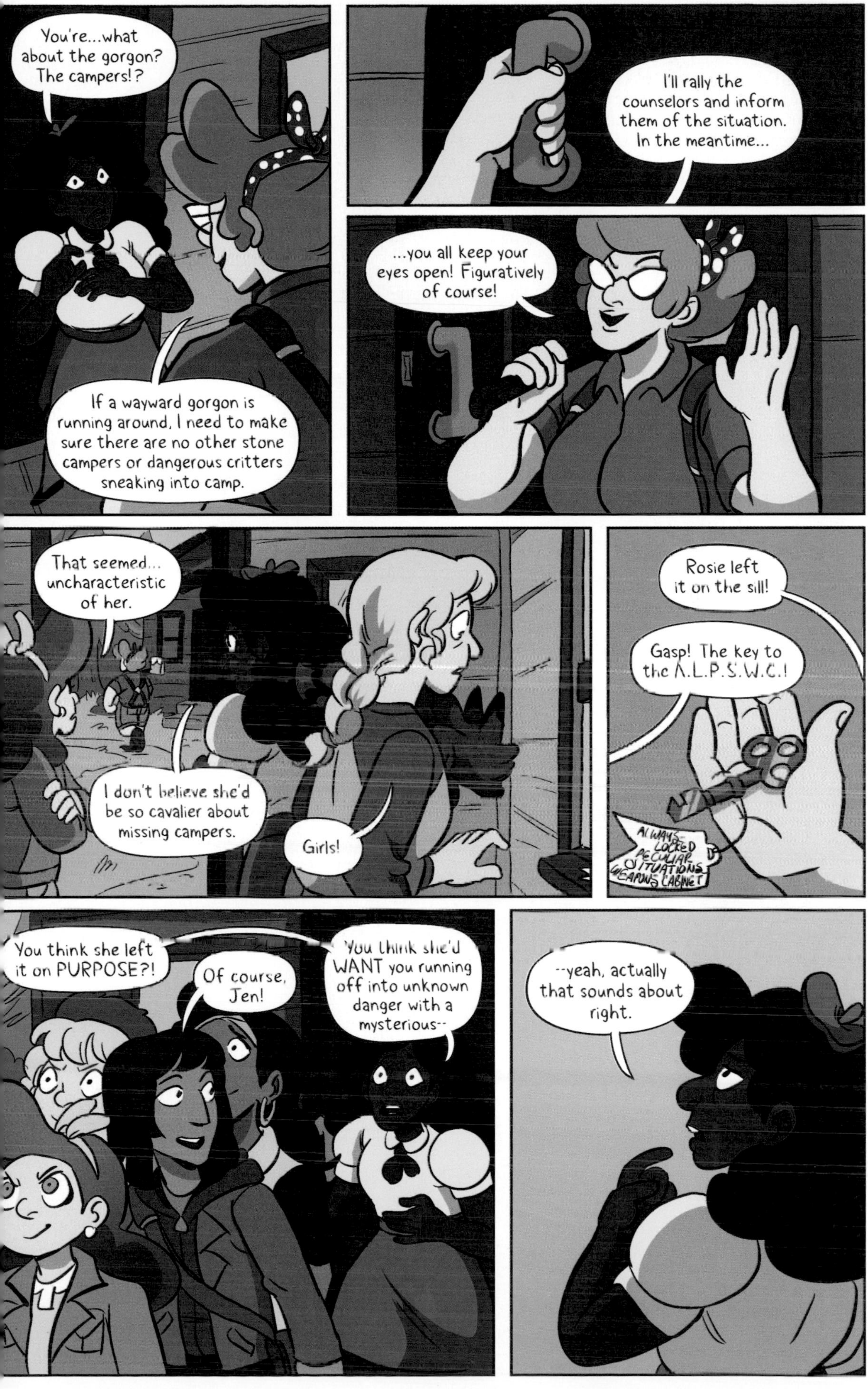
You're...what about the gorgon? The campers!?
If a wayward gorgon is running around, I need to make sure there are no other stone campers or dangerous critters sneaking into camp.
I'll rally the counselors and inform them of the situation. In the meantime...
...you all keep your eyes open! Figuratively of course!
That seemed... uncharacteristic of her.
I don't believe she'd be so cavalier about missing campers.
Girls!
Rosie left it on the sill!
Gasp! The key to the A.L.P.S.W.C.!
ALWAYS-LOCKED PECULIAR SITUATIONS WEAPONS CABINET
You think she left it on PURPOSE?!
Of course, Jen!
You think she'd WANT you running off into unknown danger with a mysterious--
--yeah, actually that sounds about right.

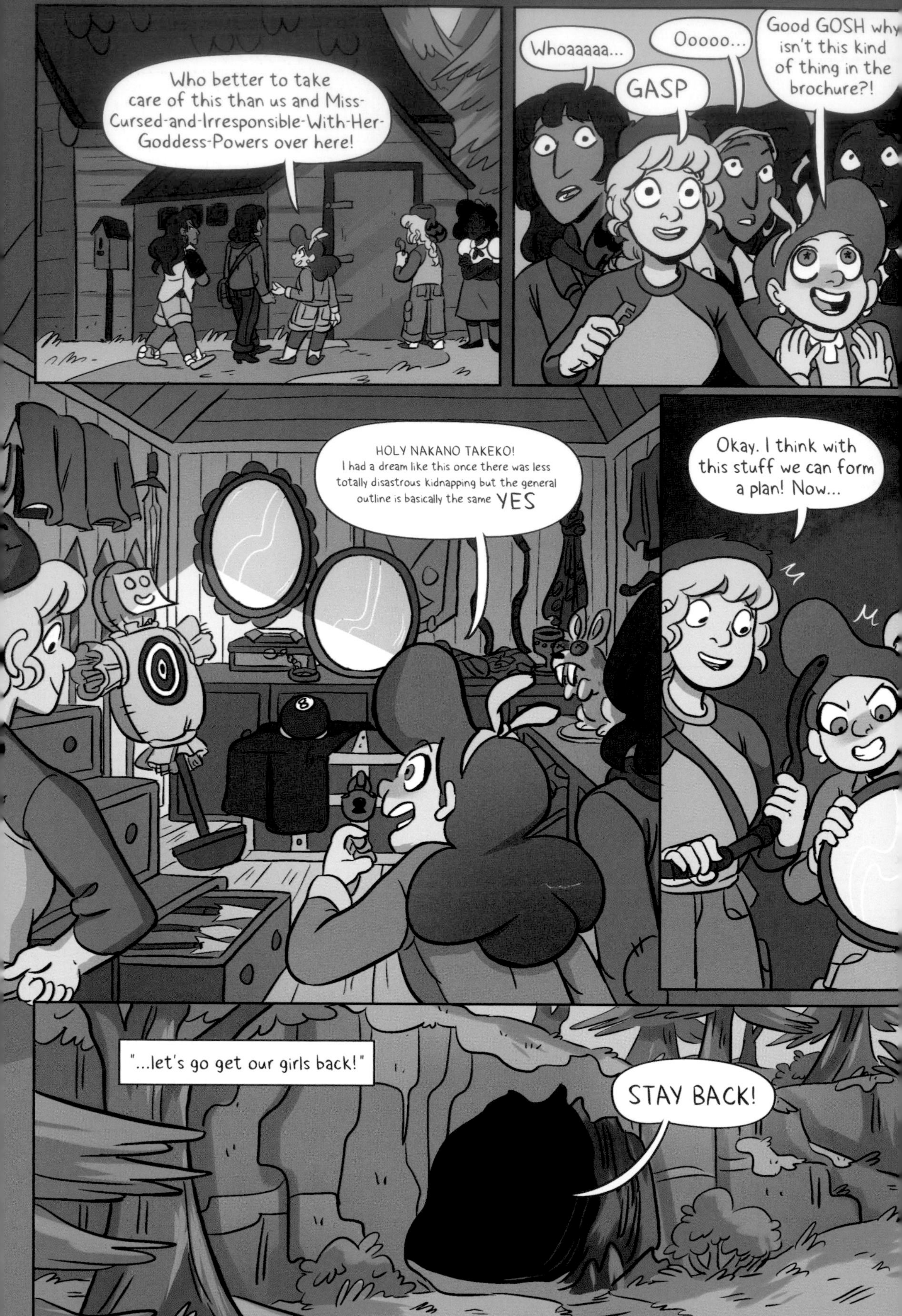
Who better to take care of this than us and Miss-Cursed-and-Irresponsible-With-Her-Goddess-Powers over here!
Whoaaaaa...
GASP
Ooooo...
Good GOSH why isn't this kind of thing in the brochure?!
HOLY NAKANO TAKEKO! I had a dream like this once there was less totally disastrous kidnapping but the general outline is basically the same YES
Okay. I think with this stuff we can form a plan! Now...
"...let's go get our girls back!"
STAY BACK!

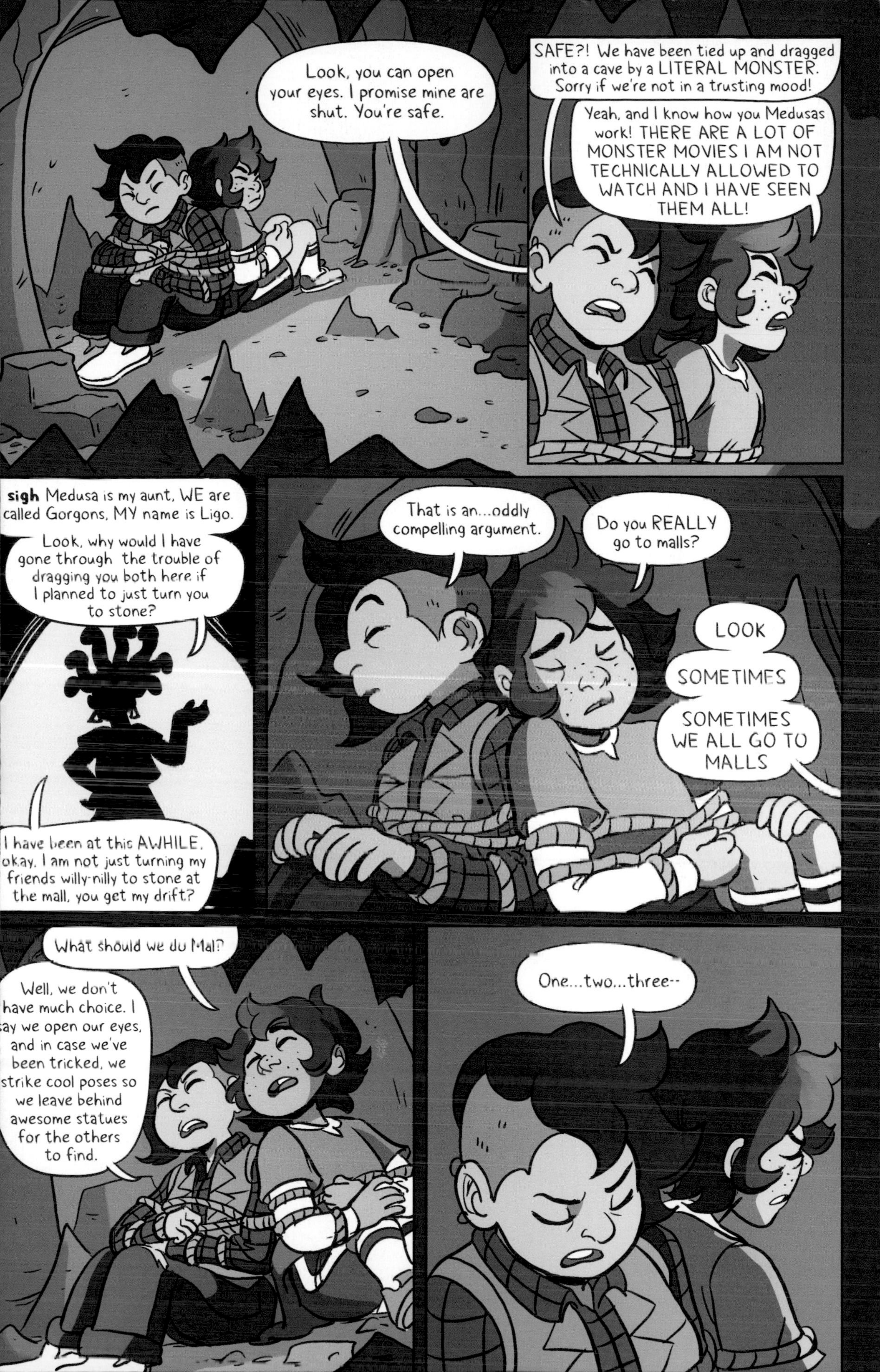
Look, you can open your eyes. I promise mine are shut. You're safe.
SAFE?! We have been tied up and dragged into a cave by a LITERAL MONSTER. Sorry if we're not in a trusting mood!
Yeah, and I know how you Medusas work! THERE ARE A LOT OF MONSTER MOVIES I AM NOT TECHNICALLY ALLOWED TO WATCH AND I HAVE SEEN THEM ALL!
sigh Medusa is my aunt, WE are called Gorgons, MY name is Ligo.
Look, why would I have gone through the trouble of dragging you both here if I planned to just turn you to stone?
I have been at this AWHILE, okay. I am not just turning my friends willy-nilly to stone at the mall, you get my drift?
That is an...oddly compelling argument.
Do you REALLY go to malls?
LOOK
SOMETIMES
SOMETIMES WE ALL GO TO MALLS
What should we do Mal?
Well, we don't have much choice. I say we open our eyes, and in case we've been tricked, we strike cool poses so we leave behind awesome statues for the others to find.
One...two...three--

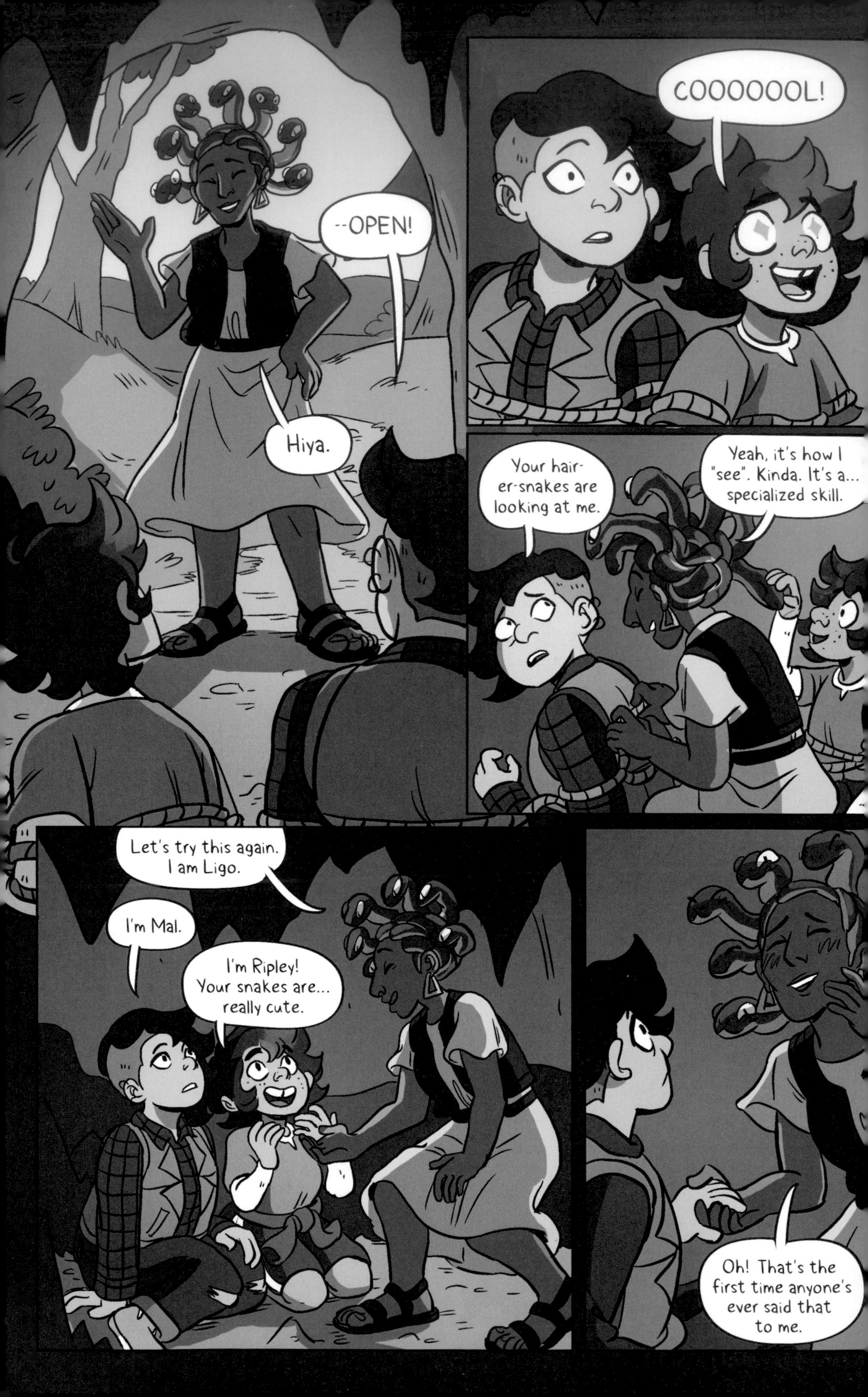
--OPEN!
Hiya.
COOOOOOL!
Your hair-er-snakes are looking at me.
Yeah, it's how I "see". Kinda. It's a... specialized skill.
Let's try this again. I am Ligo.
I'm Mal.
I'm Ripley! Your snakes are... really cute.
Oh! That's the first time anyone's ever said that to me.

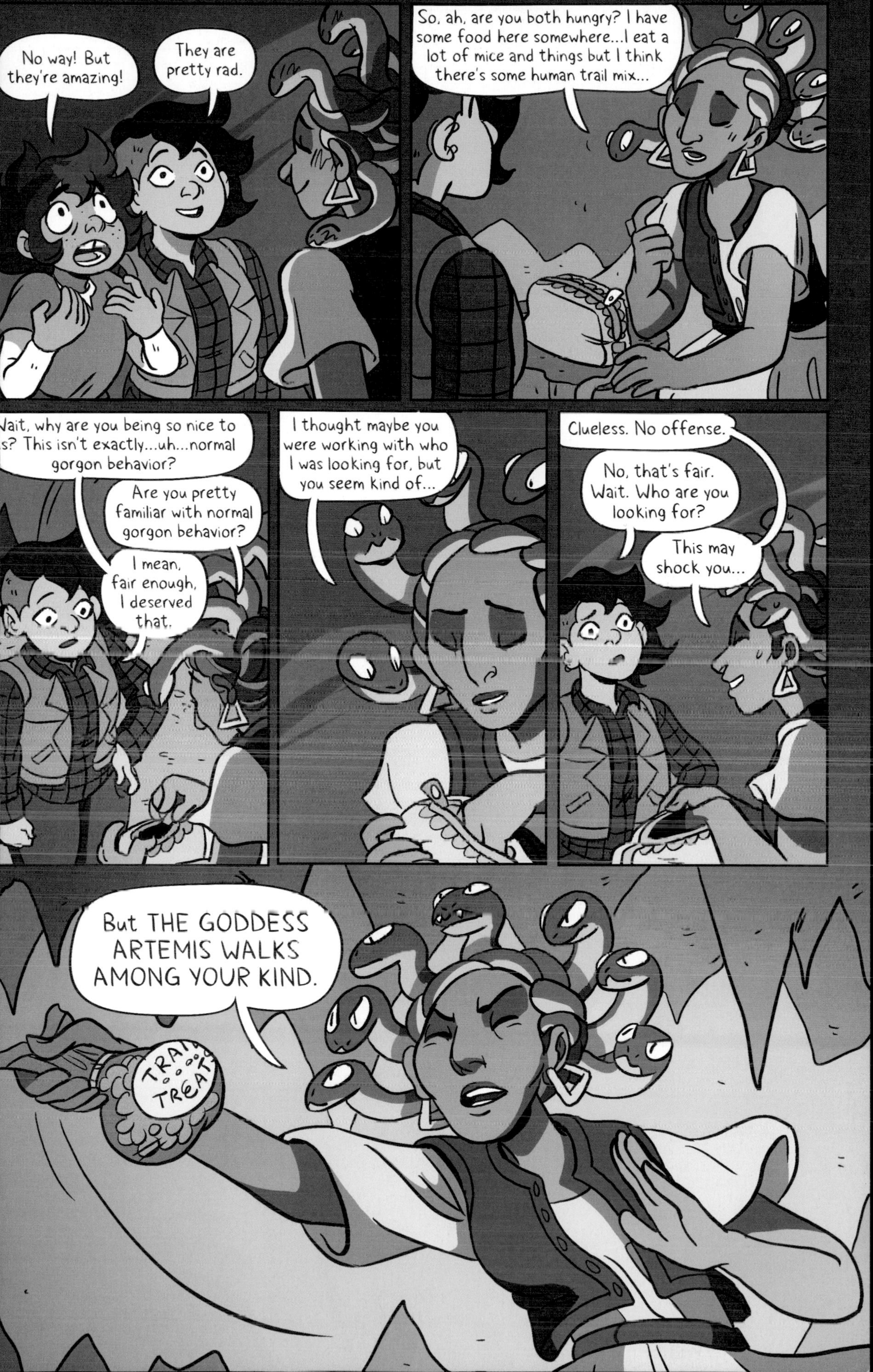
No way! But they're amazing!
They are pretty rad.
So, ah, are you both hungry? I have some food here somewhere...I eat a lot of mice and things but I think there's some human trail mix...
ait, why are you being so nice to s? This isn't exactly...uh...normal gorgon behavior?
Are you pretty familiar with normal gorgon behavior?
I mean, fair enough, I deserved that.
I thought maybe you were working with who I was looking for, but you seem kind of...
Clueless. No offense.
No, that's fair. Wait. Who are you looking for?
This may shock you...
But THE GODDESS ARTEMIS WALKS AMONG YOUR KIND.

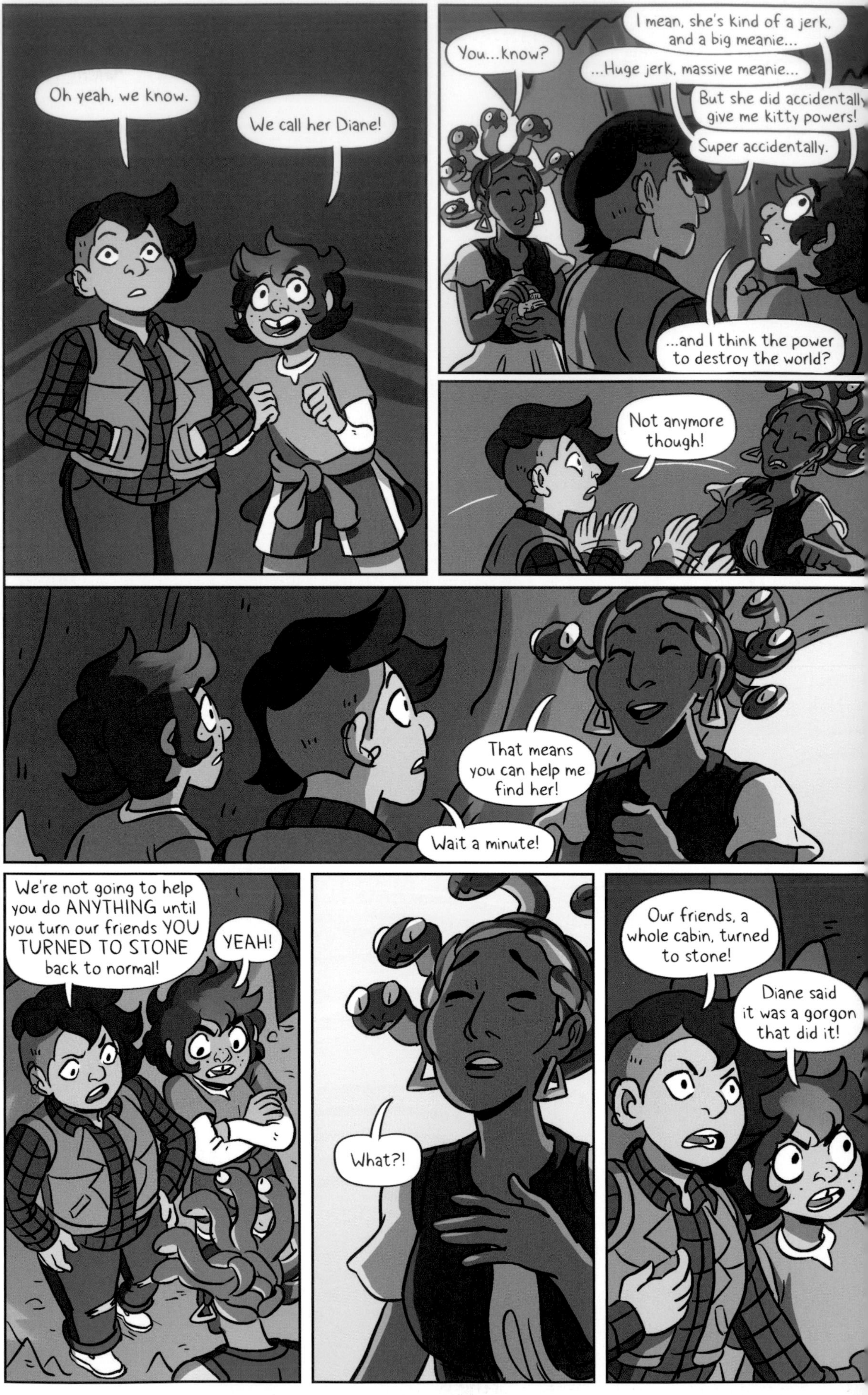
Oh yeah, we know.
We call her Diane!
You...know?
I mean, she's kind of a jerk, and a big meanie...
...Huge jerk, massive meanie...
But she did accidentally give me kitty powers!
Super accidentally.
...and I think the power to destroy the world?
Not anymore though!
That means you can help me find her!
Wait a minute!
We're not going to help you do ANYTHING until you turn our friends YOU TURNED TO STONE back to normal!
YEAH!
What?!
Our friends, a whole cabin, turned to stone!
Diane said it was a gorgon that did it!

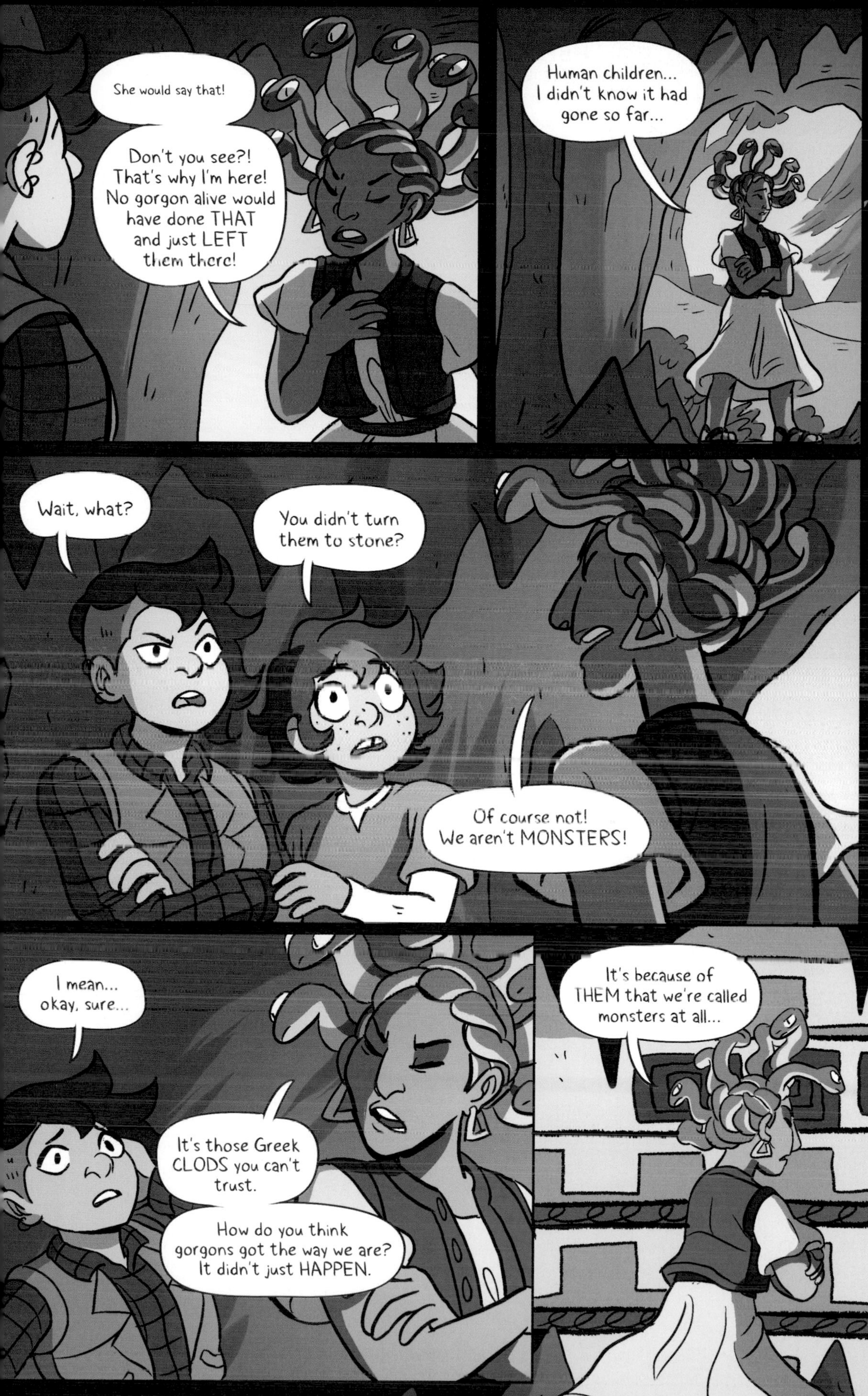
She would say that!
Don't you see?! That's why I'm here! No gorgon alive would have done THAT and just LEFT them there!
Human children... I didn't know it had gone so far...
Wait, what?
You didn't turn them to stone?
Of course not! We aren't MONSTERS!
I mean... okay, sure...
It's those Greek CLODS you can't trust.
How do you think gorgons got the way we are? It didn't just HAPPEN.
It's because of THEM that we're called monsters at all...

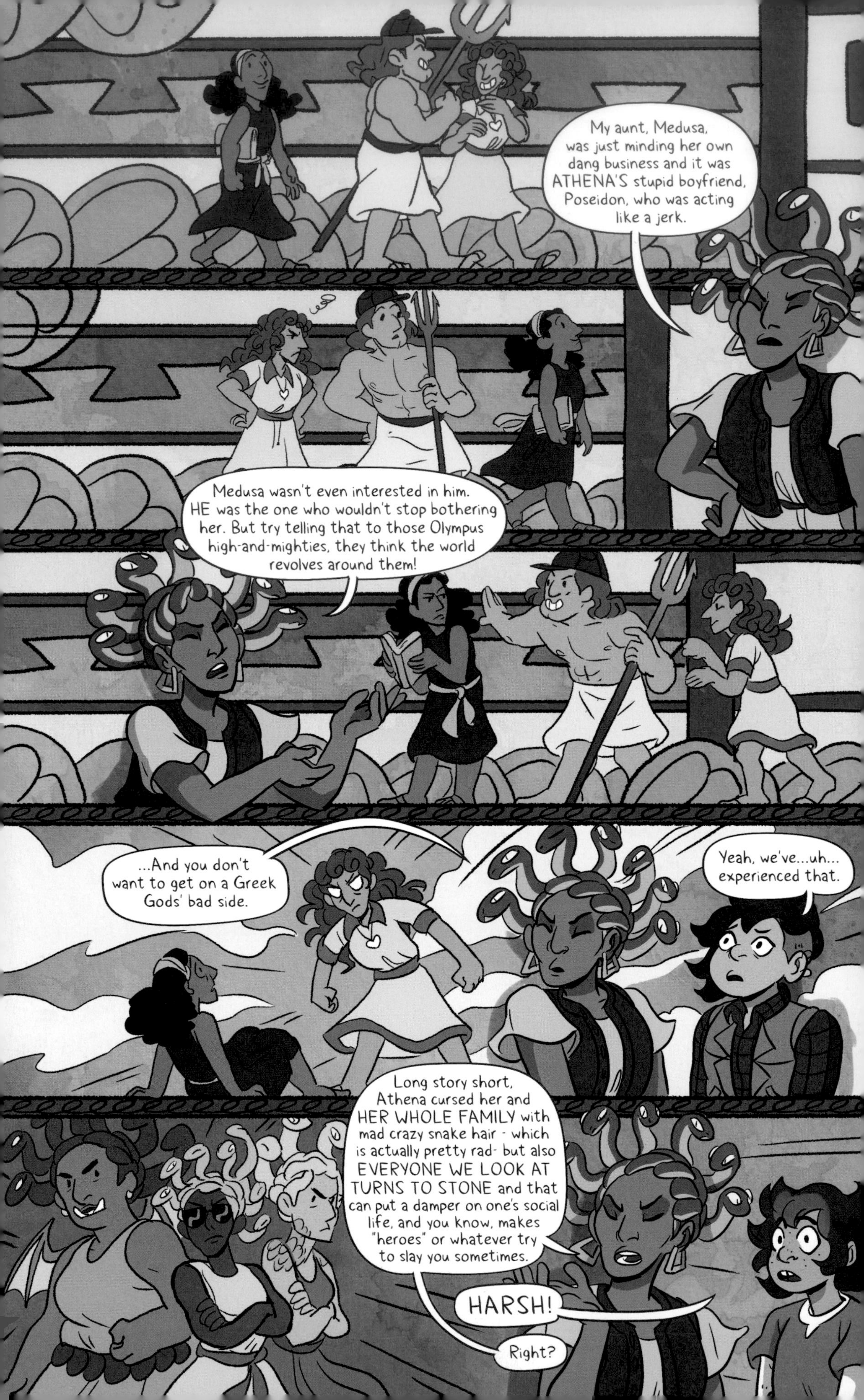
My aunt, Medusa, was just minding her own dang business and it was ATHENA'S stupid boyfriend, Poseidon, who was acting like a jerk.
Medusa wasn't even interested in him. HE was the one who wouldn't stop bothering her. But try telling that to those Olympus high-and-mighties, they think the world revolves around them!
...And you don't want to get on a Greek Gods' bad side.
Yeah, we've...uh... experienced that.
Long story short, Athena cursed her and HER WHOLE FAMILY with mad crazy snake hair - which is actually pretty rad- but also EVERYONE WE LOOK AT TURNS TO STONE and that can put a damper on one's social life, and you know, makes "heroes" or whatever try to slay you sometimes.
HARSH!
Right?

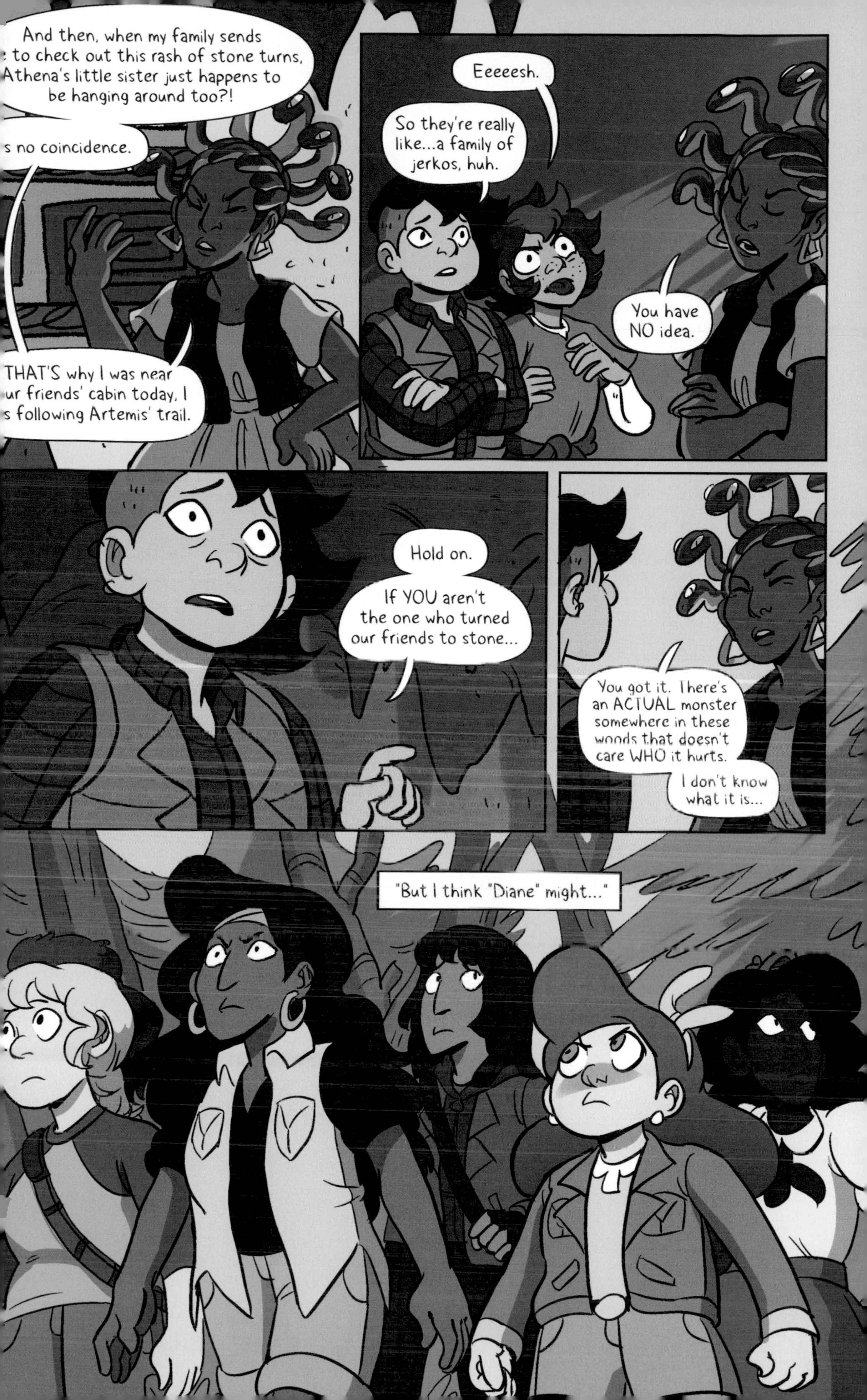
And then, when my family sends
to check out this rash of stone turns,
Athena's little sister just happens to
be hanging around too?!
s no coincidence.
THAT'S why I was near
ur friends' cabin today, I
s following Artemis' trail.
Eeeeesh.
So they're really
like...a family of
jerkos, huh.
You have
NO idea.
Hold on.
If YOU aren't
the one who turned
our friends to stone...
You got it. There's
an ACTUAL monster
somewhere in these
woods that doesn't
care WHO it hurts.
I don't know
what it is...
"But I think "Diane" might..."

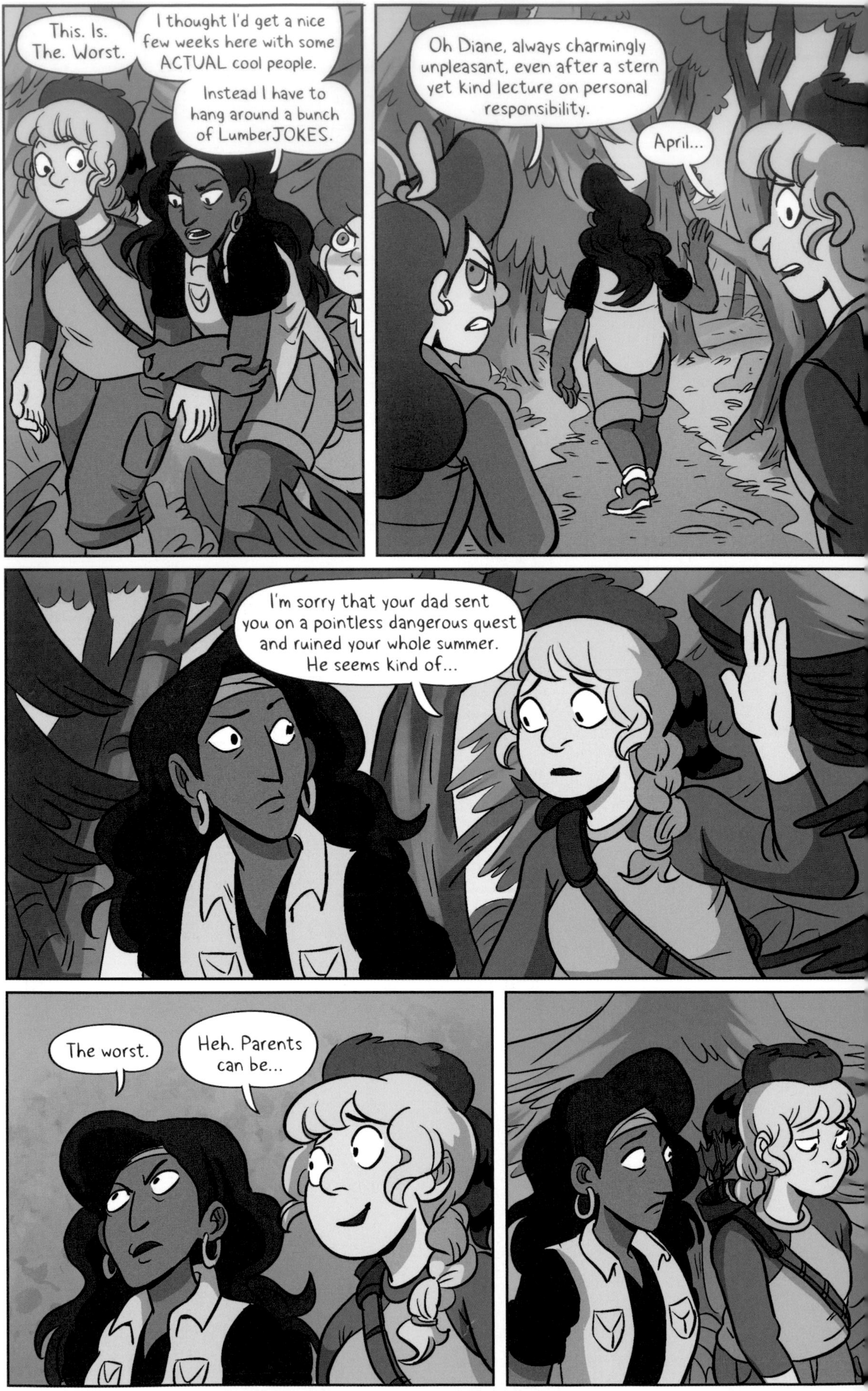
This. Is. The. Worst.
I thought I'd get a nice few weeks here with some ACTUAL cool people.
Instead I have to hang around a bunch of LumberJOKES.
Oh Diane, always charmingly unpleasant, even after a stern yet kind lecture on personal responsibility.
April...
I'm sorry that your dad sent you on a pointless dangerous quest and ruined your whole summer. He seems kind of...
The worst.
Heh. Parents can be...

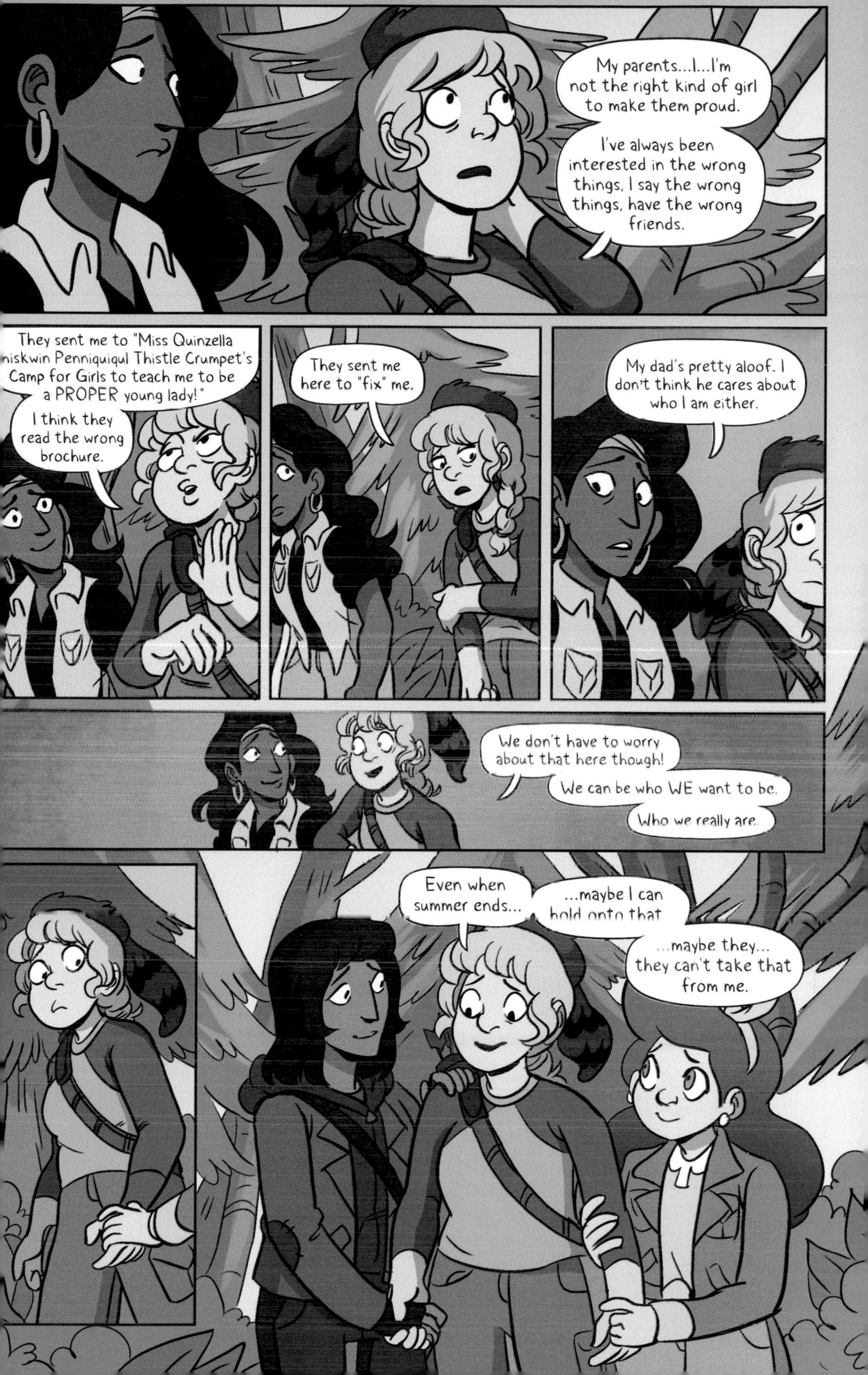

My parents...I...I'm not the right kind of girl to make them proud.
I've always been interested in the wrong things, I say the wrong things, have the wrong friends.
They sent me to "Miss Quinzella niskwin Penniquiqul Thistle Crumpet's Camp for Girls to teach me to be a PROPER young lady!"
I think they read the wrong brochure.
They sent me here to "fix" me.
My dad's pretty aloof. I don't think he cares about who I am either.
We don't have to worry about that here though!
We can be who WE want to be.
Who we really are.
Even when summer ends...
...maybe I can hold onto that
...maybe they... they can't take that from me.

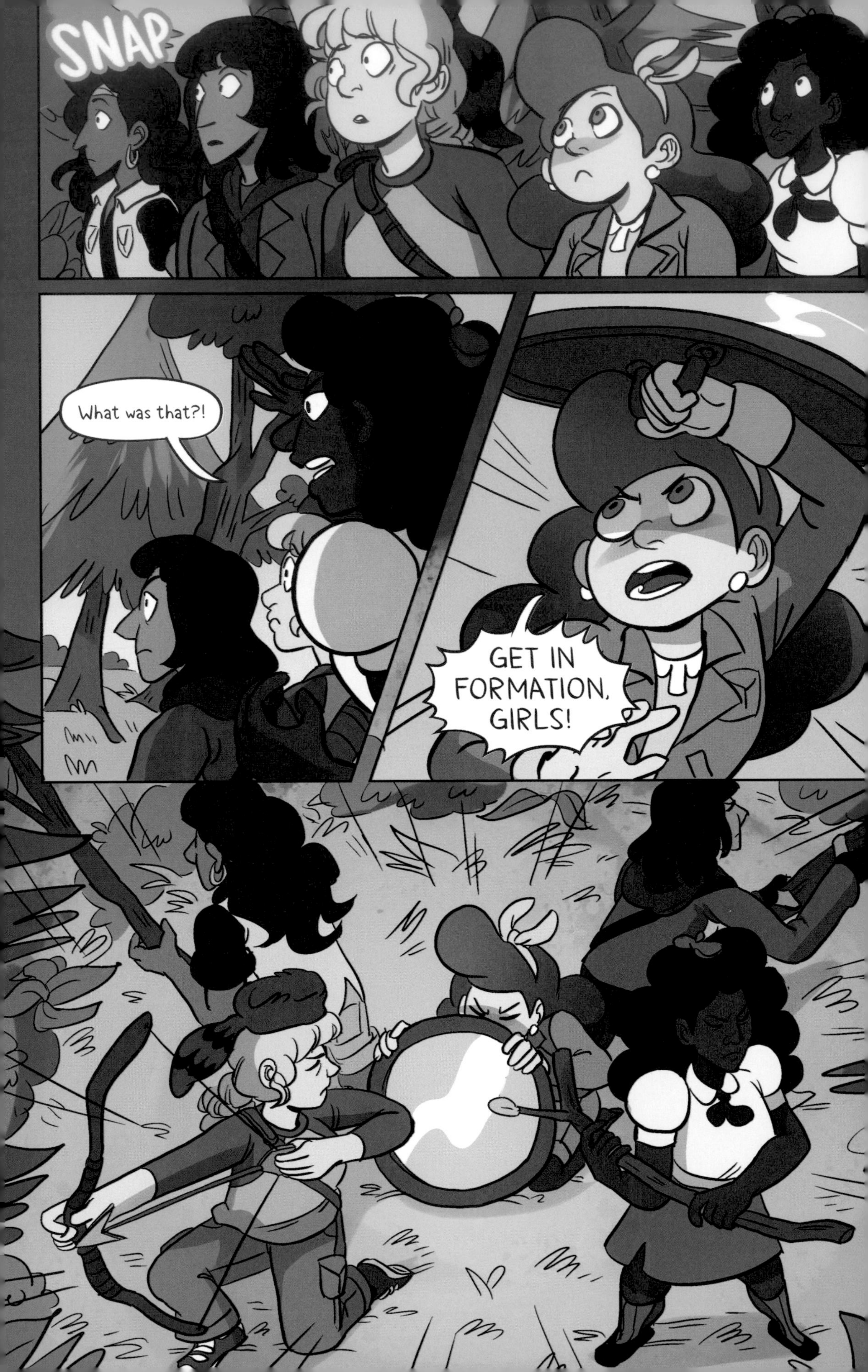
SNAP
What was that?!
GET IN FORMATION, GIRLS!

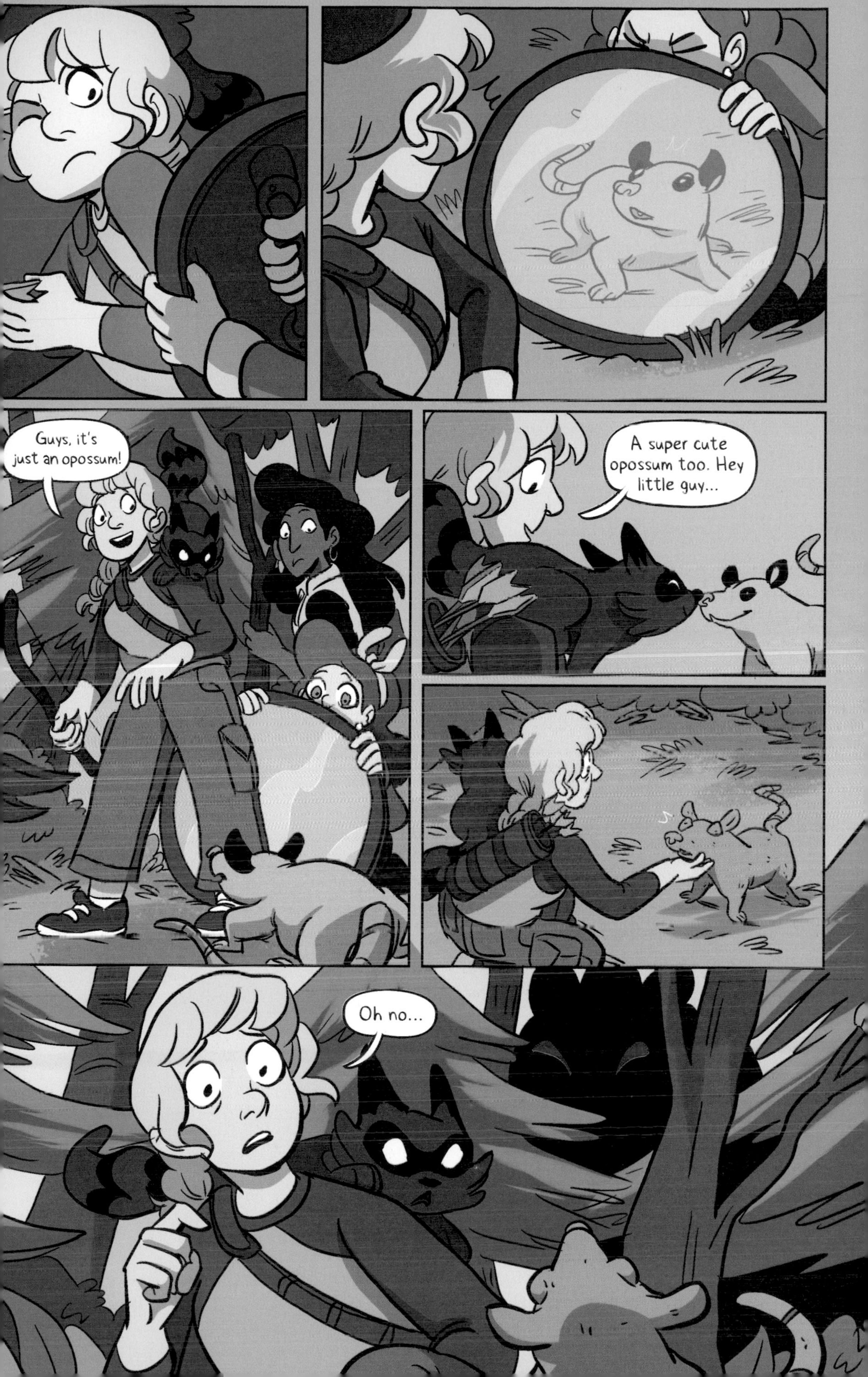
Guys, it's just an opossum!
A super cute opossum too. Hey little guy...
Oh no...

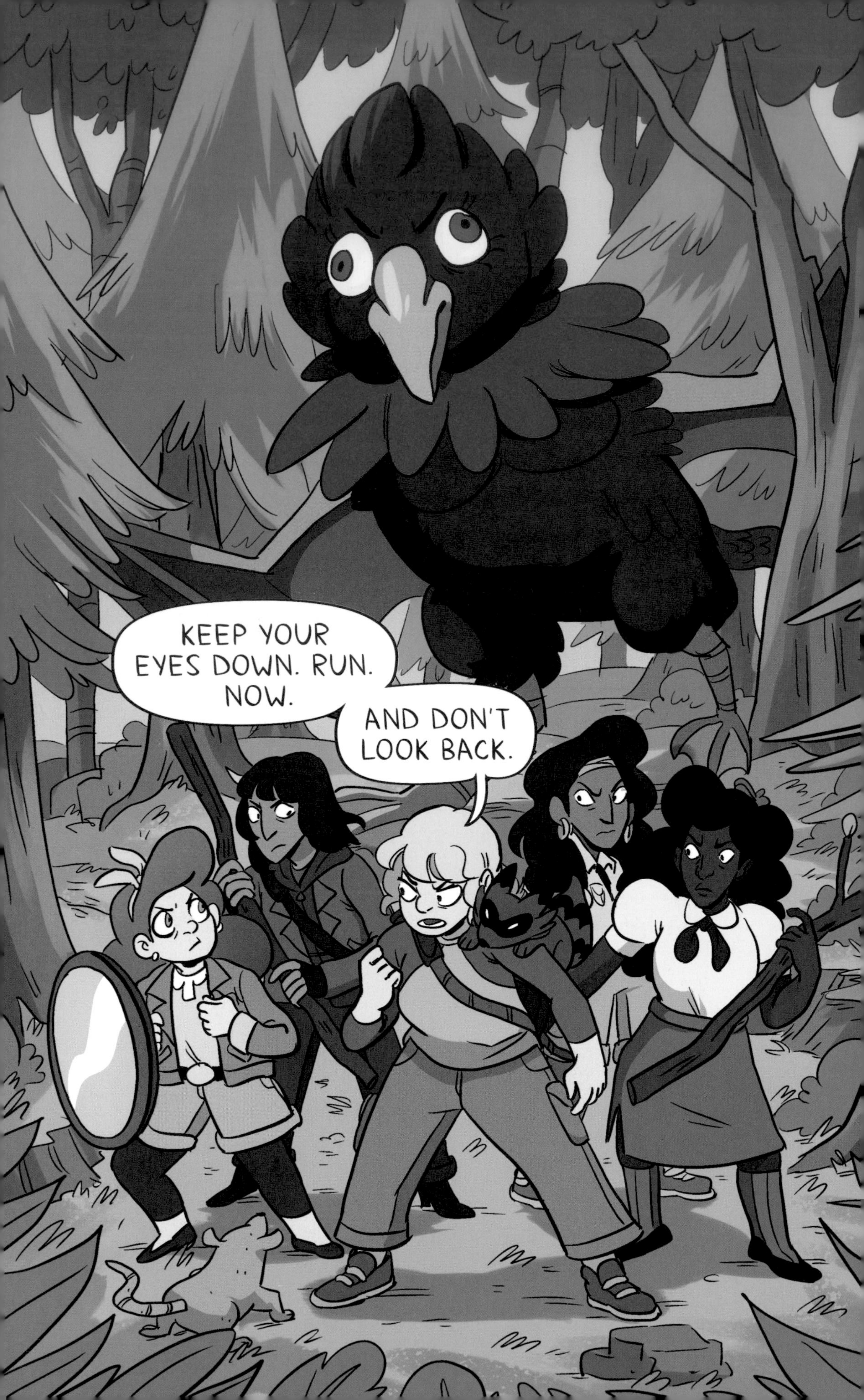
KEEP YOUR EYES DOWN. RUN. NOW.
AND DON'T LOOK BACK.

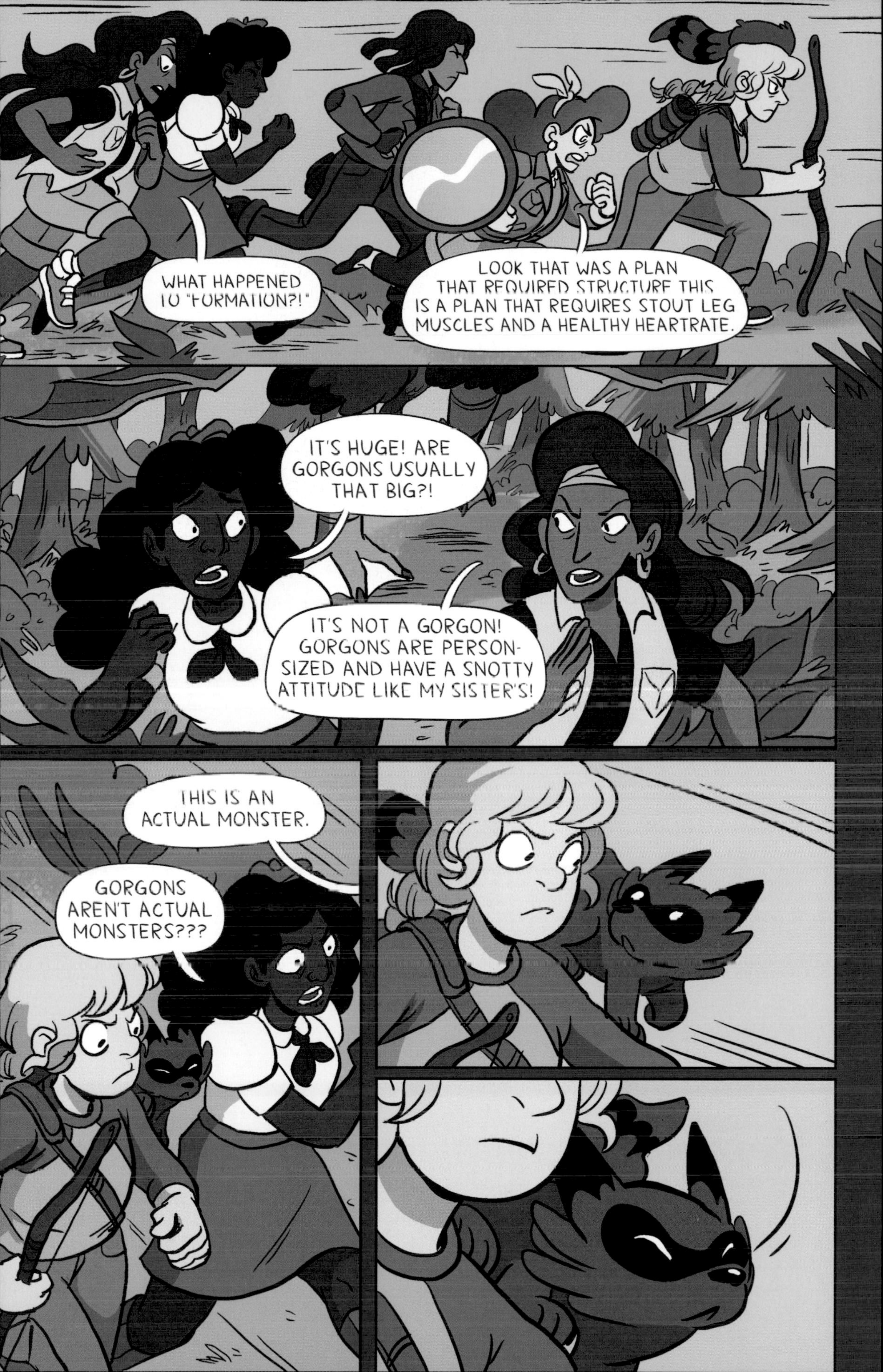
WHAT HAPPENED TO "FORMATION?!"
LOOK THAT WAS A PLAN THAT REQUIRED STRUCTURE THIS IS A PLAN THAT REQUIRES STOUT LEG MUSCLES AND A HEALTHY HEARTRATE.
IT'S HUGE! ARE GORGONS USUALLY THAT BIG?!
IT'S NOT A GORGON! GORGONS ARE PERSON-SIZED AND HAVE A SNOTTY ATTITUDE LIKE MY SISTER'S!
THIS IS AN ACTUAL MONSTER.
GORGONS AREN'T ACTUAL MONSTERS???

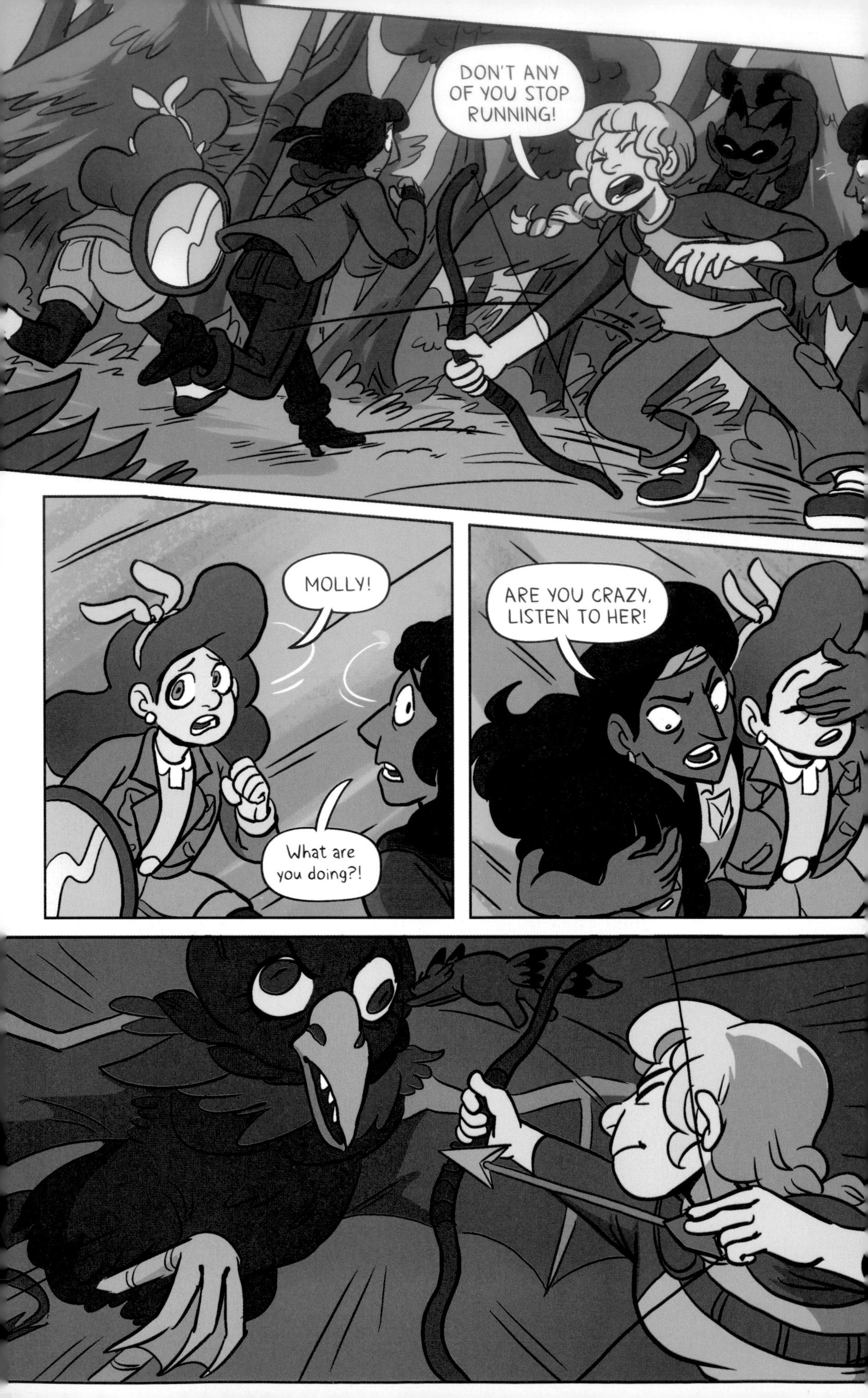

DON'T ANY OF YOU STOP RUNNING!
MOLLY!
What are you doing?!
ARE YOU CRAZY, LISTEN TO HER!

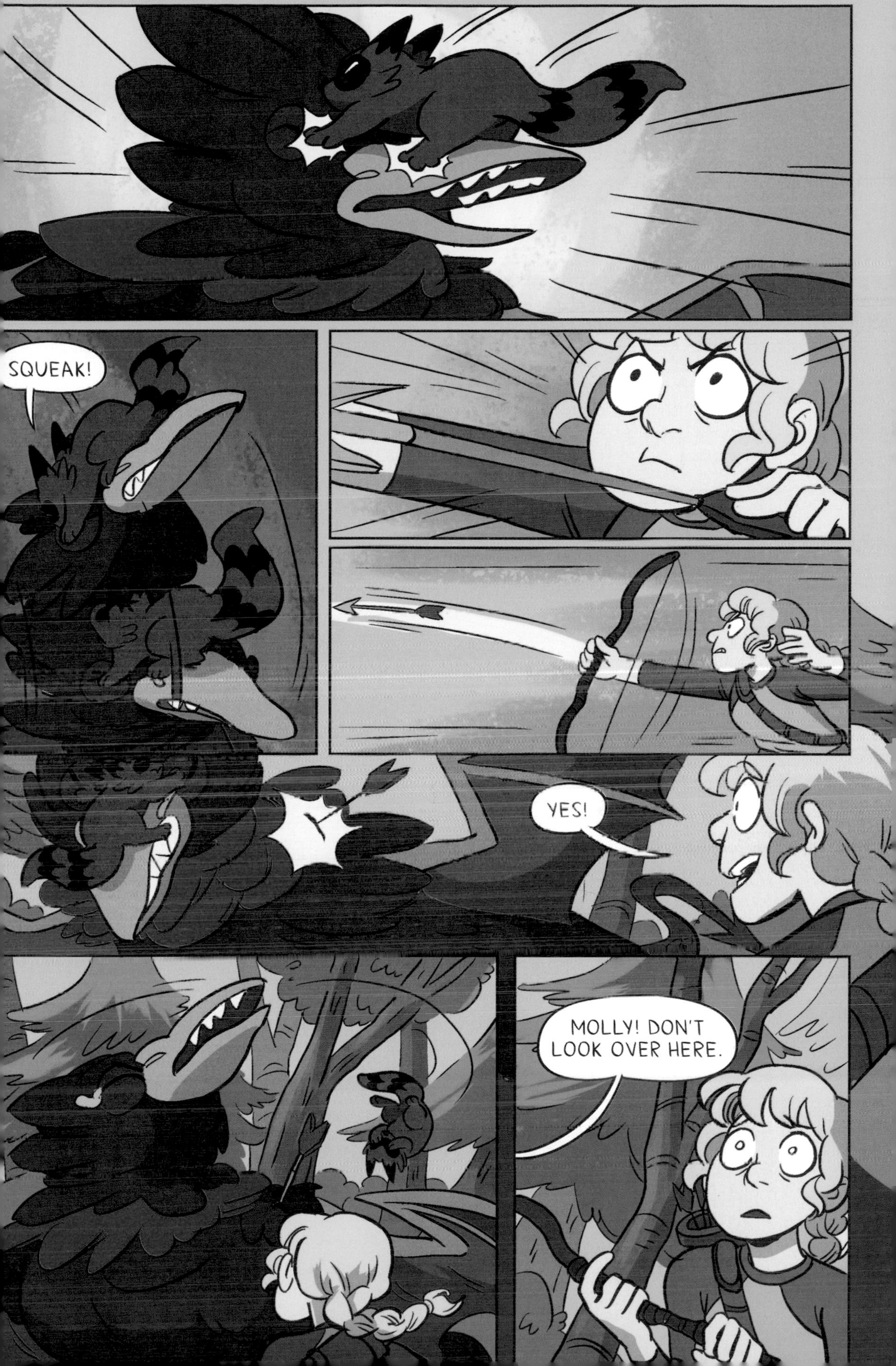
SQUEAK!
YES!
MOLLY! DON'T LOOK OVER HERE.

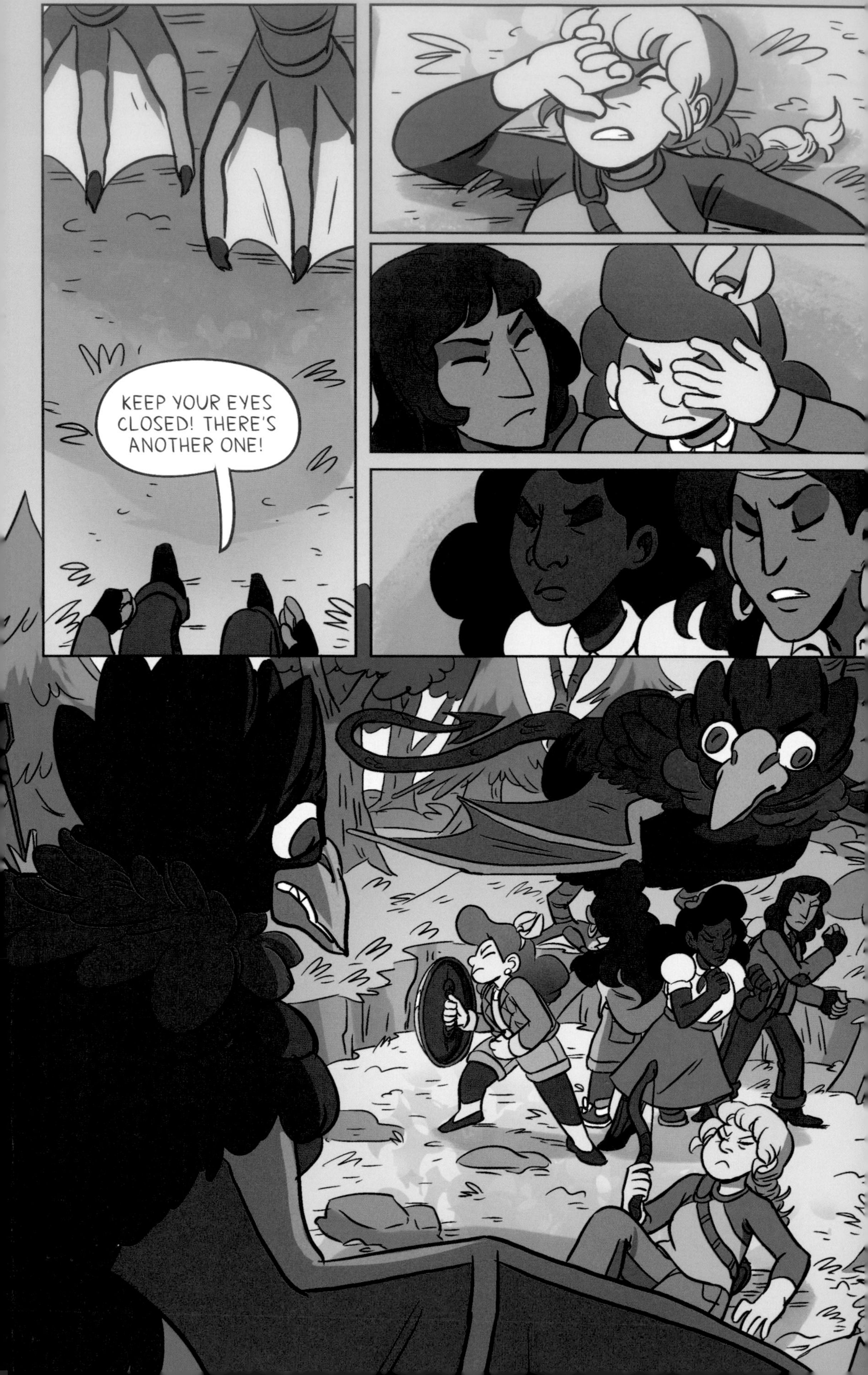
KEEP YOUR EYES CLOSED! THERE'S ANOTHER ONE!

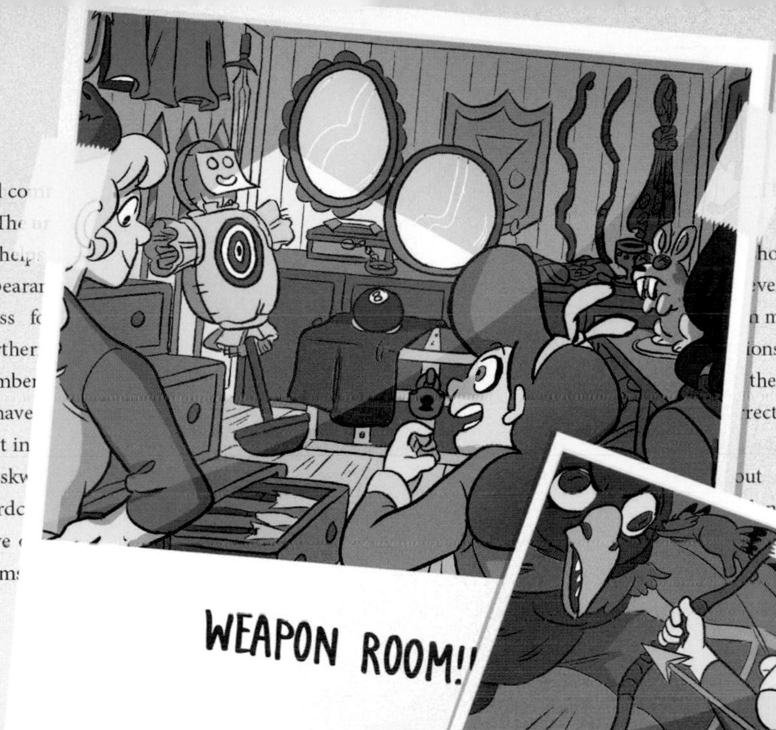
WEAPON ROOM!!

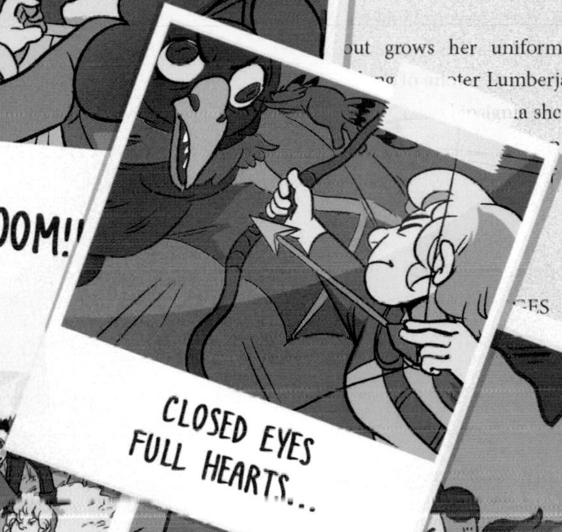
CLOSED EYES
FULL HEARTS...

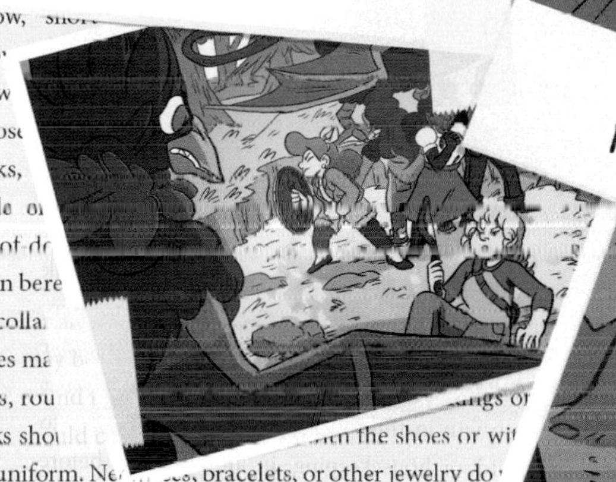

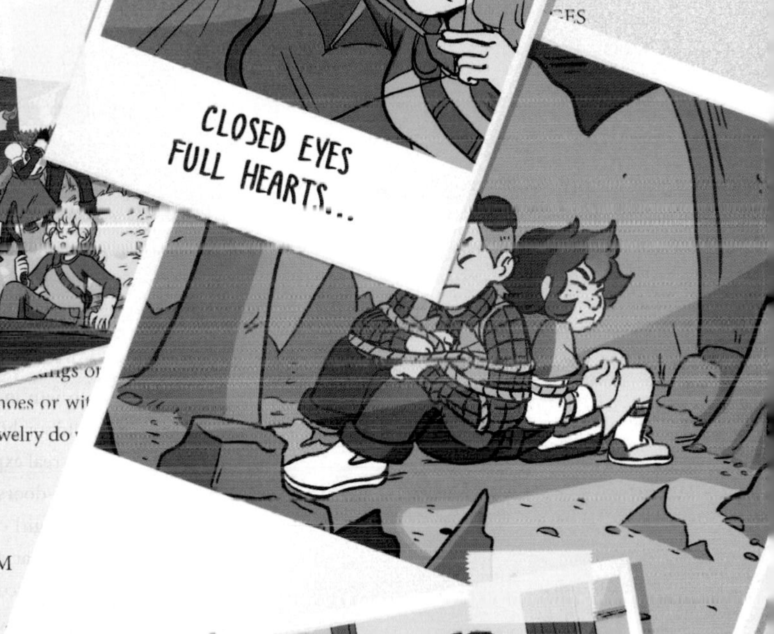

will com

The u

It helps

appearan

dress fo

Further

Lumber

to have

part in

Thiskw

Hardc

have

thems

HE UNIFORM

hould be worn at camp vents when Lumberjanes n may also be worn at other ions. It should be worn as a the uniform dress with rrect shoes, and stocking or

out grows her uniform or ng to another Lumberjane. a she has her her

The yellow, emb the w choose slacks, made o out-of-d green bere the colla Shoes ma heels, rou ings or socks shou with the shoes or wi the uniform. Ne ces, bracelets, or other jewelry do belong with a Lumberjane uniform.

HOW TO WEAR THE UNIFORM

To look well in a uniform demans first of uniform be kept in good condition—clean pressed. See that the skirt is the right length for your own height and build, that the belt is adjusted to your waist, that your shoes and stockings are in keeping with the uniform, that you watch your posture and carry yourself with dignity and grace. If the beret is removed indoors, be sure that your hair is neat and kept in place with an insonspicuous clip or ribbon. When you wear a Lumberjane uniform you are identified as a member of this organization and you should be doubly careful to conduct yourself in a way that will show everyone that courtesy and thoughtfullness are part of being a Lumberjane. People are likely to judge a whole nation by the selfishness of a few individuals, to criticize a whole family because of the misconduct of one member, and to feel unkindly toward and organization because of the

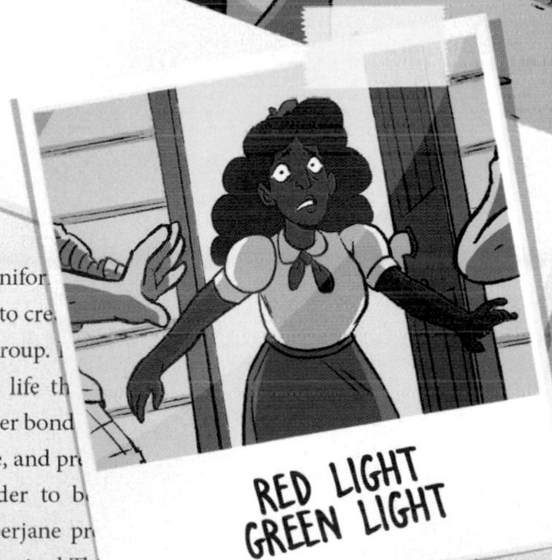
RED LIGHT
GREEN LIGHT

The unifor helps to cre in a group. active life th another bond future, and pr in order to b Lumberjane pr Penniquiqul Thi Lady Types, but m will wish to have one. They can either bu the uniform, or make it themselves from materials available at the trading post.

LUMBERJANES FIELD MANUAL

CHAPTER
THIRTY-ONE

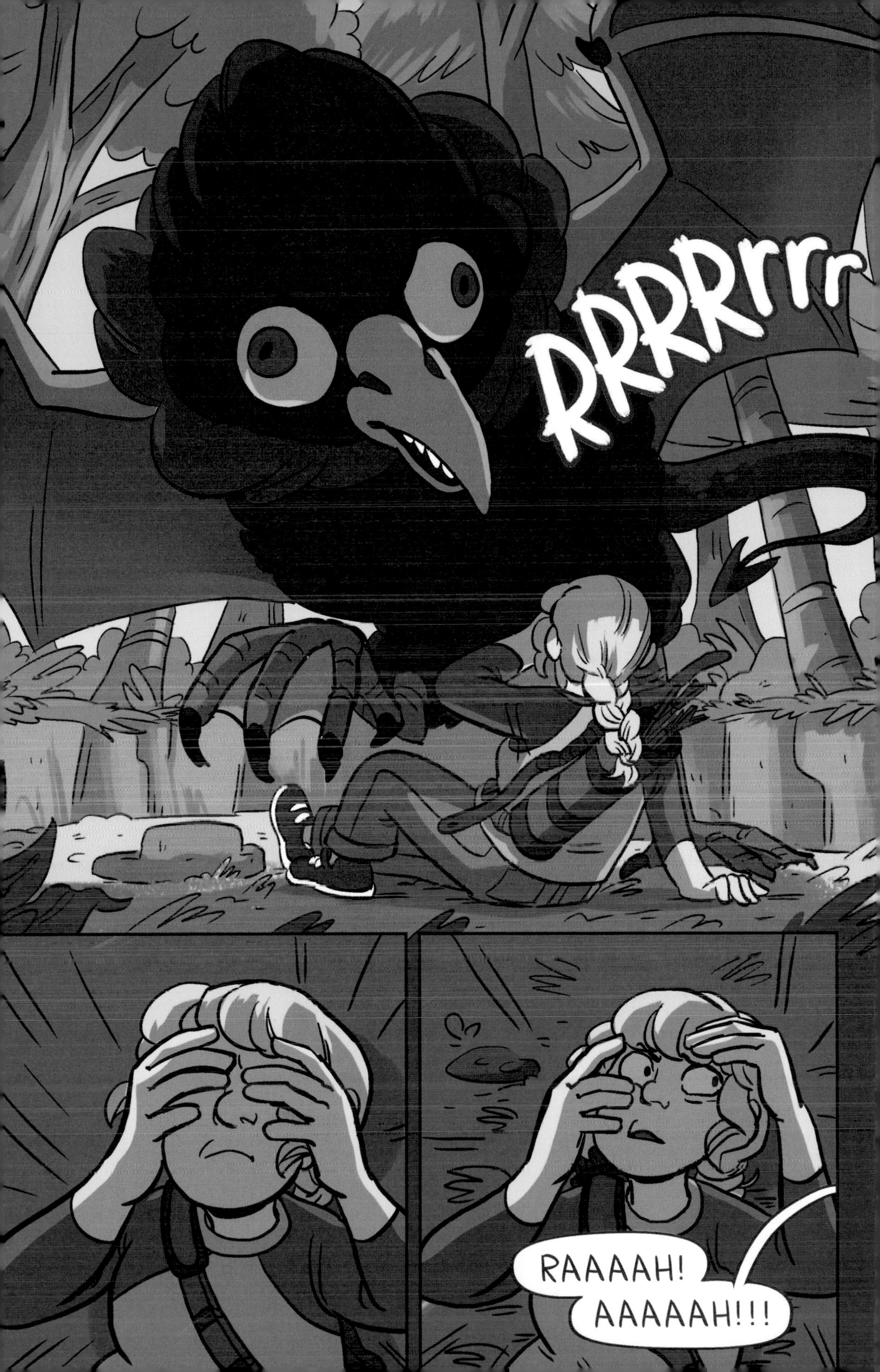
RRRRrrr
RAAAAH! AAAAAH!!!

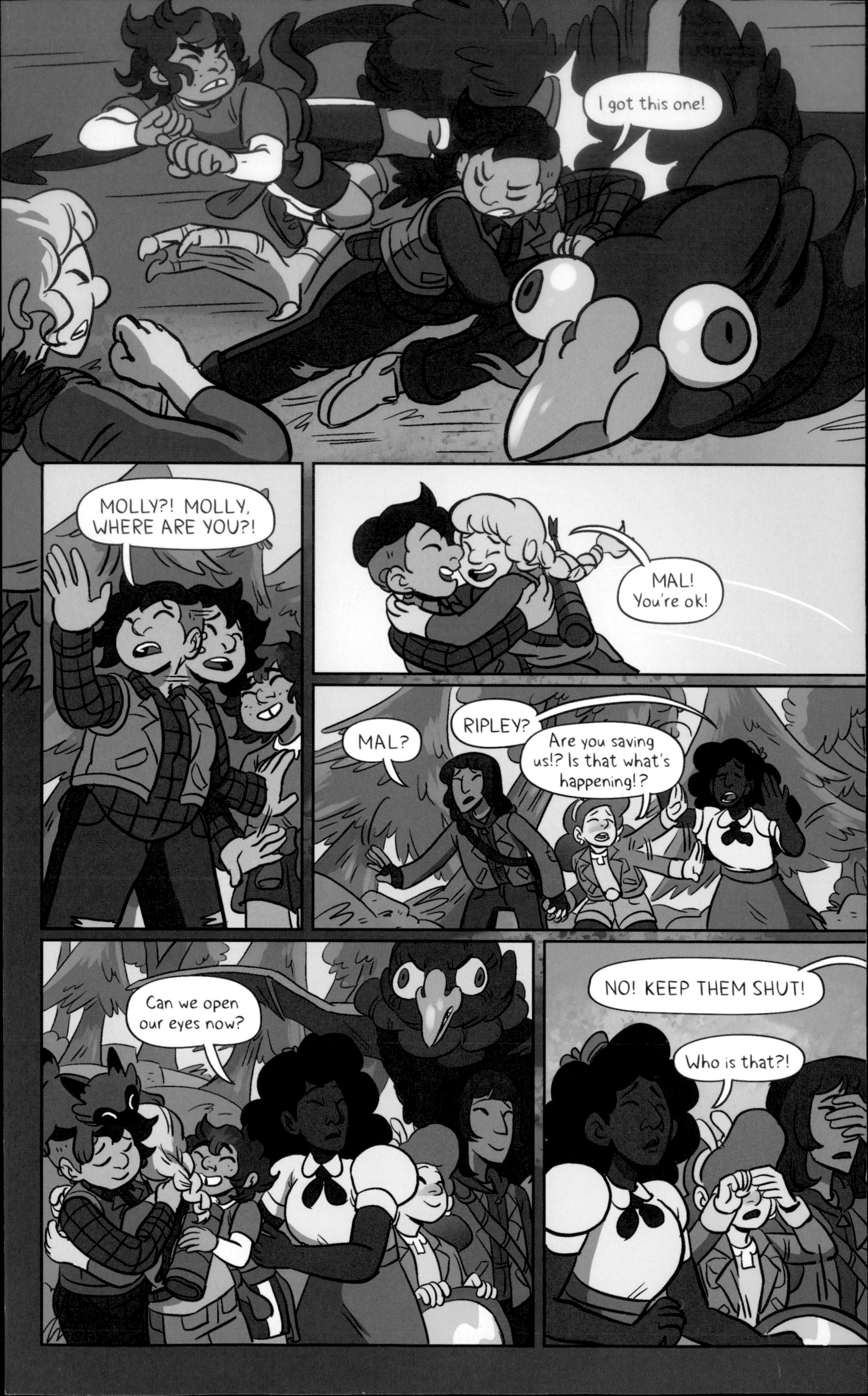
I got this one!
MOLLY?! MOLLY, WHERE ARE YOU?!
MAL! You're ok!
MAL?
RIPLEY?
Are you saving us!? Is that what's happening!?
Can we open our eyes now?
NO! KEEP THEM SHUT!
Who is that?!

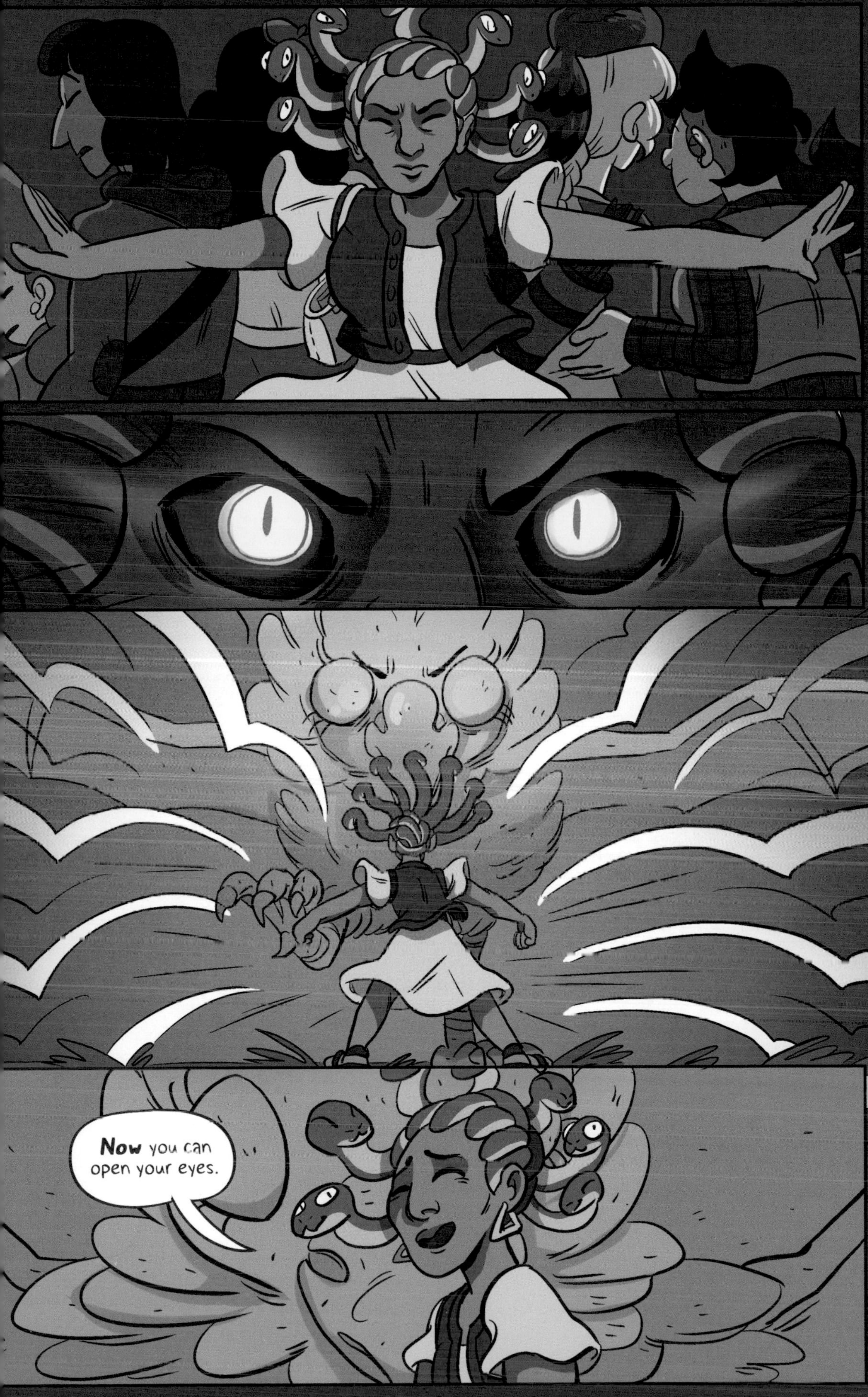
Now you can open your eyes.

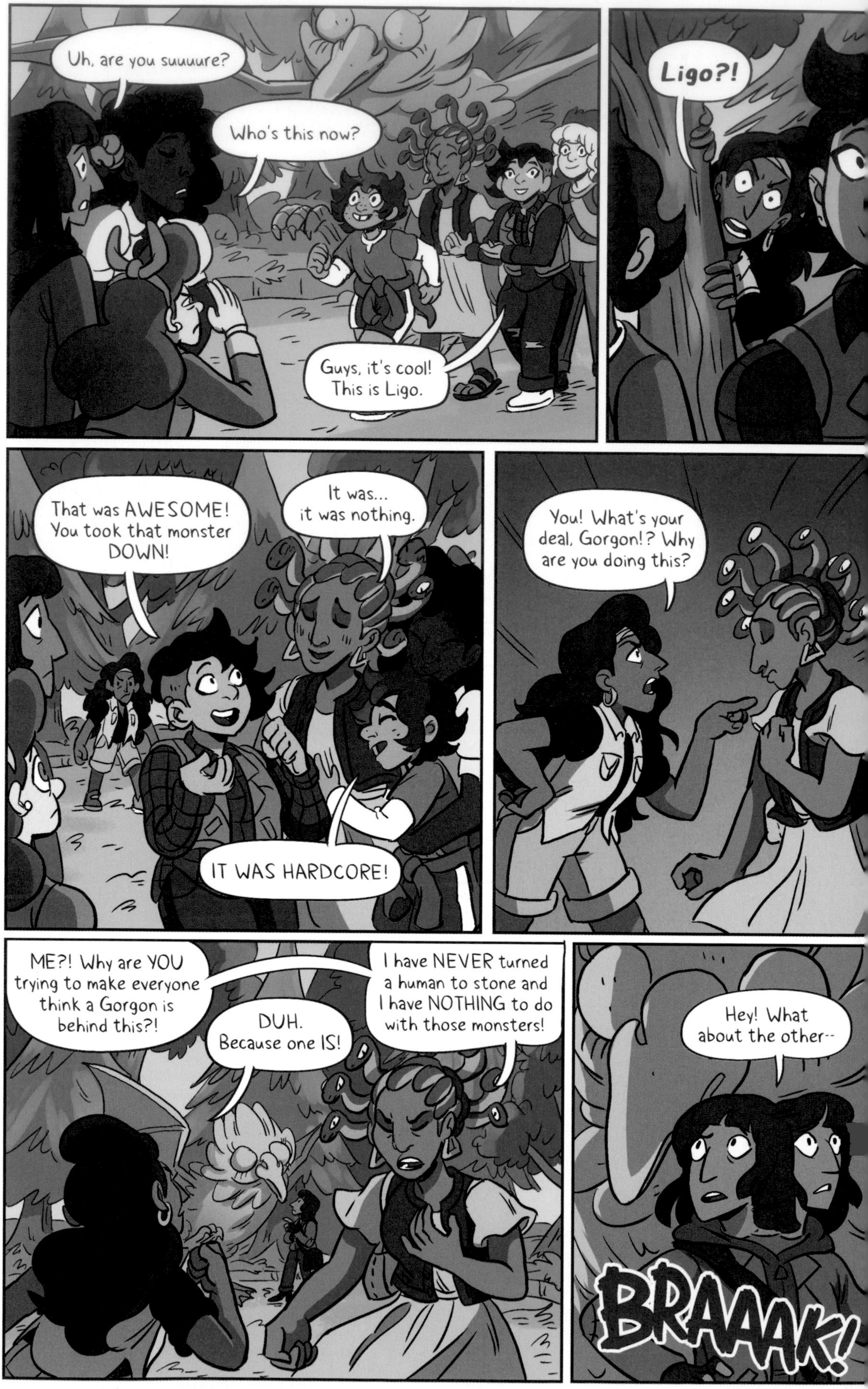
Uh, are you suuuure?
Who's this now?
Guys, it's cool! This is Ligo.
Ligo?!
That was AWESOME! You took that monster DOWN!
It was... it was nothing.
IT WAS HARDCORE!
You! What's your deal, Gorgon!? Why are you doing this?
ME?! Why are YOU trying to make everyone think a Gorgon is behind this?!
DUH. Because one IS!
I have NEVER turned a human to stone and I have NOTHING to do with those monsters!
Hey! What about the other--
BRAAAK!

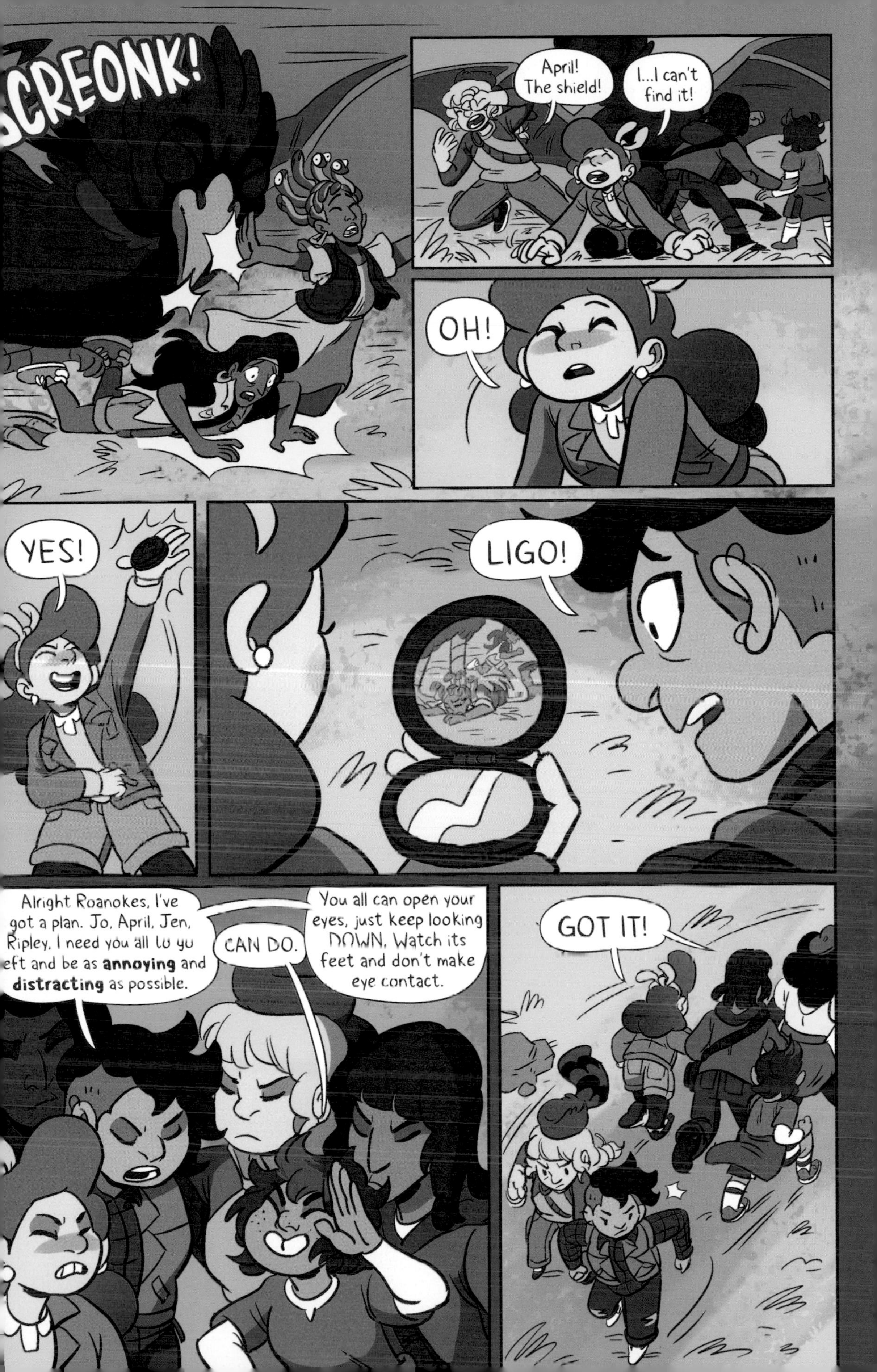
SCREONK!
April! The shield!
I...I can't find it!
OH!
YES!
LIGO!
Alright Roanokes, I've got a plan. Jo, April, Jen, Ripley, I need you all to go left and be as **annoying** and **distracting** as possible.
CAN DO.
You all can open your eyes, just keep looking DOWN. Watch its feet and don't make eye contact.
GOT IT!

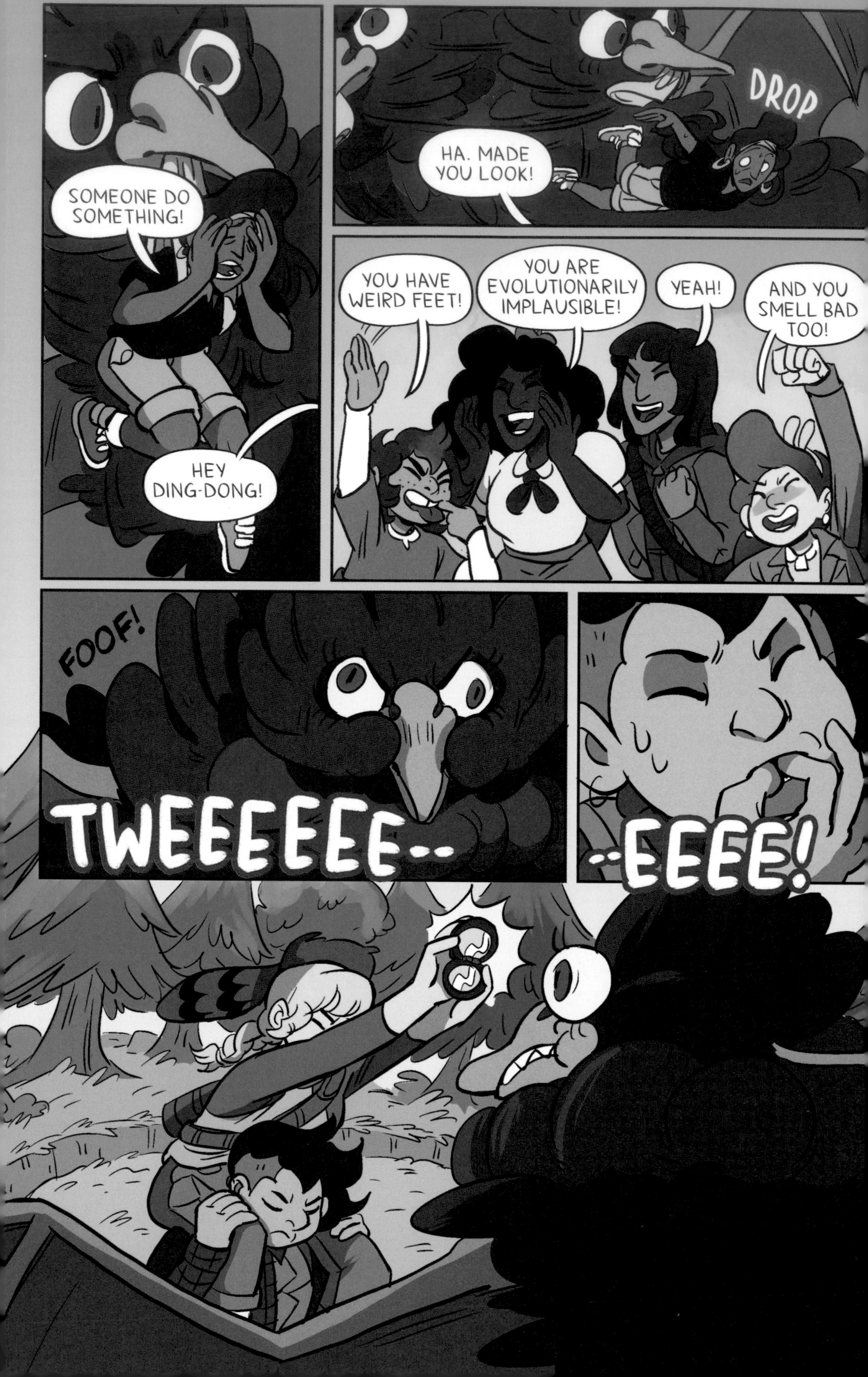
SOMEONE DO SOMETHING!
HEY DING-DONG!
HA. MADE YOU LOOK!
DROP
YOU HAVE WEIRD FEET!
YOU ARE EVOLUTIONARILY IMPLAUSIBLE!
YEAH!
AND YOU SMELL BAD TOO!
FOOF!
TWEEEEEE--
--EEEE!

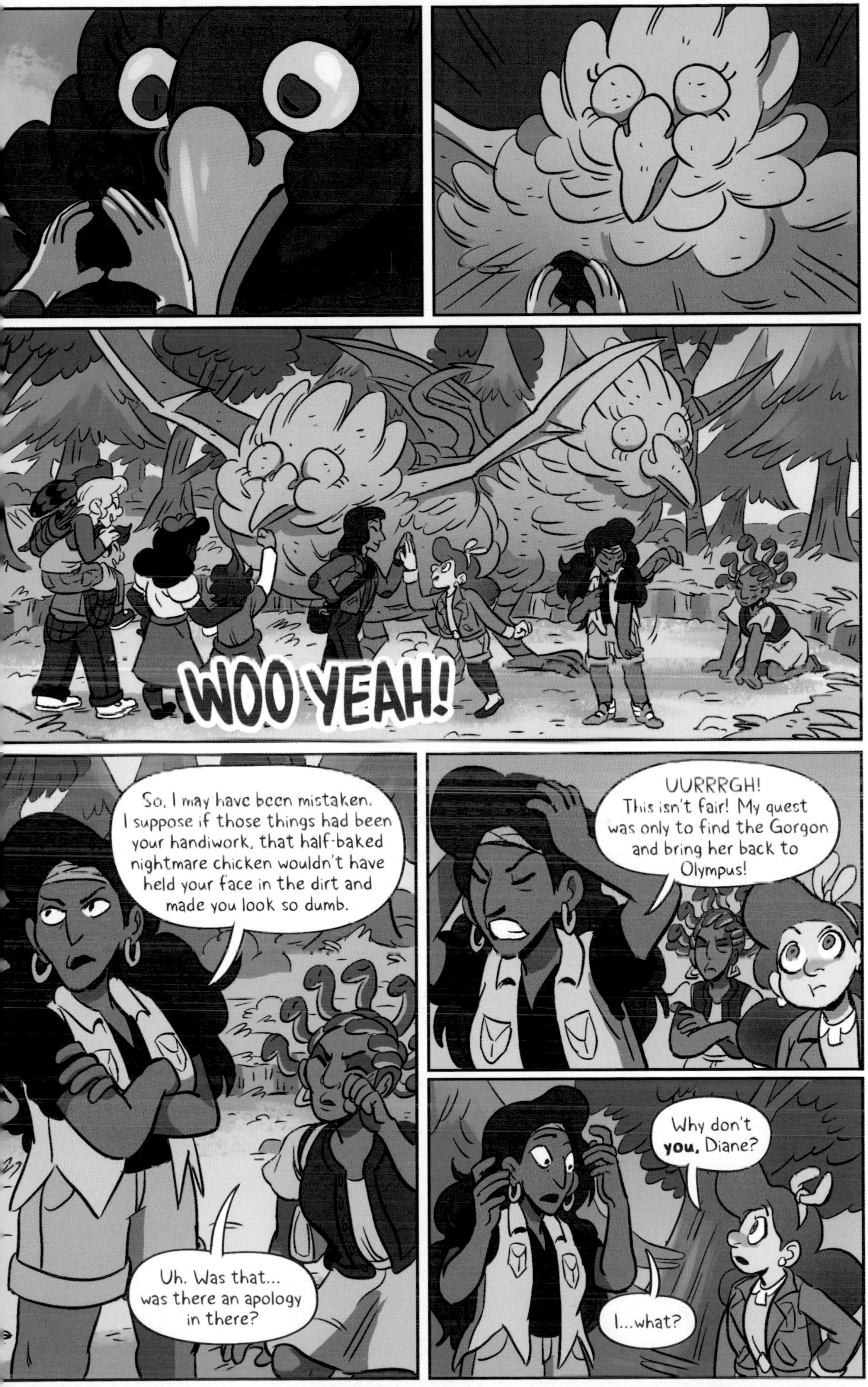
WOO YEAH!
So, I may have been mistaken. I suppose if those things had been your handiwork, that half-baked nightmare chicken wouldn't have held your face in the dirt and made you look so dumb.
Uh. Was that... was there an apology in there?
UURRRGH! This isn't fair! My quest was only to find the Gorgon and bring her back to Olympus!
Why don't **you,** Diane?
I...what?

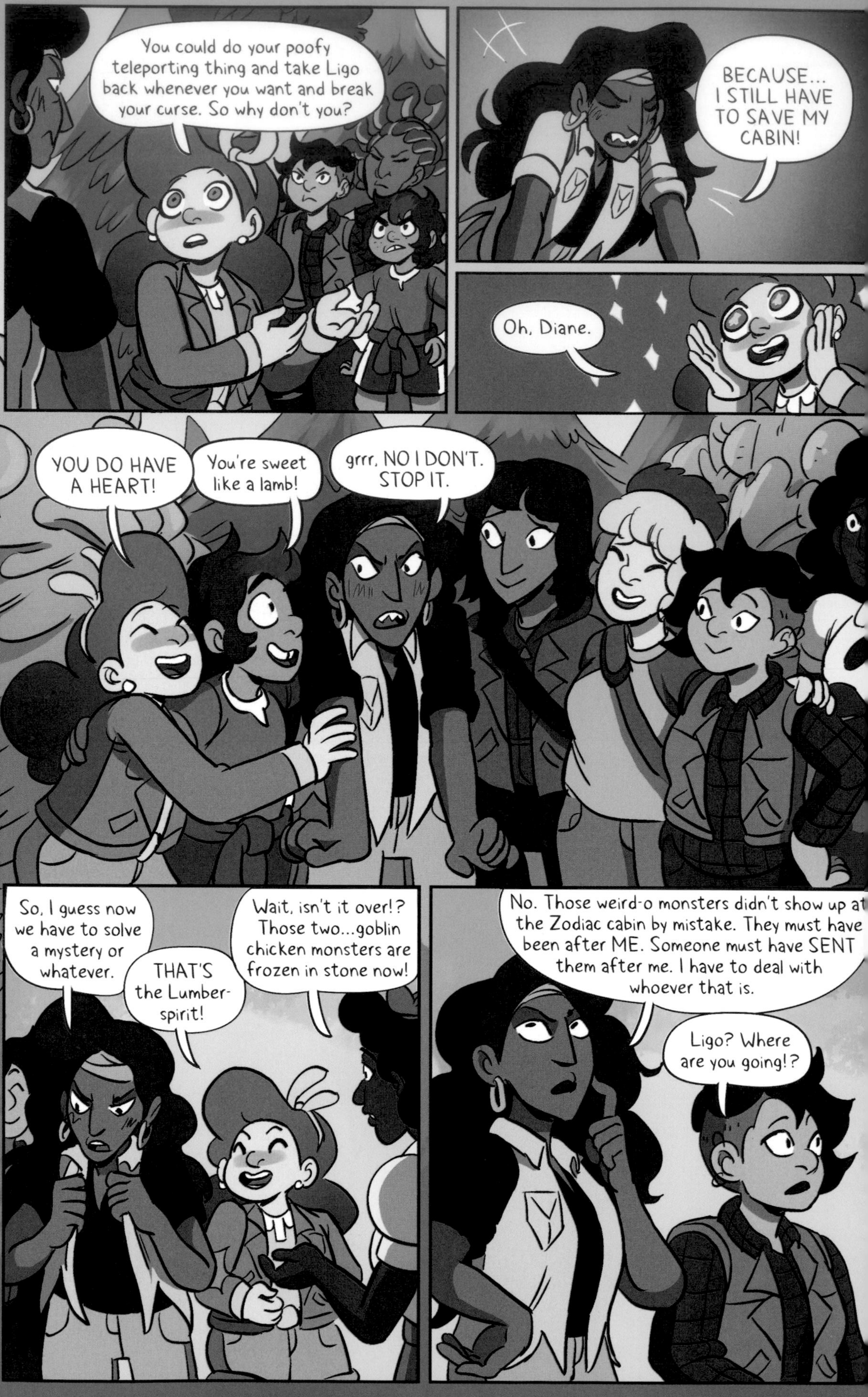
You could do your poofy teleporting thing and take Ligo back whenever you want and break your curse. So why don't you?
BECAUSE... I STILL HAVE TO SAVE MY CABIN!
Oh, Diane.
YOU DO HAVE A HEART!
You're sweet like a lamb!
grrr, NO I DON'T. STOP IT.
So, I guess now we have to solve a mystery or whatever.
THAT'S the Lumber-spirit!
Wait, isn't it over!? Those two...goblin chicken monsters are frozen in stone now!
No. Those weird-o monsters didn't show up at the Zodiac cabin by mistake. They must have been after ME. Someone must have SENT them after me. I have to deal with whoever that is.
Ligo? Where are you going!?

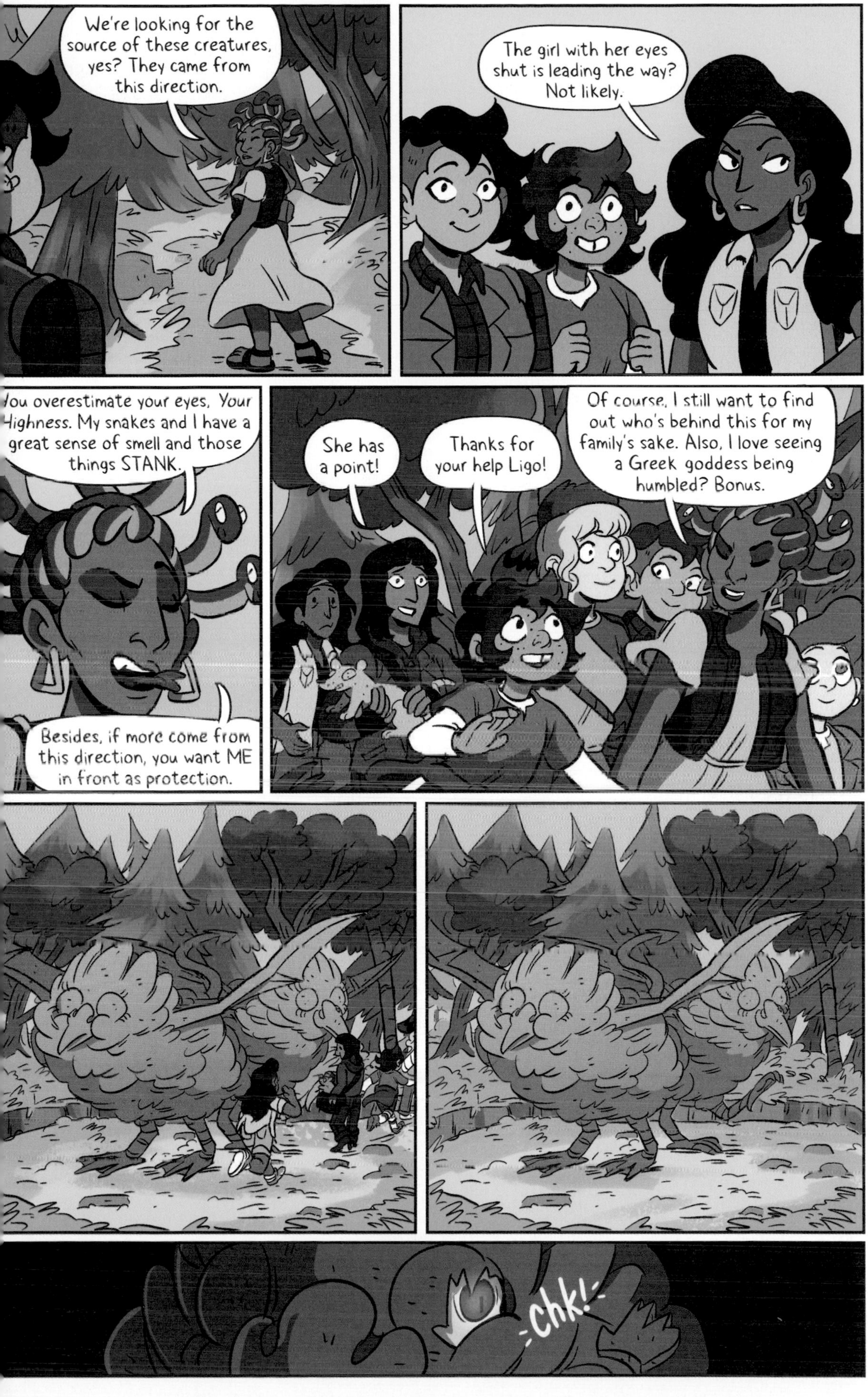
We're looking for the source of these creatures, yes? They came from this direction.
The girl with her eyes shut is leading the way? Not likely.
You overestimate your eyes, Your Highness. My snakes and I have a great sense of smell and those things STANK.
Besides, if more come from this direction, you want ME in front as protection.
She has a point!
Thanks for your help Ligo!
Of course, I still want to find out who's behind this for my family's sake. Also, I love seeing a Greek goddess being humbled? Bonus.
Chk!

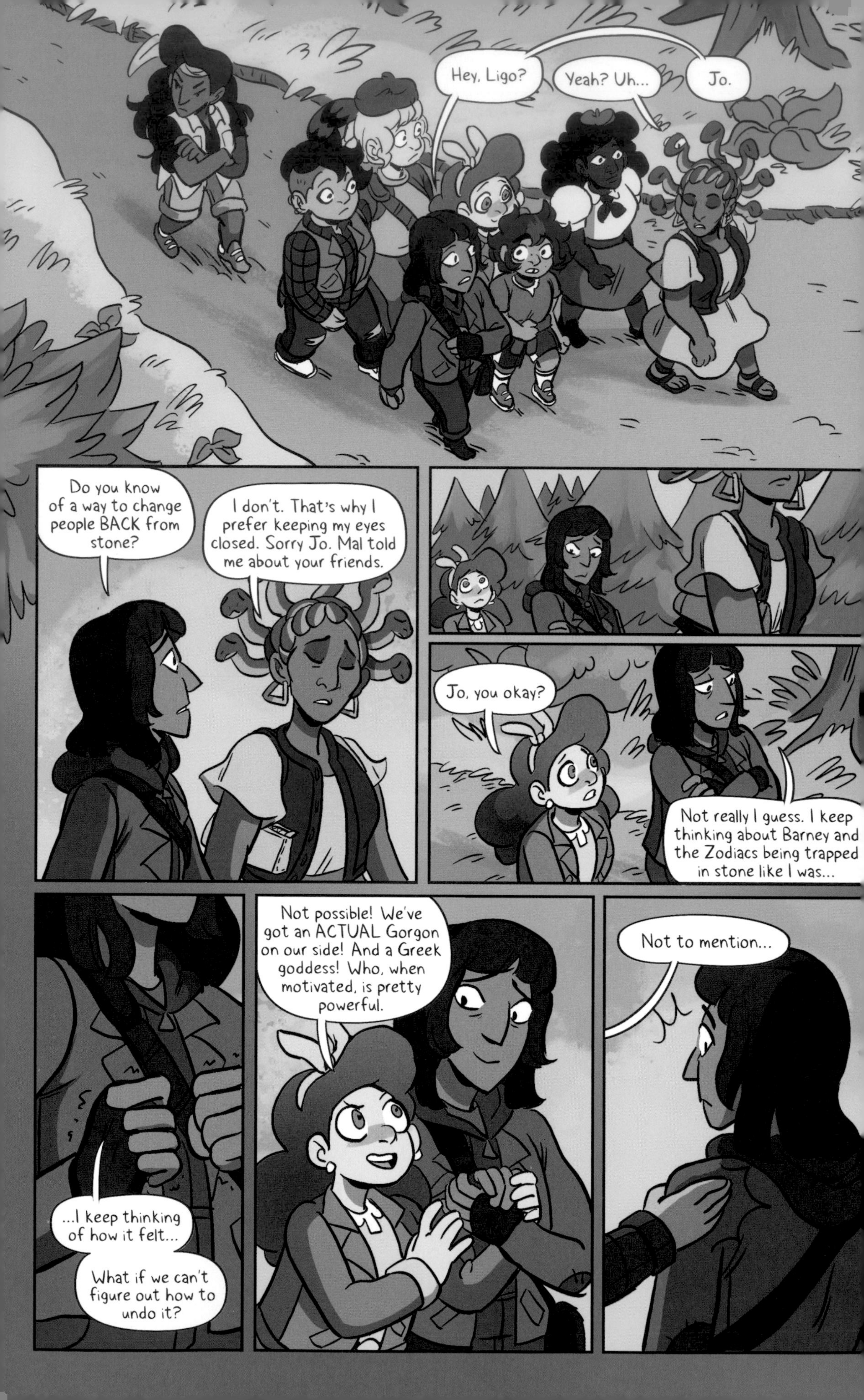
Hey, Ligo?
Yeah? Uh...
Jo.
Do you know of a way to change people BACK from stone?
I don't. That's why I prefer keeping my eyes closed. Sorry Jo. Mal told me about your friends.
Jo, you okay?
Not really I guess. I keep thinking about Barney and the Zodiacs being trapped in stone like I was...
...I keep thinking of how it felt...
What if we can't figure out how to undo it?
Not possible! We've got an ACTUAL Gorgon on our side! And a Greek goddess! Who, when motivated, is pretty powerful.
Not to mention...

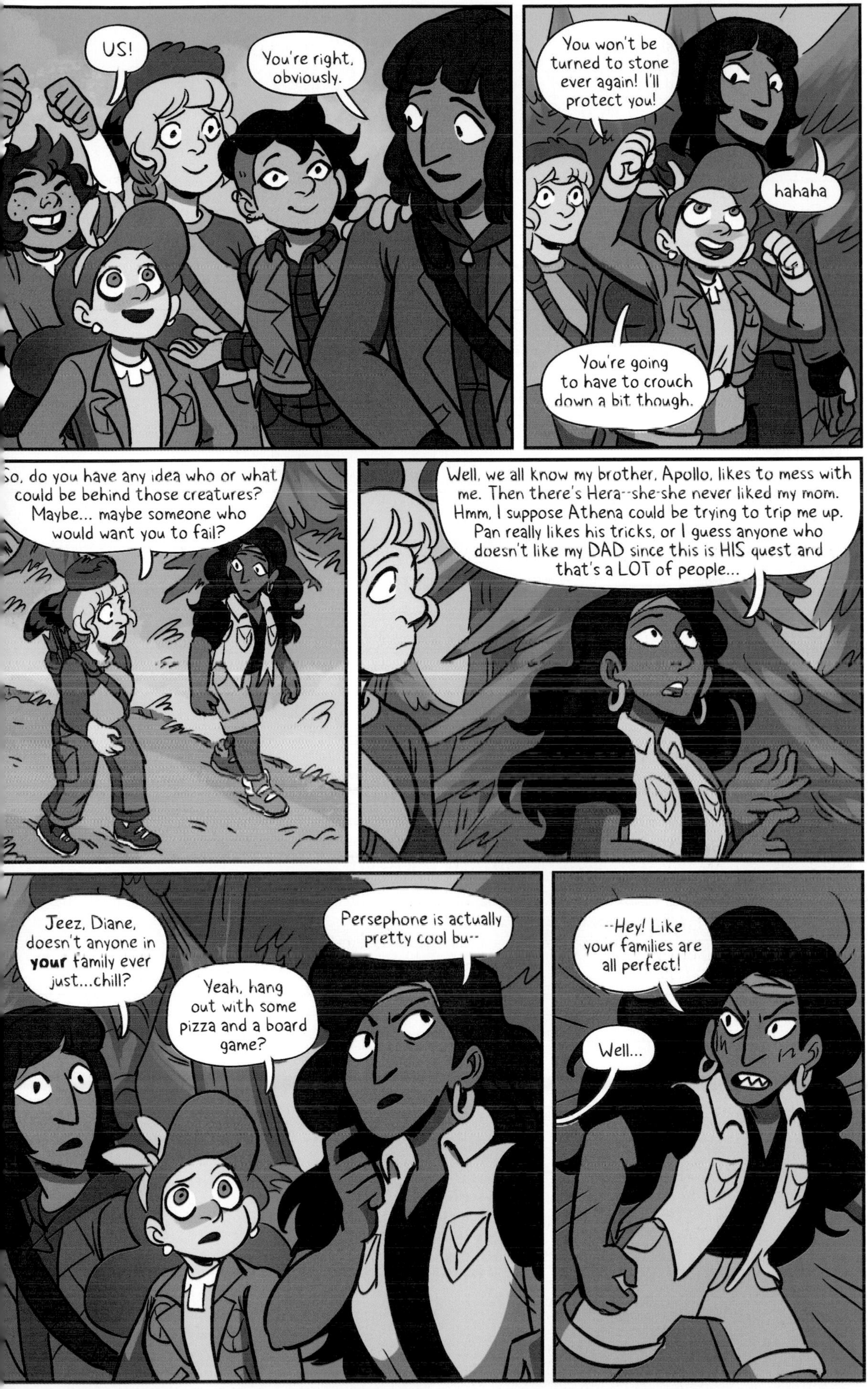
US!
You're right, obviously.
You won't be turned to stone ever again! I'll protect you!
hahaha
You're going to have to crouch down a bit though.
So, do you have any idea who or what could be behind those creatures? Maybe... maybe someone who would want you to fail?
Well, we all know my brother, Apollo, likes to mess with me. Then there's Hera--she-she never liked my mom. Hmm, I suppose Athena could be trying to trip me up. Pan really likes his tricks, or I guess anyone who doesn't like my DAD since this is HIS quest and that's a LOT of people...
Jeez, Diane, doesn't anyone in **your** family ever just...chill?
Yeah, hang out with some pizza and a board game?
Persephone is actually pretty cool bu--
--Hey! Like your families are all perfect!
Well...

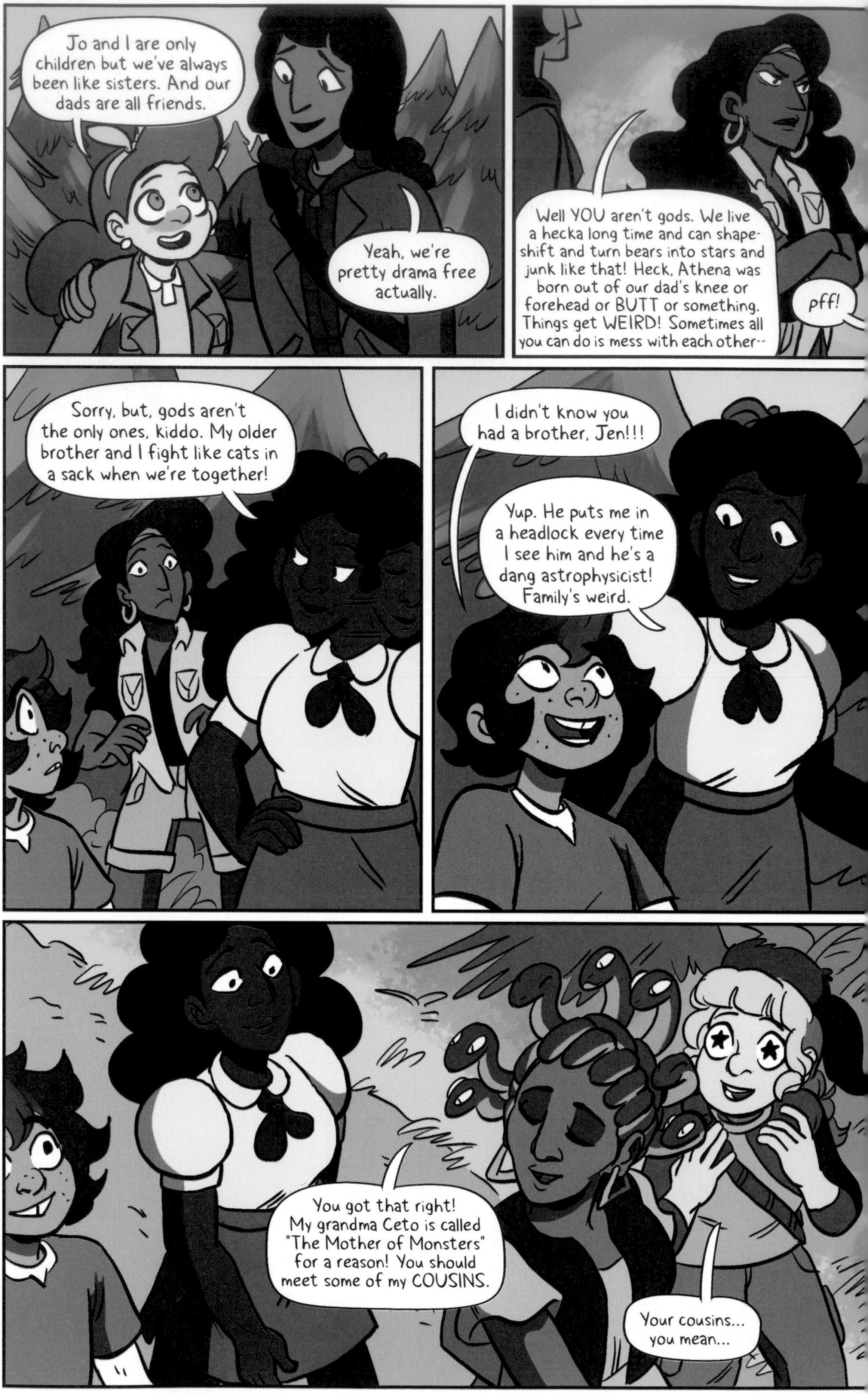
Jo and I are only children but we've always been like sisters. And our dads are all friends.
Yeah, we're pretty drama free actually.
Well YOU aren't gods. We live a hecka long time and can shape-shift and turn bears into stars and junk like that! Heck, Athena was born out of our dad's knee or forehead or BUTT or something. Things get WEIRD! Sometimes all you can do is mess with each other--
pff!
Sorry, but, gods aren't the only ones, kiddo. My older brother and I fight like cats in a sack when we're together!
I didn't know you had a brother, Jen!!!
Yup. He puts me in a headlock every time I see him and he's a dang astrophysicist! Family's weird.
You got that right! My grandma Ceto is called "The Mother of Monsters" for a reason! You should meet some of my COUSINS.
Your cousins... you mean...

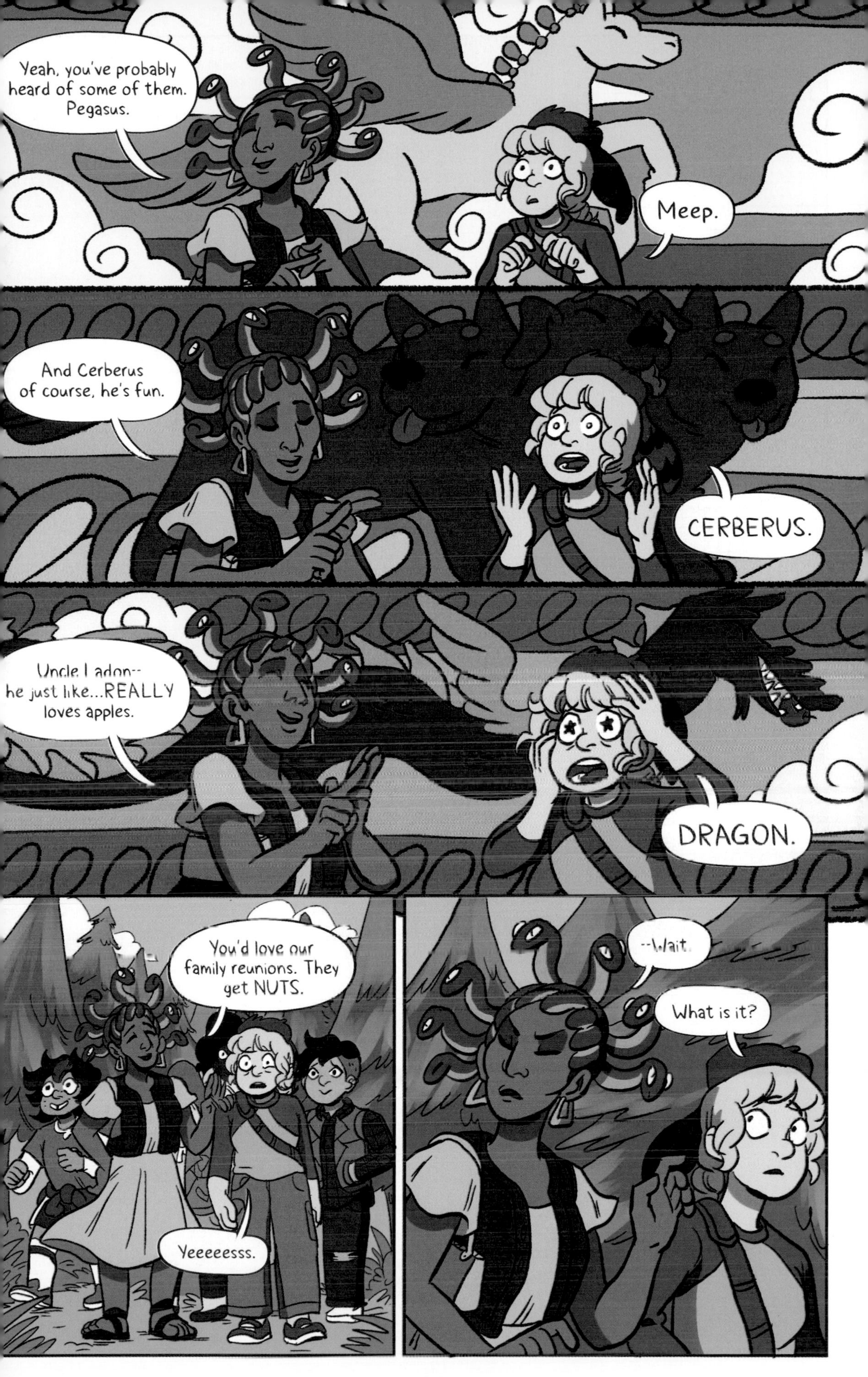
Yeah, you've probably heard of some of them. Pegasus.
Meep.
And Cerberus of course, he's fun.
CERBERUS.
Uncle Ladon-- he just like...REALLY loves apples.
DRAGON.
You'd love our family reunions. They get NUTS.
Yeeeeesss.
--Wait.
What is it?

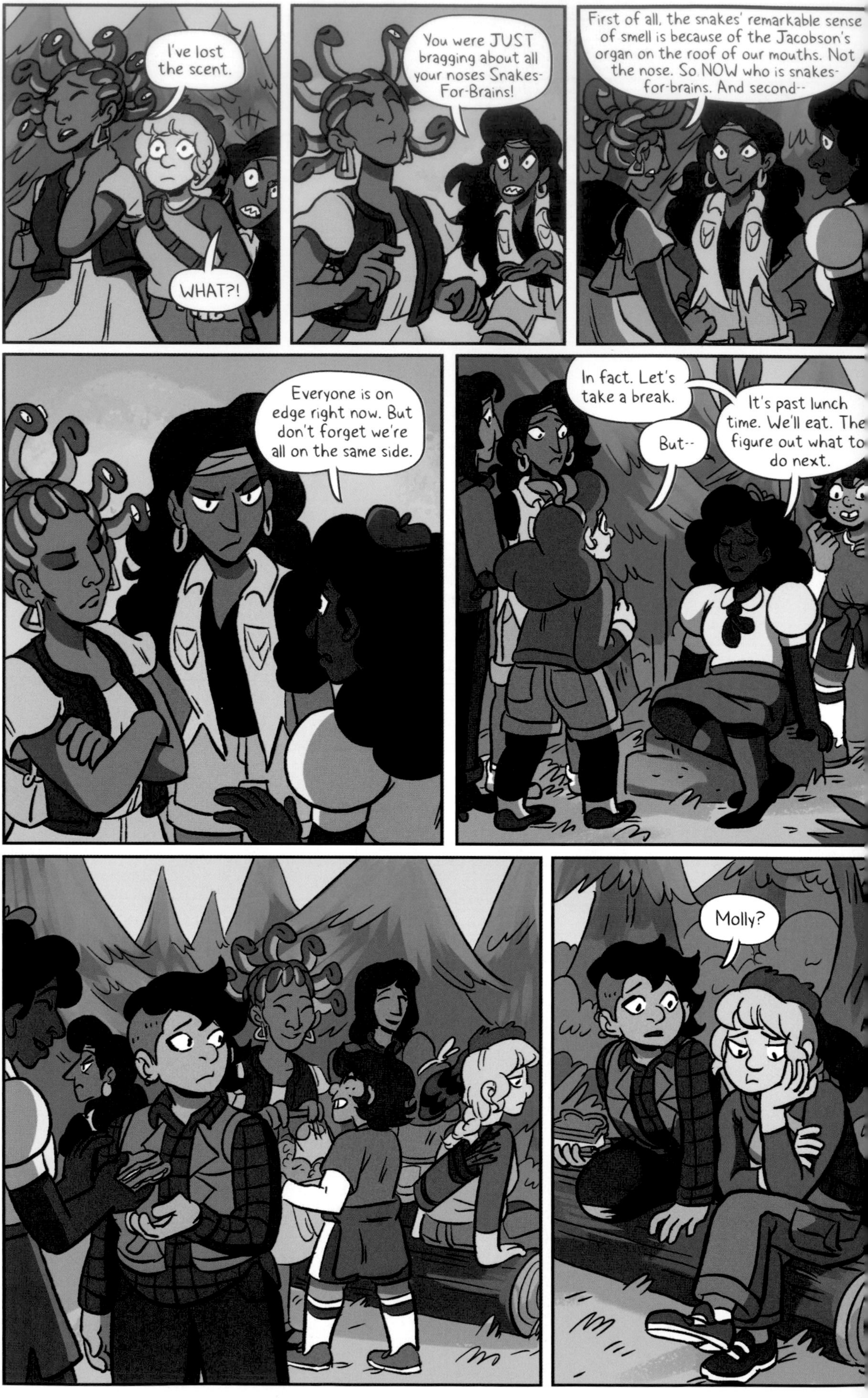
I've lost the scent.
WHAT?!
You were JUST bragging about all your noses Snakes-For-Brains!
First of all, the snakes' remarkable sense of smell is because of the Jacobson's organ on the roof of our mouths. Not the nose. So NOW who is snakes-for-brains. And second--
Everyone is on edge right now. But don't forget we're all on the same side.
In fact. Let's take a break.
But--
It's past lunch time. We'll eat. The figure out what to do next.
Molly?

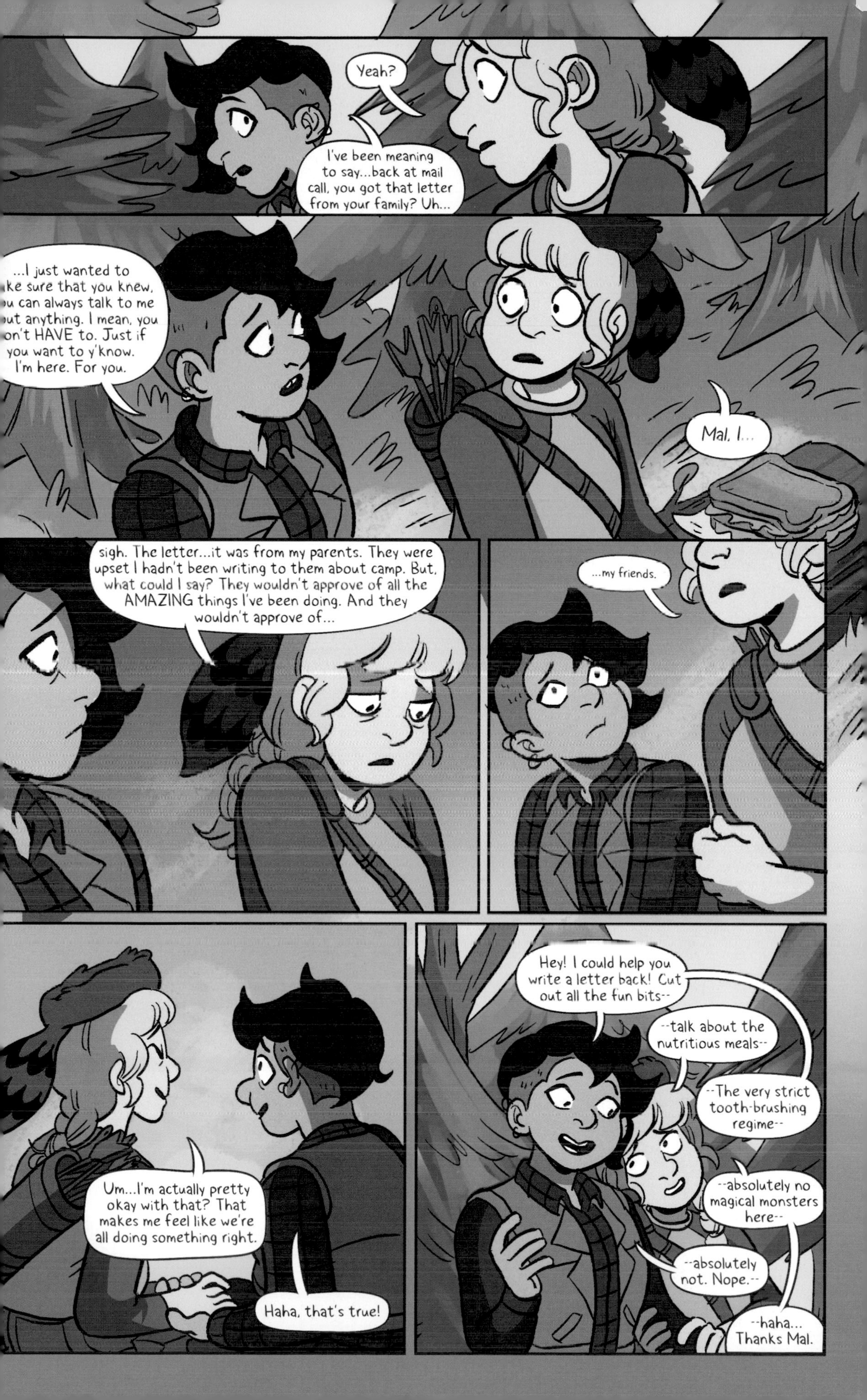
Yeah?
I've been meaning to say...back at mail call, you got that letter from your family? Uh...
...I just wanted to ke sure that you knew, u can always talk to me out anything. I mean, you on't HAVE to. Just if you want to y'know. I'm here. For you.
Mal, I...
sigh. The letter...it was from my parents. They were upset I hadn't been writing to them about camp. But, what could I say? They wouldn't approve of all the AMAZING things I've been doing. And they wouldn't approve of...
...my friends.
Um...I'm actually pretty okay with that? That makes me feel like we're all doing something right.
Haha, that's true!
Hey! I could help you write a letter back! Cut out all the fun bits--
--talk about the nutritious meals--
--The very strict tooth-brushing regime--
--absolutely no magical monsters here--
--absolutely not. Nope.--
--haha... Thanks Mal.

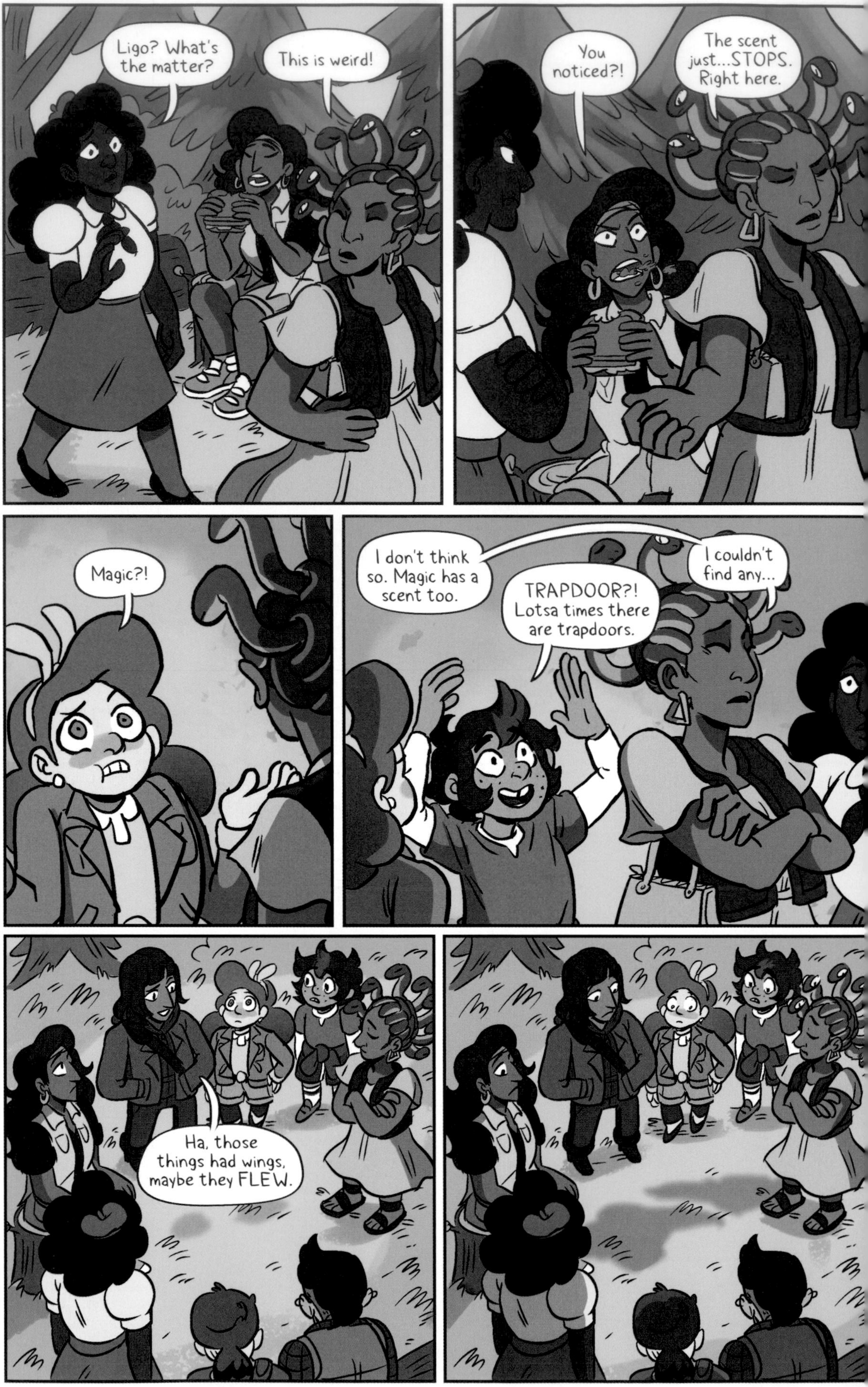
Ligo? What's the matter?
This is weird!
You noticed?!
The scent just...STOPS. Right here.
Magic?!
I don't think so. Magic has a scent too.
I couldn't find any...
TRAPDOOR?! Lotsa times there are trapdoors.
Ha, those things had wings, maybe they FLEW.

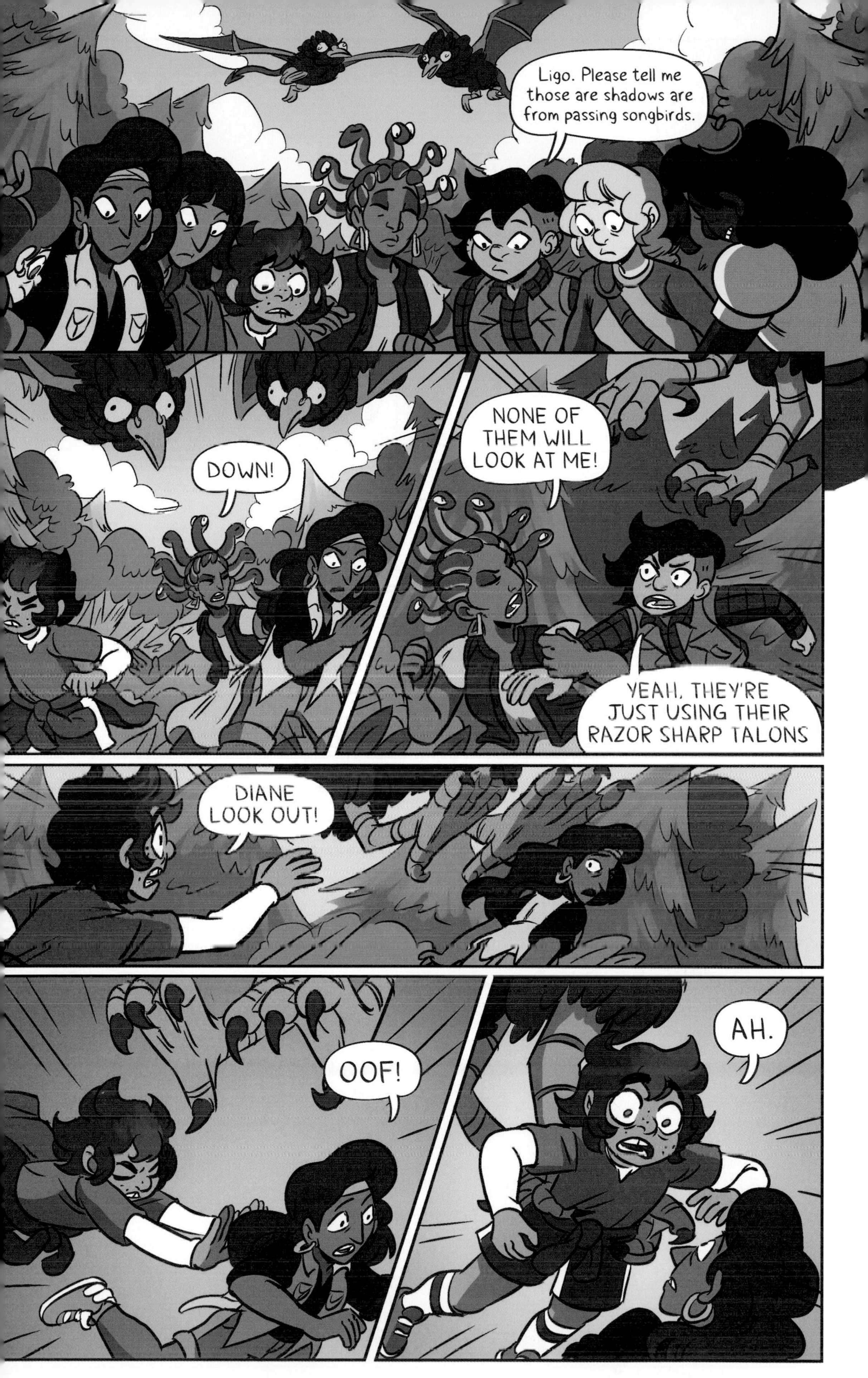
Ligo. Please tell me those are shadows are from passing songbirds.
DOWN!
NONE OF THEM WILL LOOK AT ME!
YEAH, THEY'RE JUST USING THEIR RAZOR SHARP TALONS
DIANE LOOK OUT!
OOF!
AH.

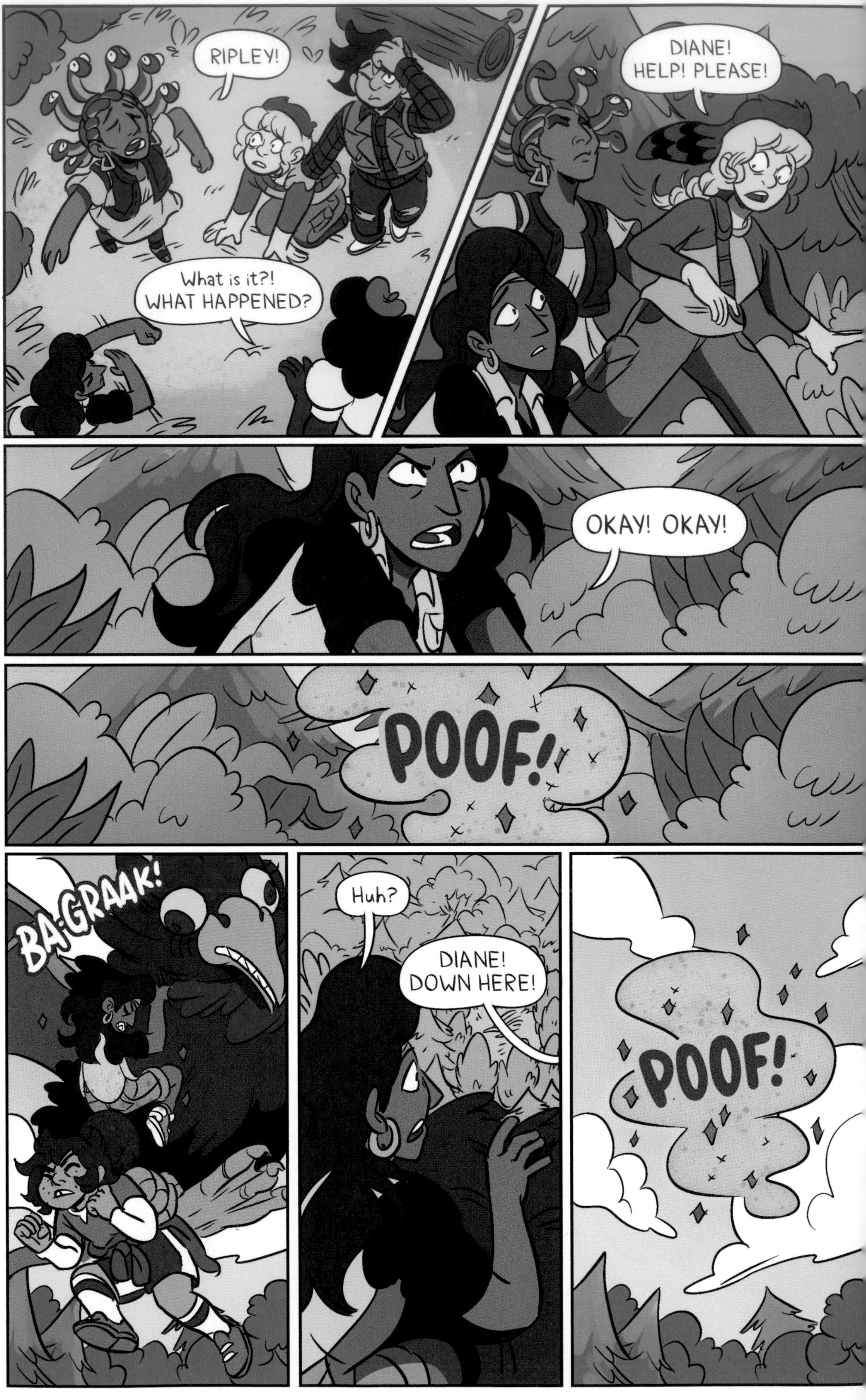
RIPLEY!
What is it?! WHAT HAPPENED?
DIANE! HELP! PLEASE!
OKAY! OKAY!
POOF!
BA-GRAAK!
Huh?
DIANE! DOWN HERE!
POOF!

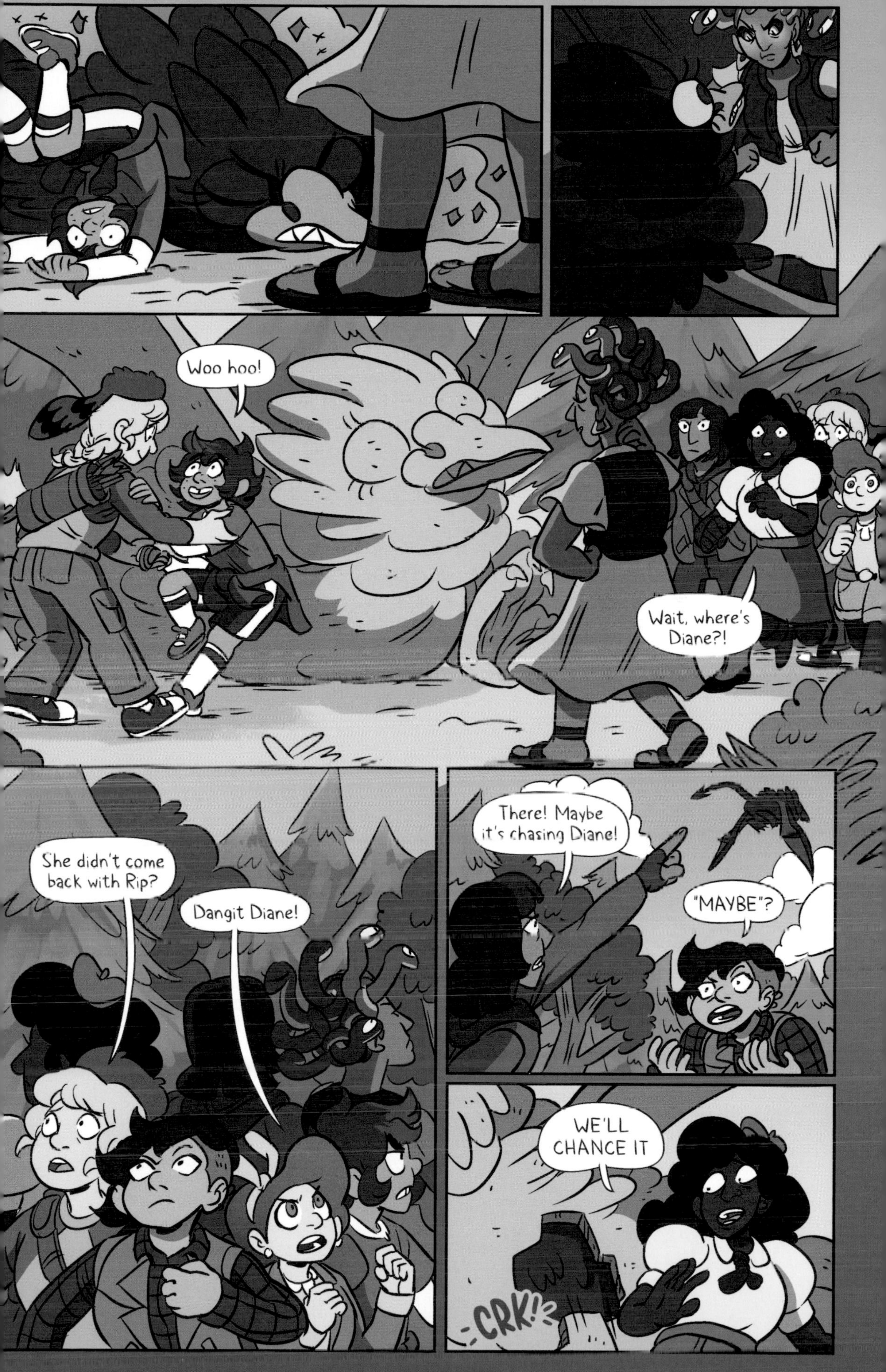
Woo hoo!
Wait, where's Diane?!
She didn't come back with Rip?
Dangit Diane!
There! Maybe it's chasing Diane!
"MAYBE"?
WE'LL CHANCE IT
CRK!

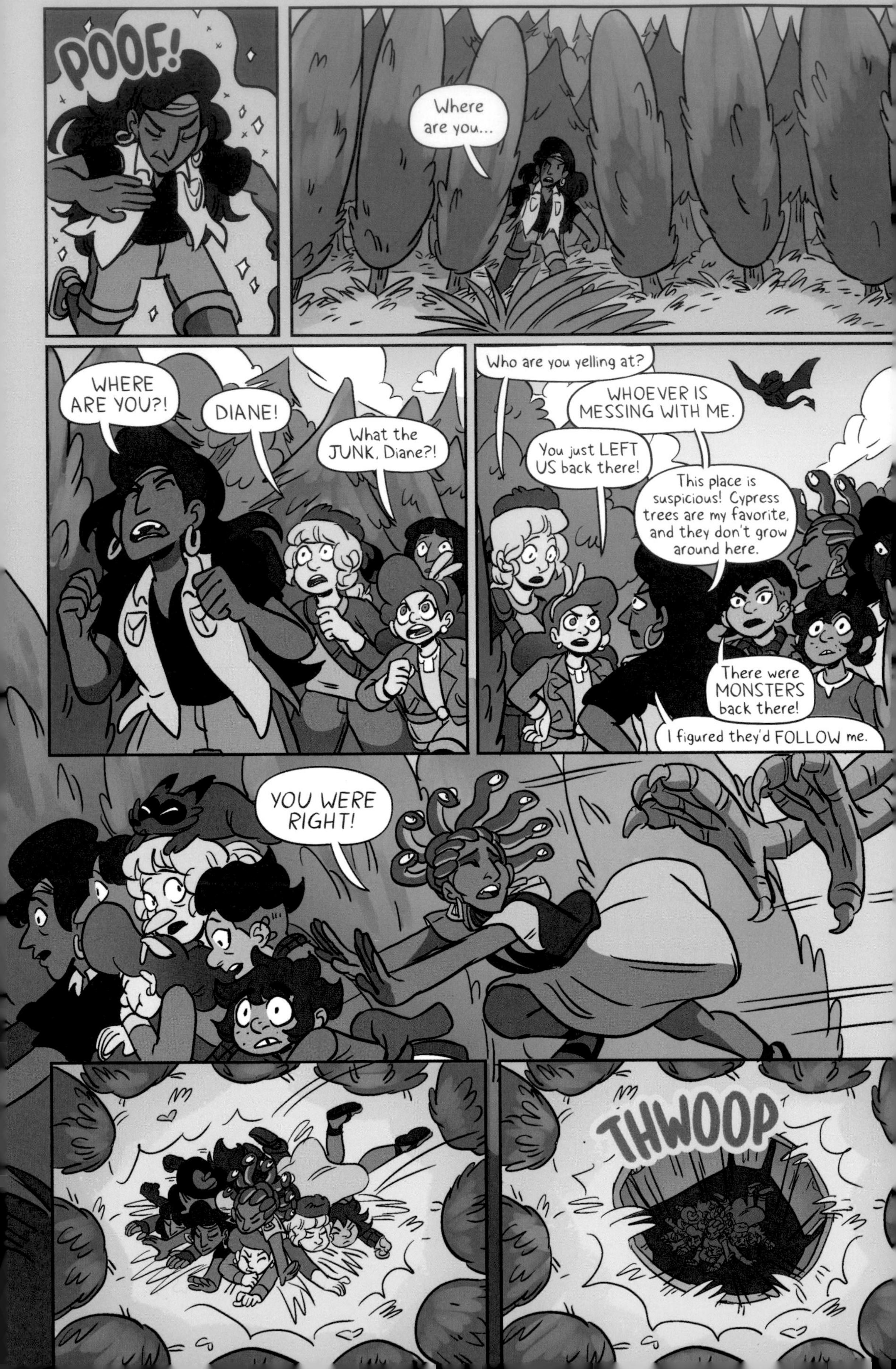
POOF!
Where are you...
WHERE ARE YOU?!
DIANE!
What the JUNK, Diane?!
Who are you yelling at?
WHOEVER IS MESSING WITH ME.
You just LEFT US back there!
This place is suspicious! Cypress trees are my favorite, and they don't grow around here.
There were MONSTERS back there!
I figured they'd FOLLOW me.
YOU WERE RIGHT!
THWOOP

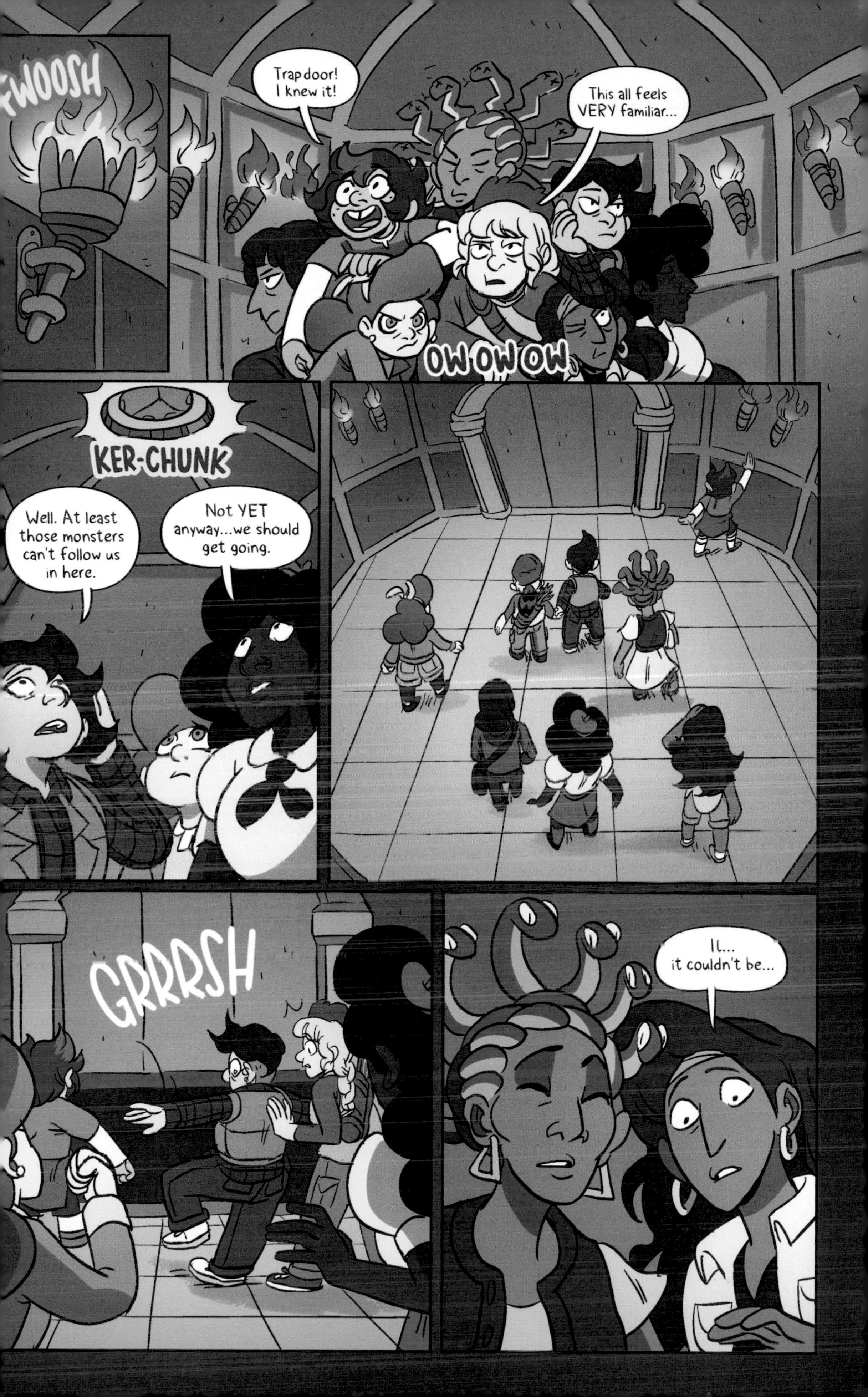

FWOOSH
Trap door! I knew it!
This all feels VERY familiar...
OW OW OW
KER-CHUNK
Well. At least those monsters can't follow us in here.
Not YET anyway...we should get going.
GRRRSH
II... it couldn't be...

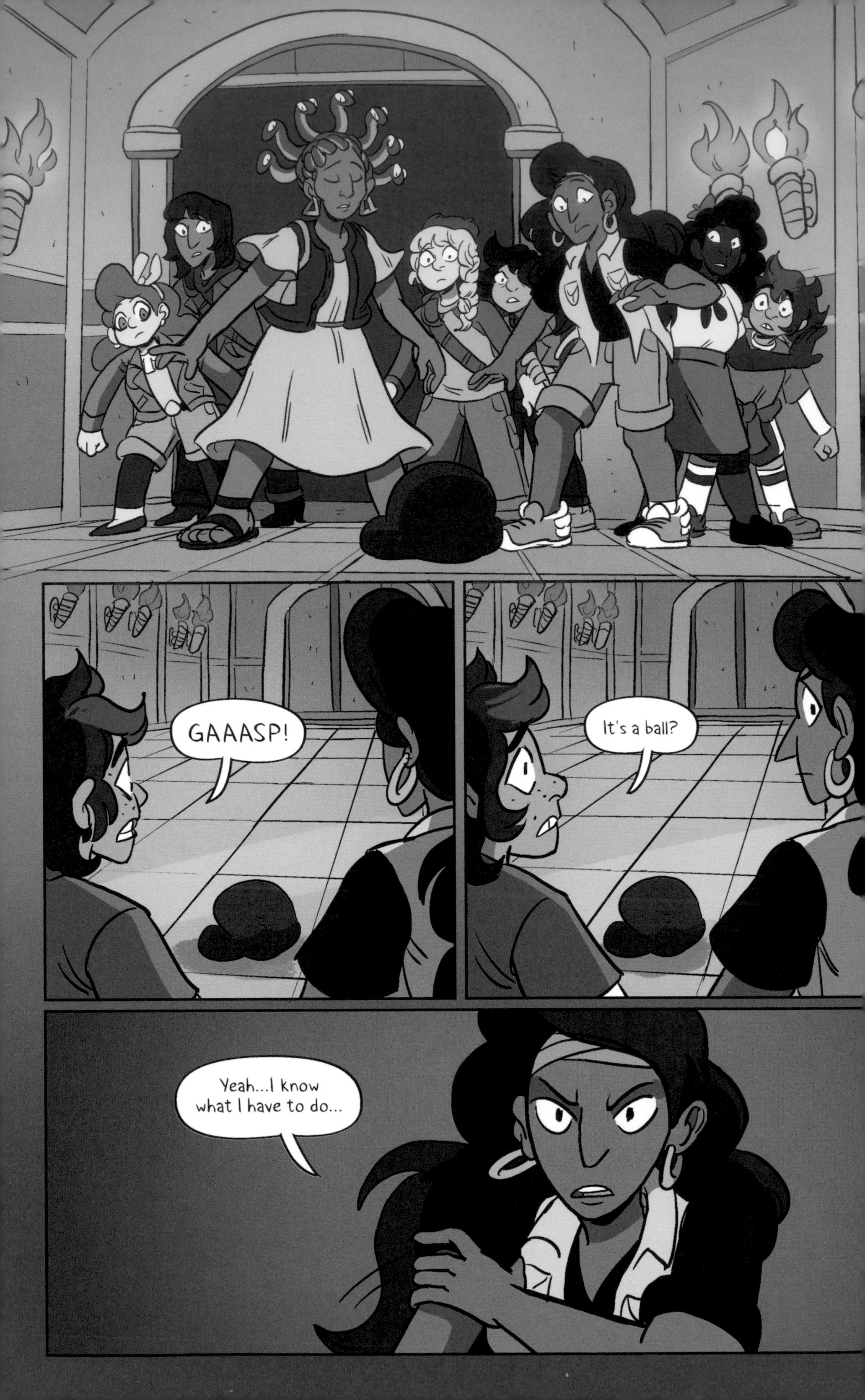
GAAASP!
It's a ball?
Yeah...I know what I have to do...

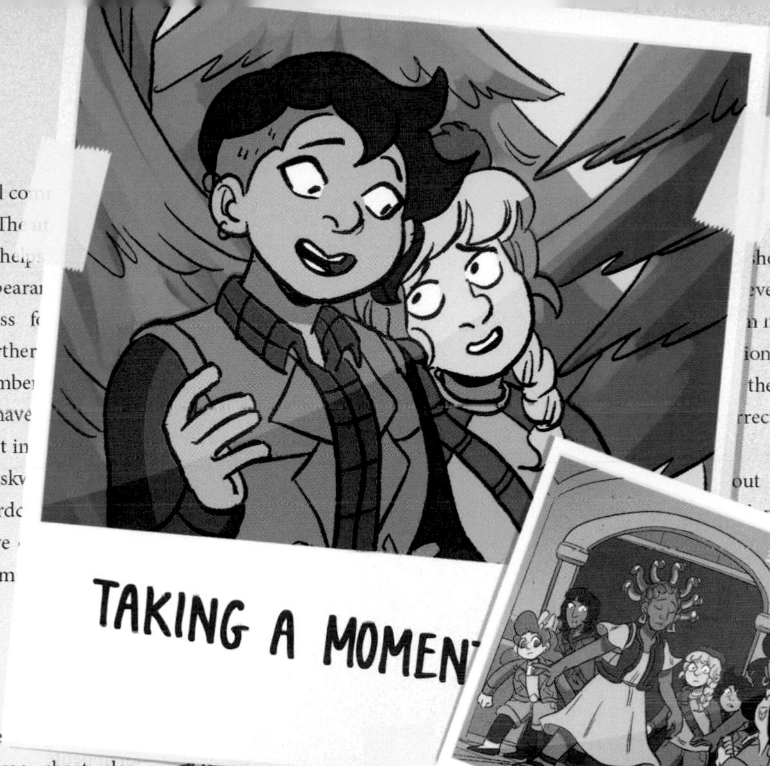
TAKING A MOMENT

will co…

The …
It help…
appeara…
dress f…
Further…
Lumbe…
to have…
part in…
Thiskv…
Hardc…
have …
them…

…E UNIFORM

…hould be worn at camp …events when Lumberjanes …n may also be worn at other …ions. It should be worn as a … the uniform dress with …rrect shoes, and stocking or

… out grows her uniform or …ng to another Lumberjane. …nsignia she has … her … her

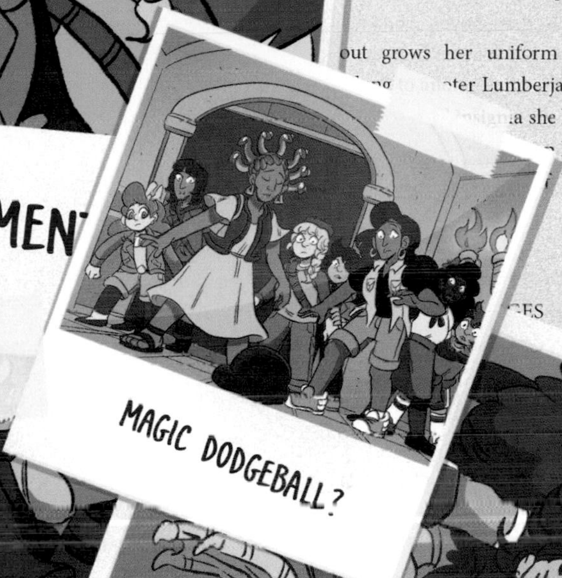
MAGIC DODGEBALL?

…GES

The …
yellow, short sl…
emb…
the w…
choos…
slacks, …
made o…
out-of-do…
green bere…
the colla…
Shoes ma…
heels, rou… …ings or
socks shou… …with the shoes or wit…
the uniform. Ne… …bracelets, or other jewelry do …
belong with a Lumberjane uniform.

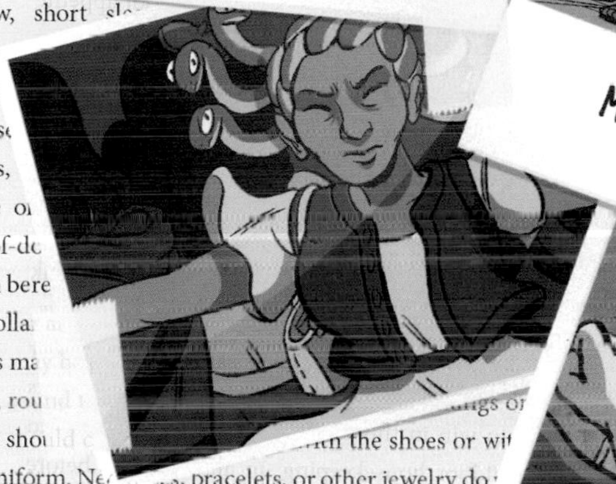

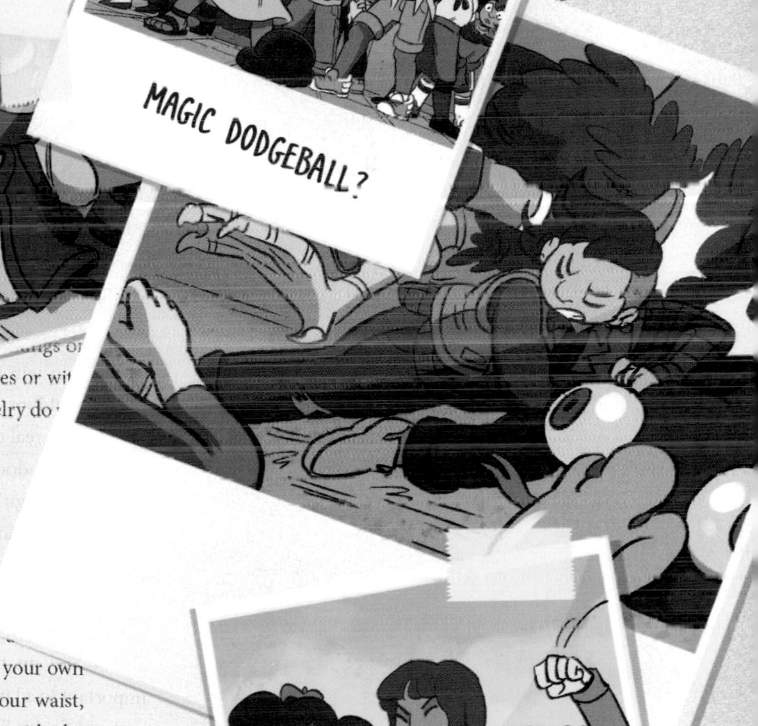

HOW TO WEAR THE UNIFORM

To look well in a uniform demans first of … uniform be kept in good condition—clean … pressed. See that the skirt is the right length for your own height and build, that the belt is adjusted to your waist, that your shoes and stockings are in keeping with the uniform, that you watch your posture and carry yourself with dignity and grace. If the beret is removed indoors, be sure that your hair is neat and kept in place with an insonspicuous clip or ribbon. When you wear a Lumberjane uniform you are identified as a member of this organization and you should be doubly careful to conduct yourself in a way that will show everyone that courtesy and thoughtfullness are part of being a Lumberjane. People are likely to judge a whole nation by the selfishness of a few individuals, to criticize a whole family because of the misconduct of one member, and to feel unkindly toward and organization because of the

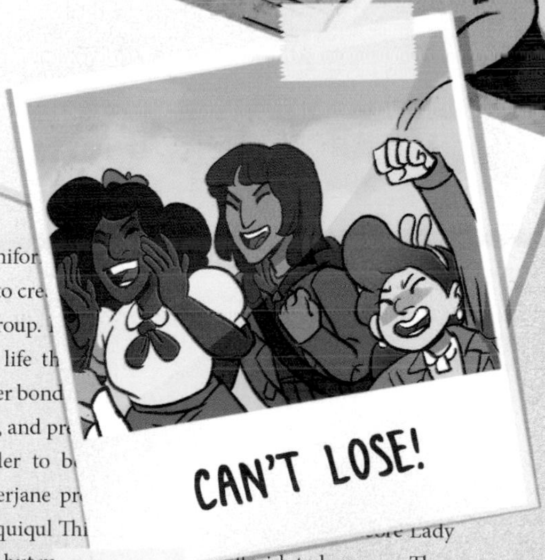
CAN'T LOSE!

The unifor…
helps to cre…
in a group. …
active life th…
another bond…
future, and pr…
in order to b…
Lumberjane pr…
Penniquiqul Th… …ore Lady
Types, but m… …s will wish to have one. They
can either bu… …, or make it themselves from
materials available at the trading post.

LUMBERJANES FIELD MANUAL

CHAPTER
THIRTY-TWO

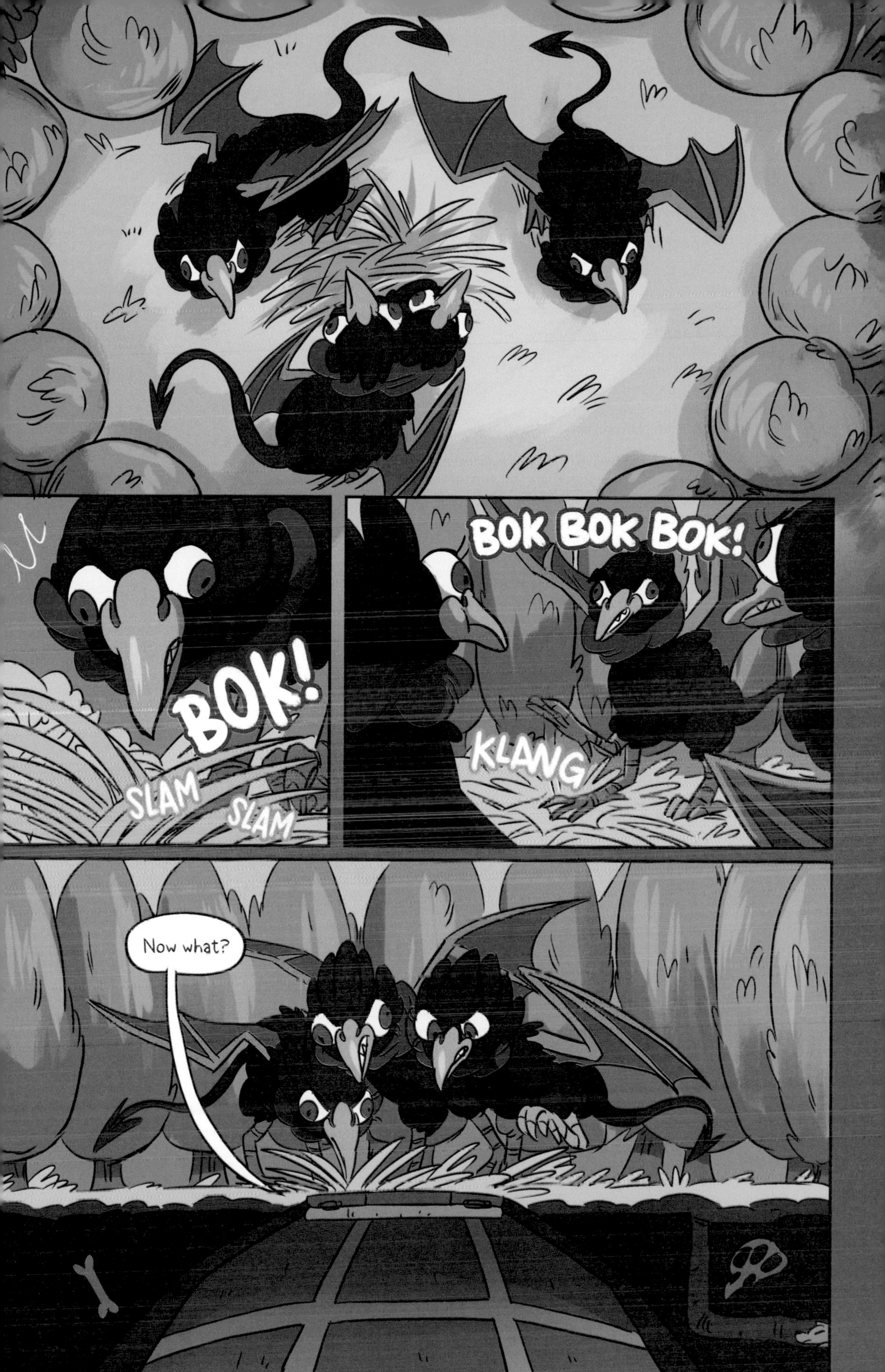
BOK!
SLAM
SLAM
BOK BOK BOK!
KLANG
Now what?

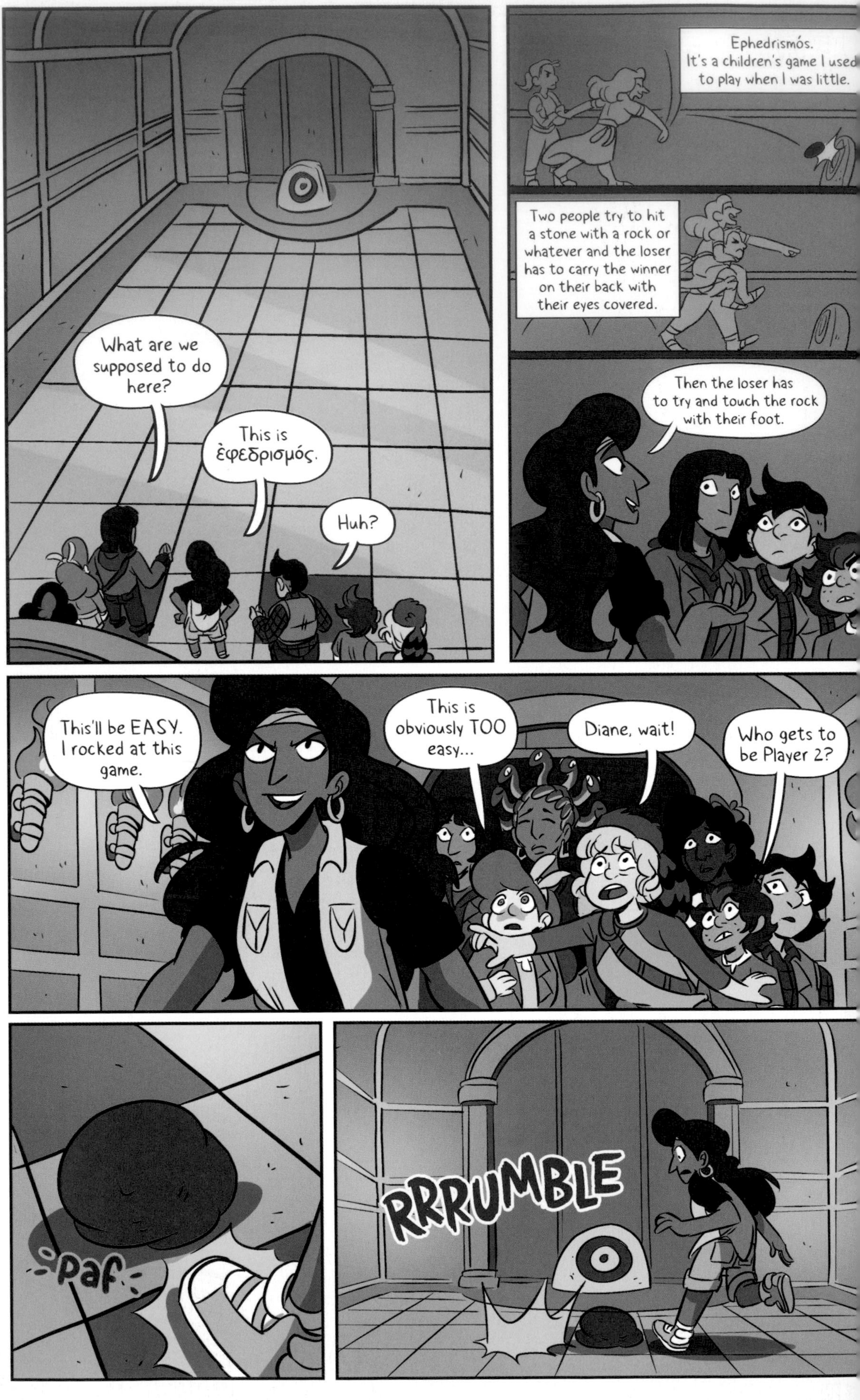
What are we supposed to do here?
This is ἐφεδρισμός.
Huh?
Ephedrismós. It's a children's game I used to play when I was little.
Two people try to hit a stone with a rock or whatever and the loser has to carry the winner on their back with their eyes covered.
Then the loser has to try and touch the rock with their foot.
This'll be EASY. I rocked at this game.
This is obviously TOO easy...
Diane, wait!
Who gets to be Player 2?
paf
RRRUMBLE

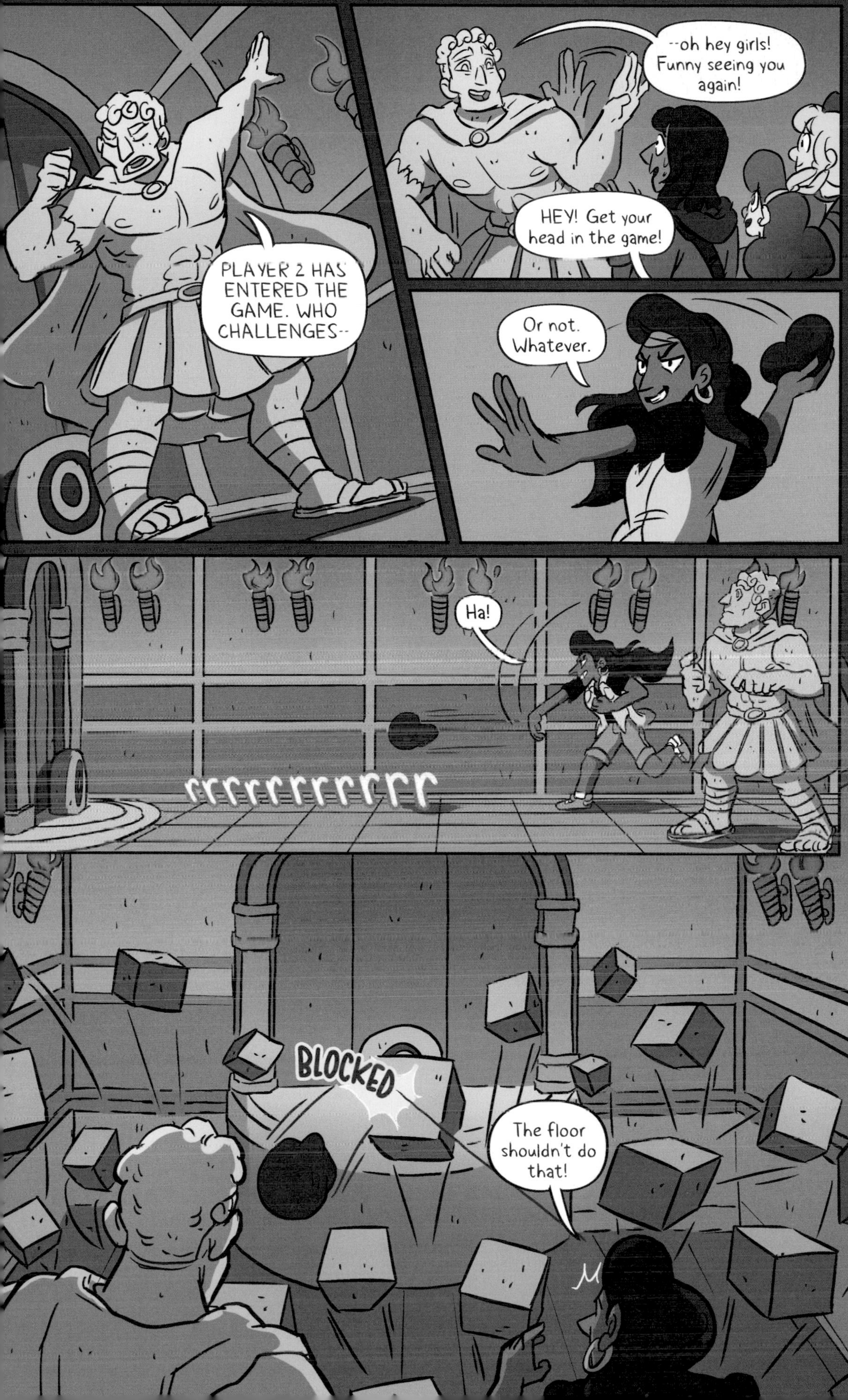
PLAYER 2 HAS ENTERED THE GAME. WHO CHALLENGES--
--oh hey girls! Funny seeing you again!
HEY! Get your head in the game!
Or not. Whatever.
Ha!
rrrrrrrrrrrr
BLOCKED
The floor shouldn't do that!

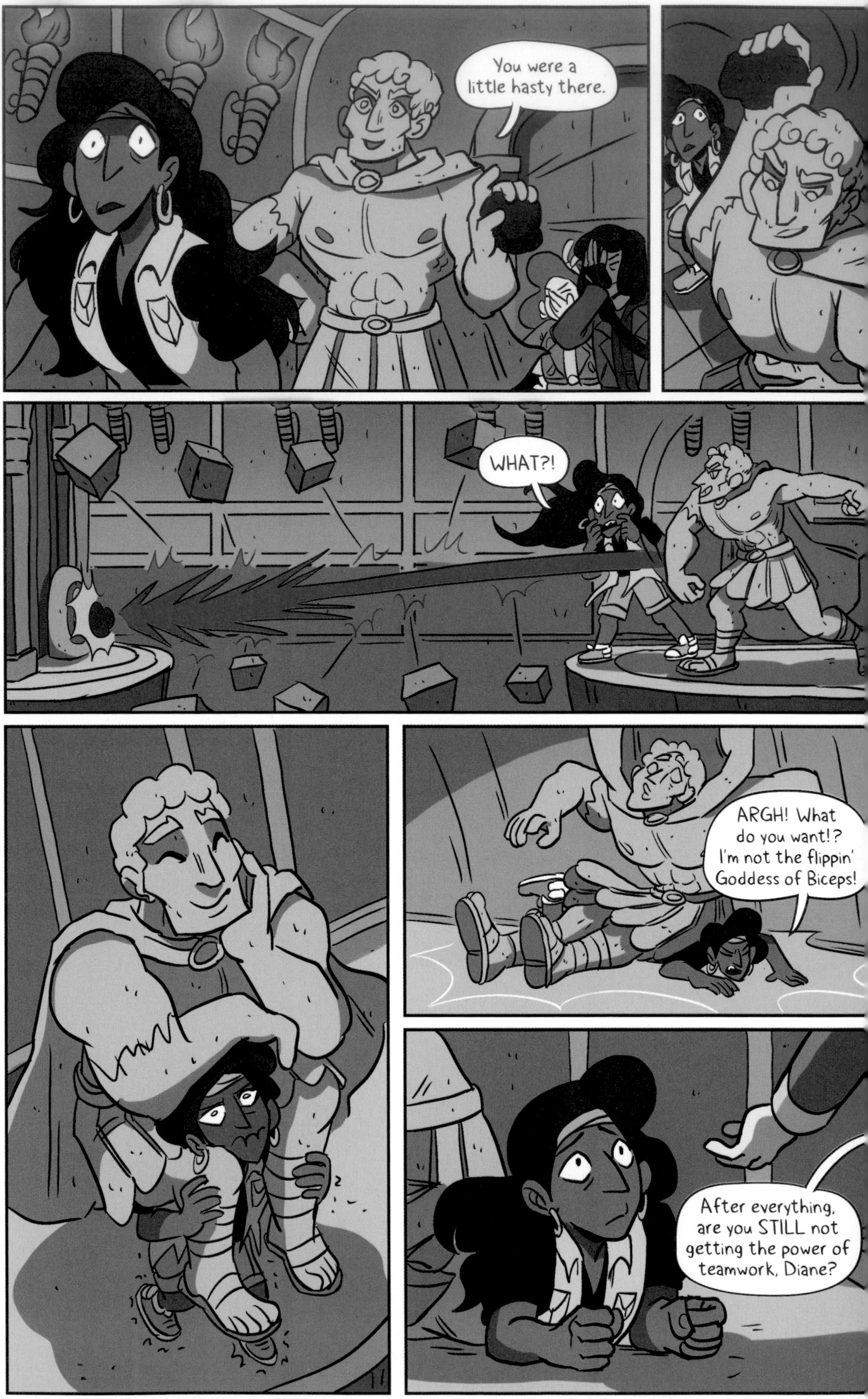
You were a little hasty there.
WHAT?!
ARGH! What do you want!? I'm not the flippin' Goddess of Biceps!
After everything, are you STILL not getting the power of teamwork, Diane?

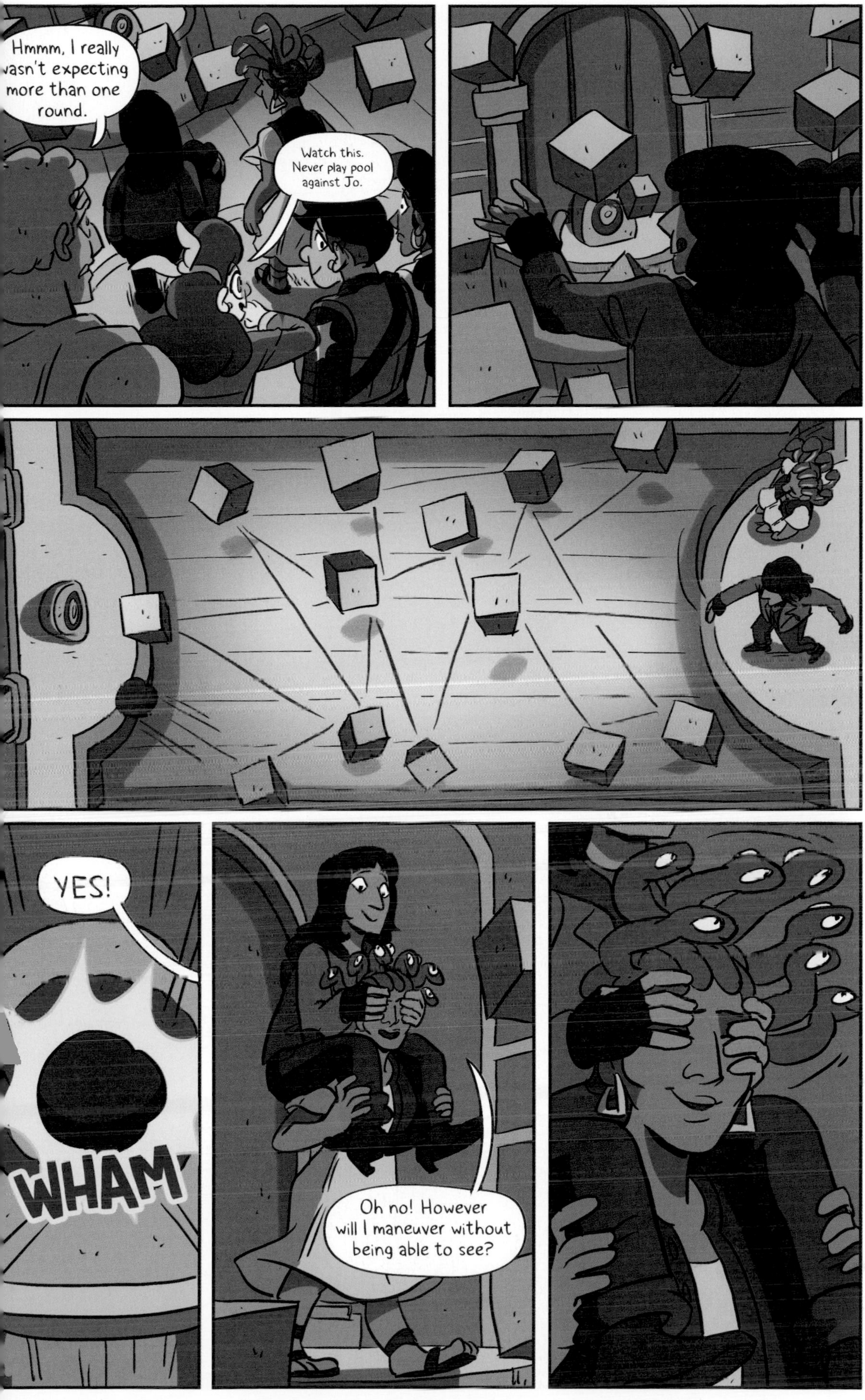
Hmmm, I really wasn't expecting more than one round.
Watch this. Never play pool against Jo.
YES!
WHAM
Oh no! However will I maneuver without being able to see?

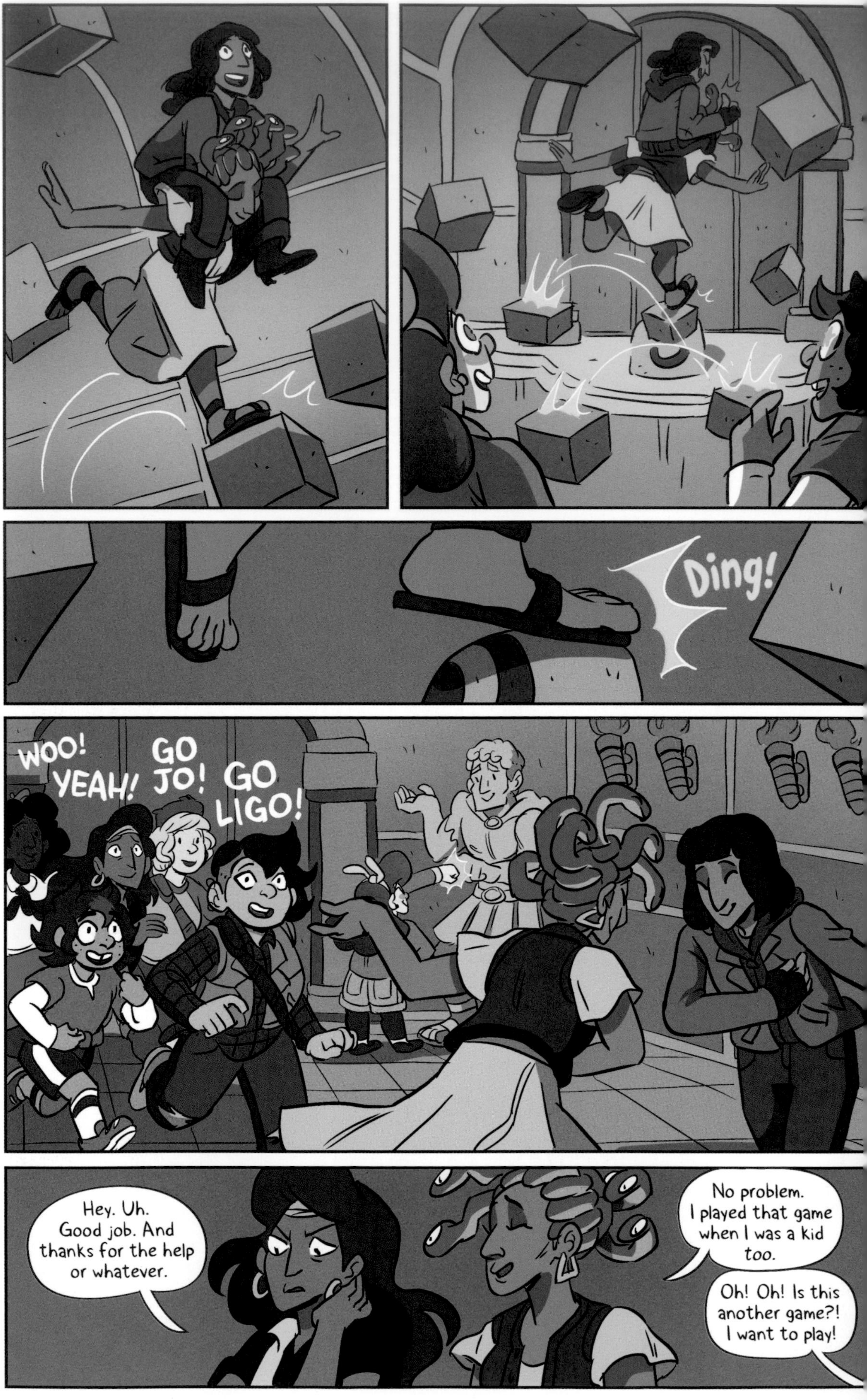
Ding!
WOO!
YEAH!
GO JO!
GO LIGO!
Hey. Uh. Good job. And thanks for the help or whatever.
No problem. I played that game when I was a kid too.
Oh! Oh! Is this another game?! I want to play!

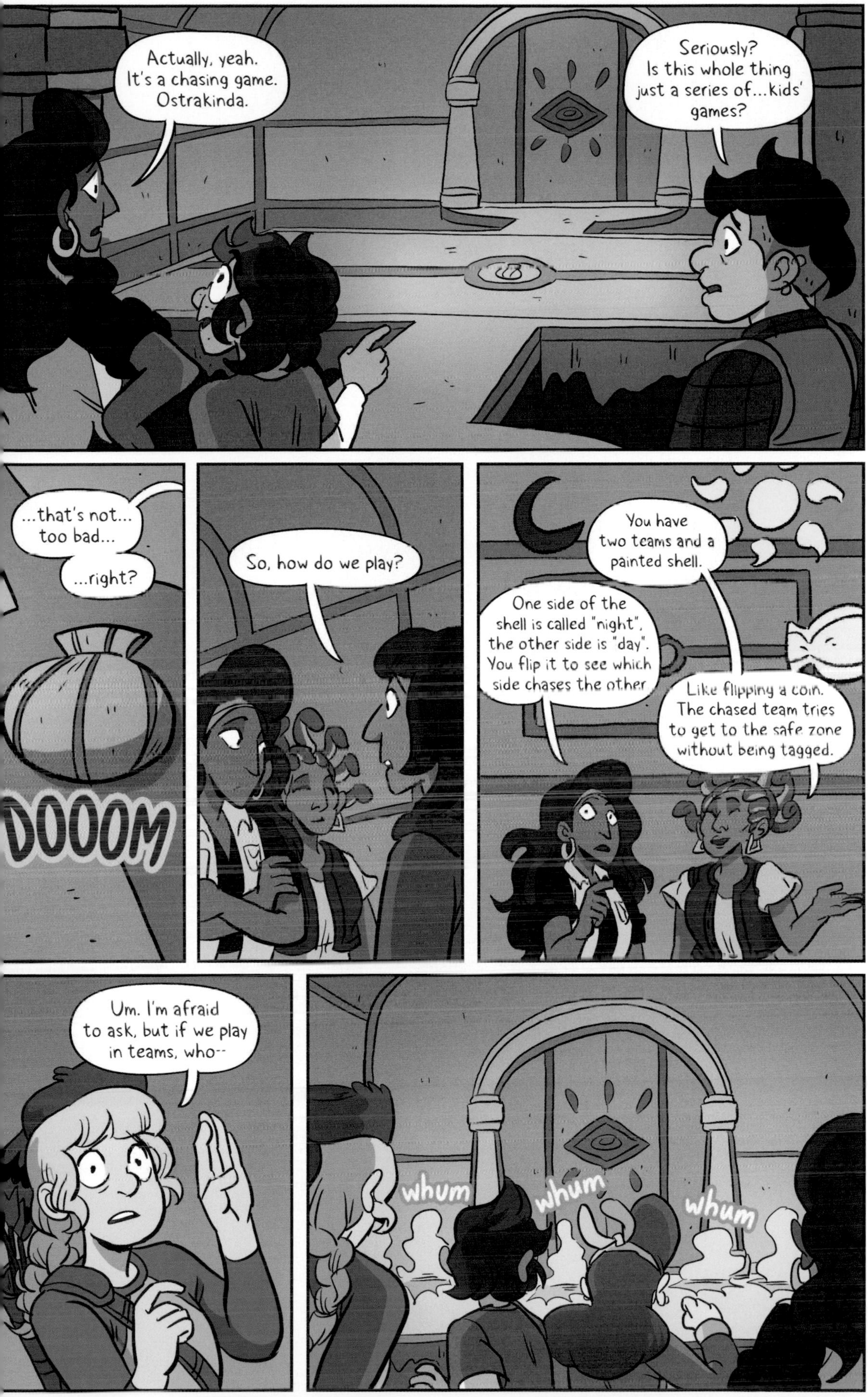
Actually, yeah.
It's a chasing game.
Ostrakinda.
Seriously?
Is this whole thing just a series of...kids' games?
...that's not... too bad...
...right?
DOOOM
So, how do we play?
You have two teams and a painted shell.
One side of the shell is called "night", the other side is "day". You flip it to see which side chases the other.
Like flipping a coin. The chased team tries to get to the safe zone without being tagged.
Um. I'm afraid to ask, but if we play in teams, who--
whum
whum
whum

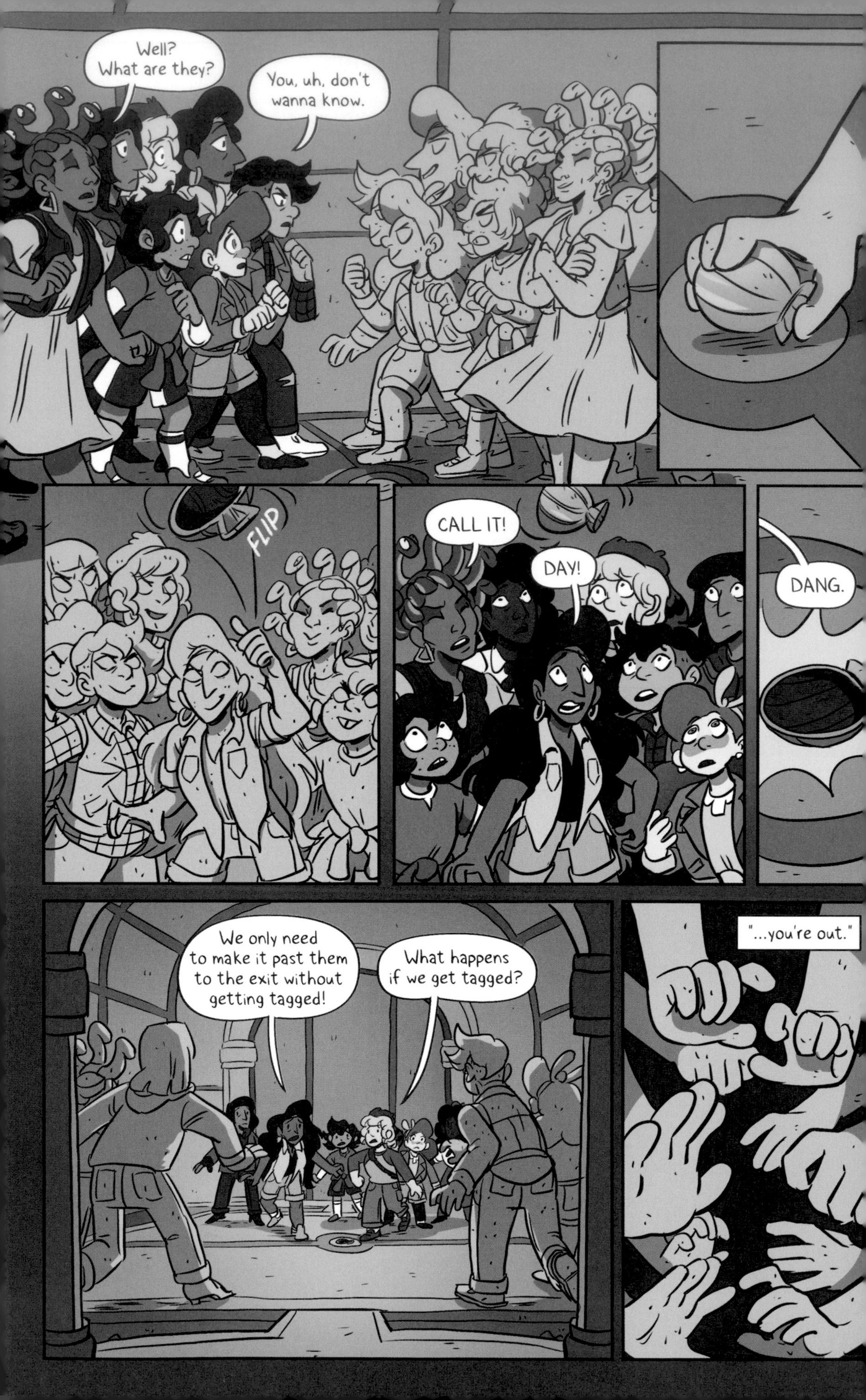
Well? What are they?
You, uh, don't wanna know.
FLIP
CALL IT!
DAY!
DANG.
We only need to make it past them to the exit without getting tagged!
What happens if we get tagged?
"...you're out."

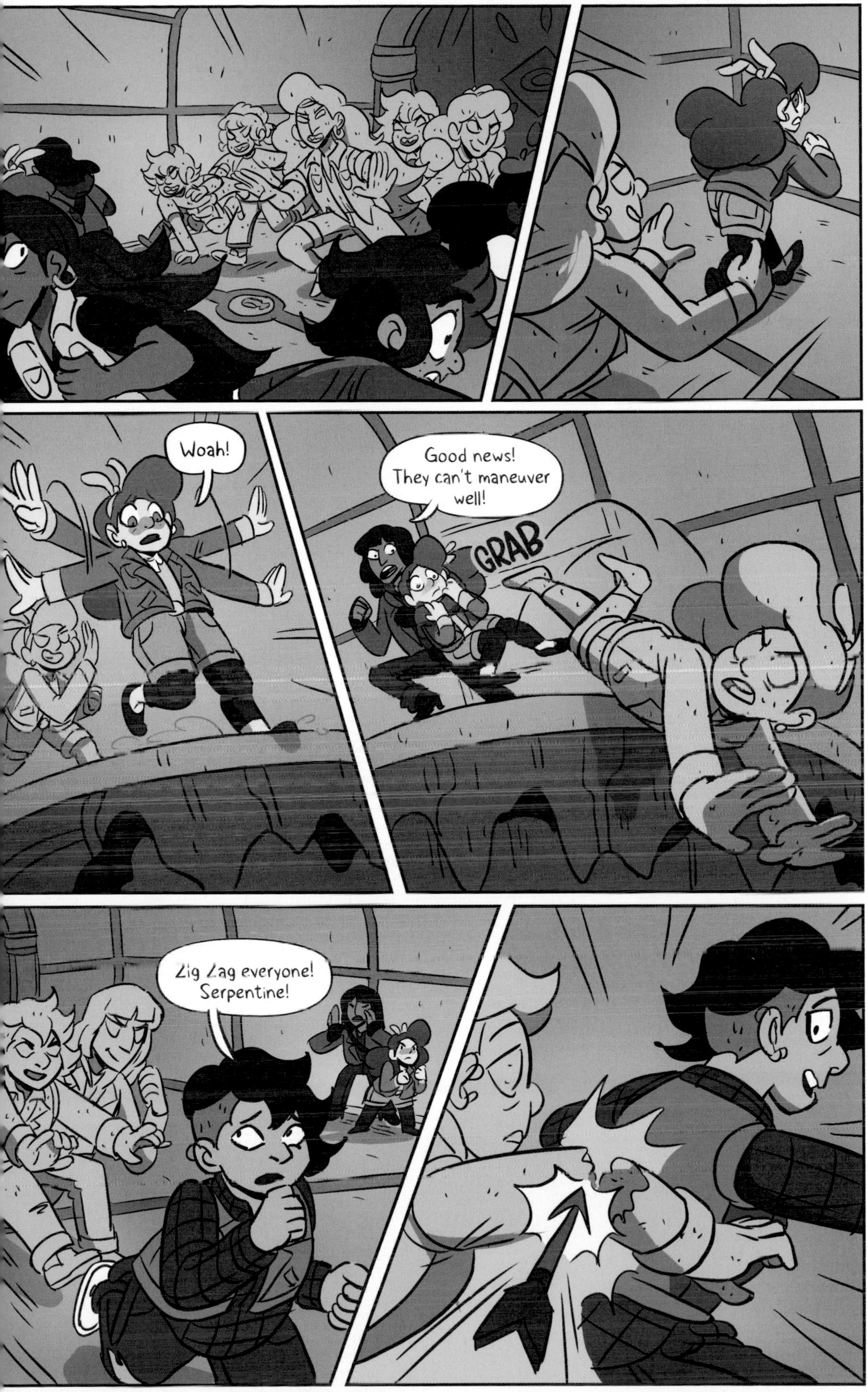
Woah!
Good news! They can't maneuver well!
GRAB
Zig Zag everyone! Serpentine!

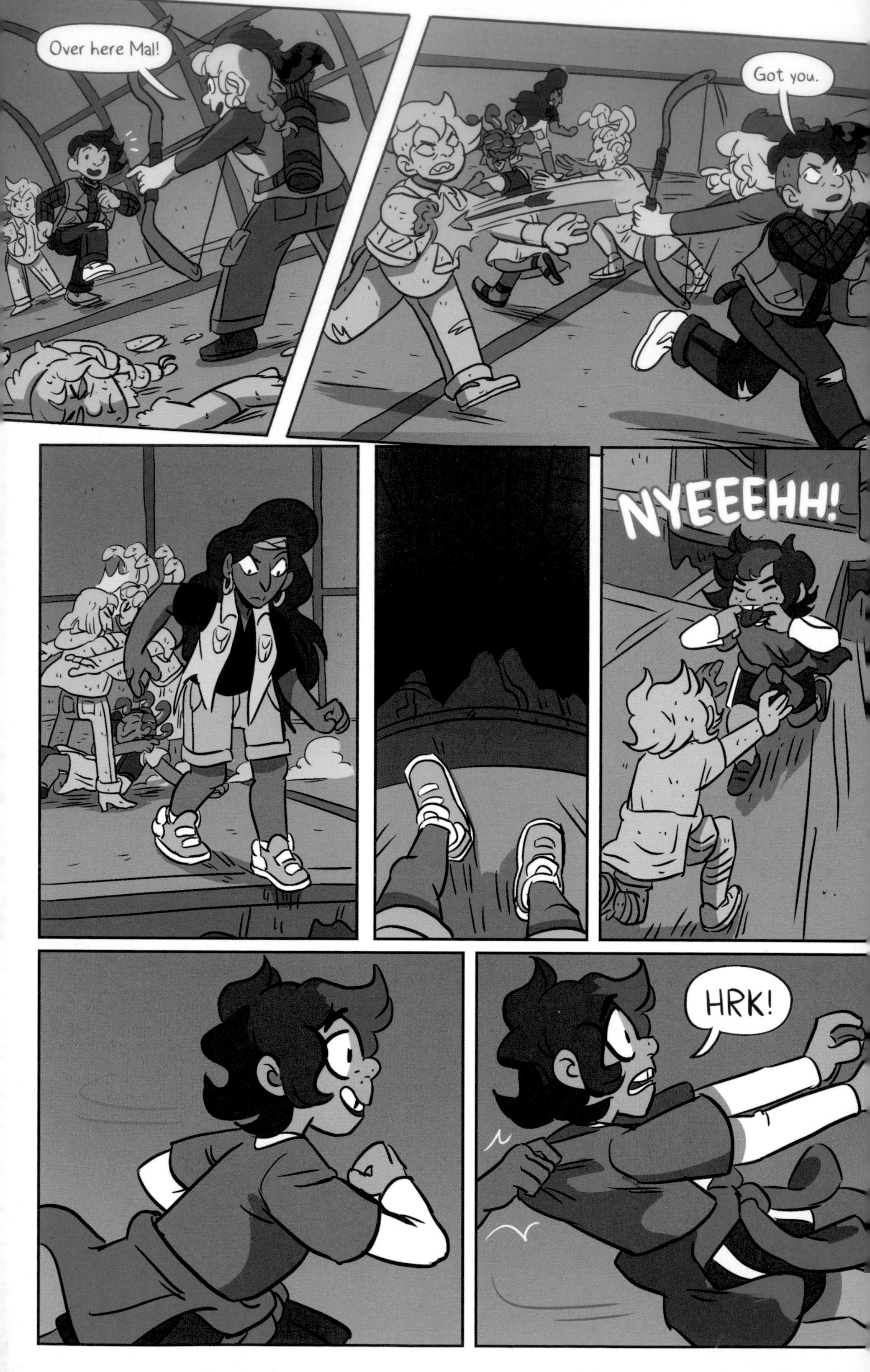
Over here Mal!
Got you.
NYEEEHH!
HRK!

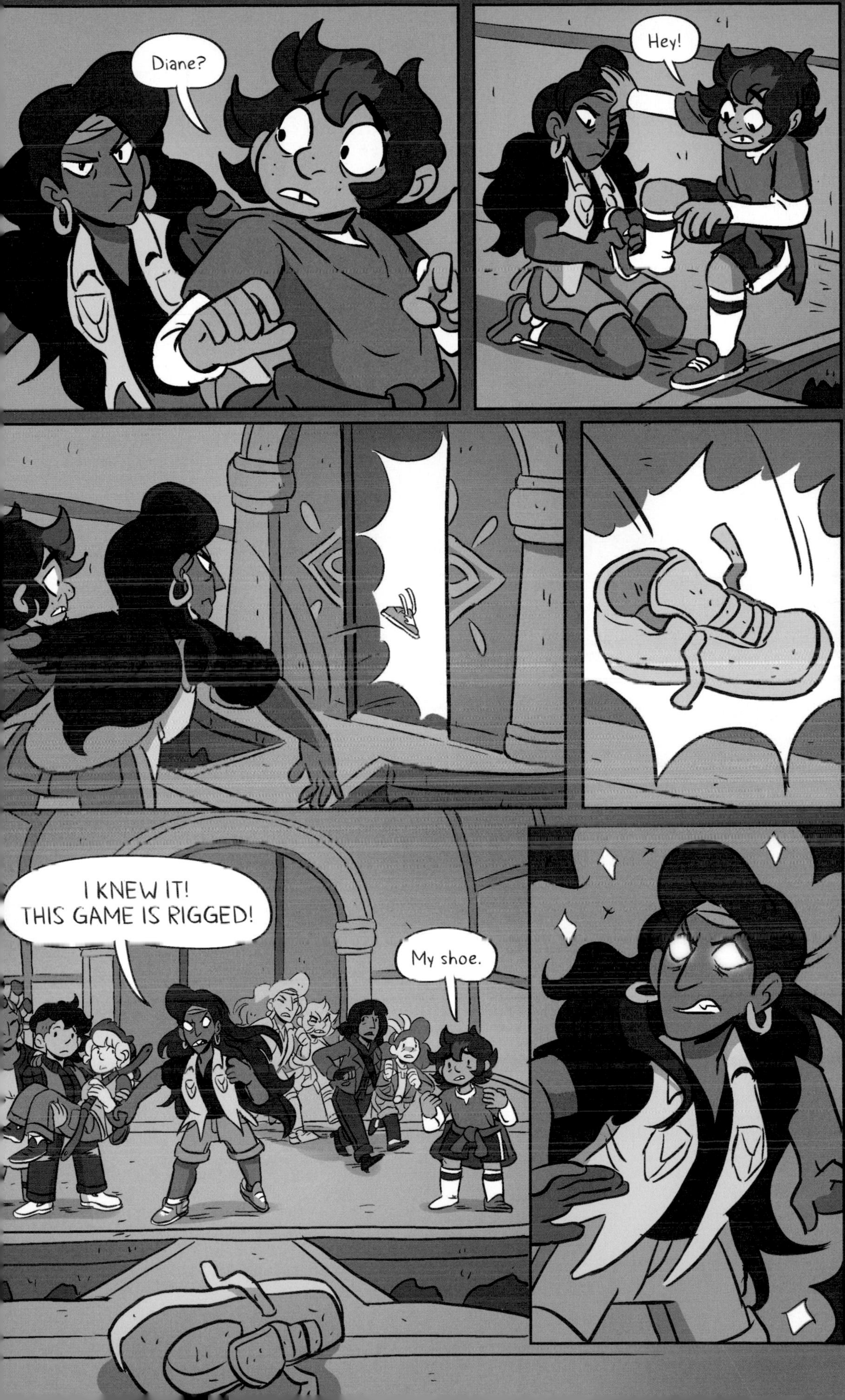
Diane?
Hey!
I KNEW IT! THIS GAME IS RIGGED!
My shoe.

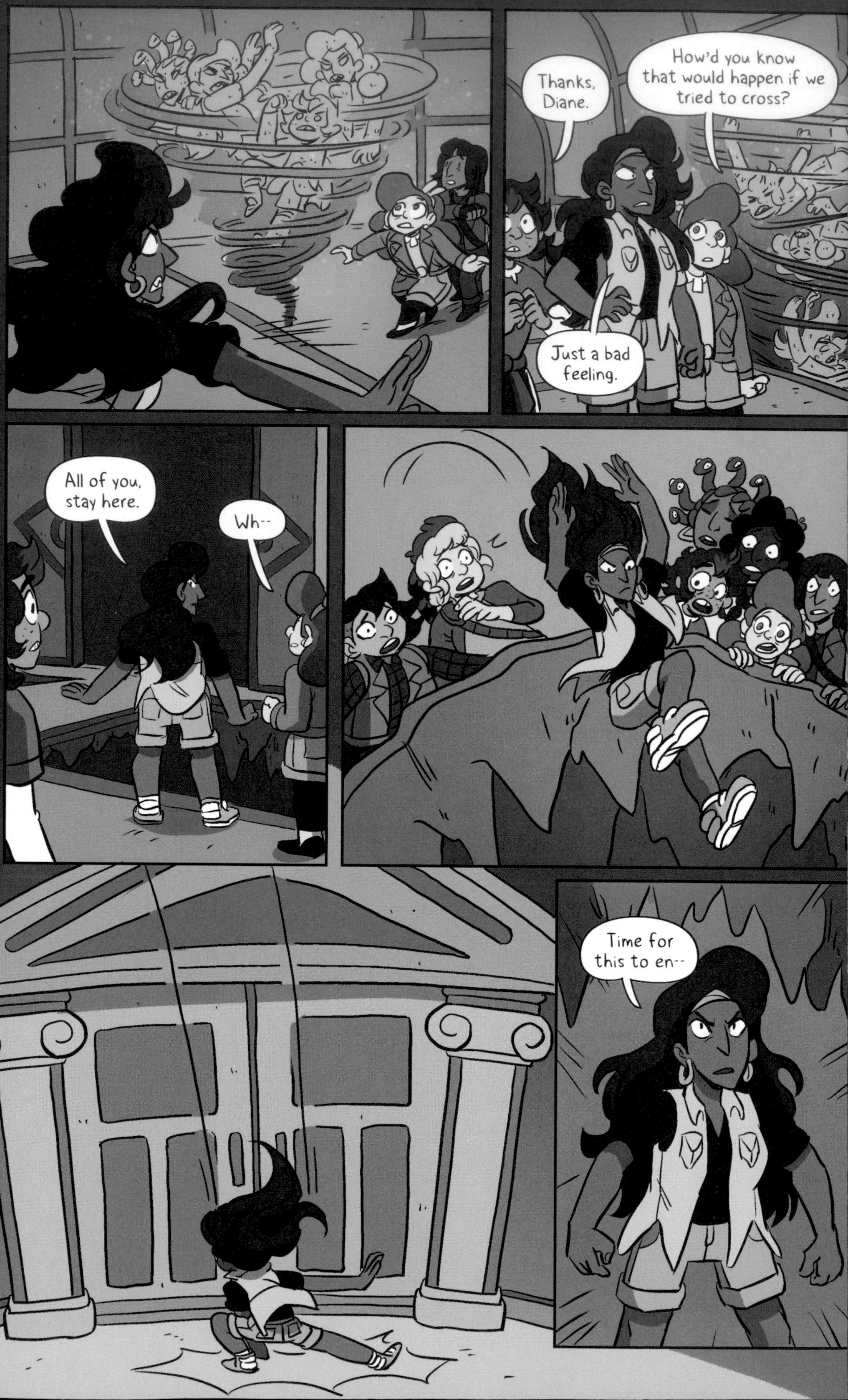
Thanks, Diane.
How'd you know that would happen if we tried to cross?
Just a bad feeling.
All of you, stay here.
Wh--
Time for this to en--

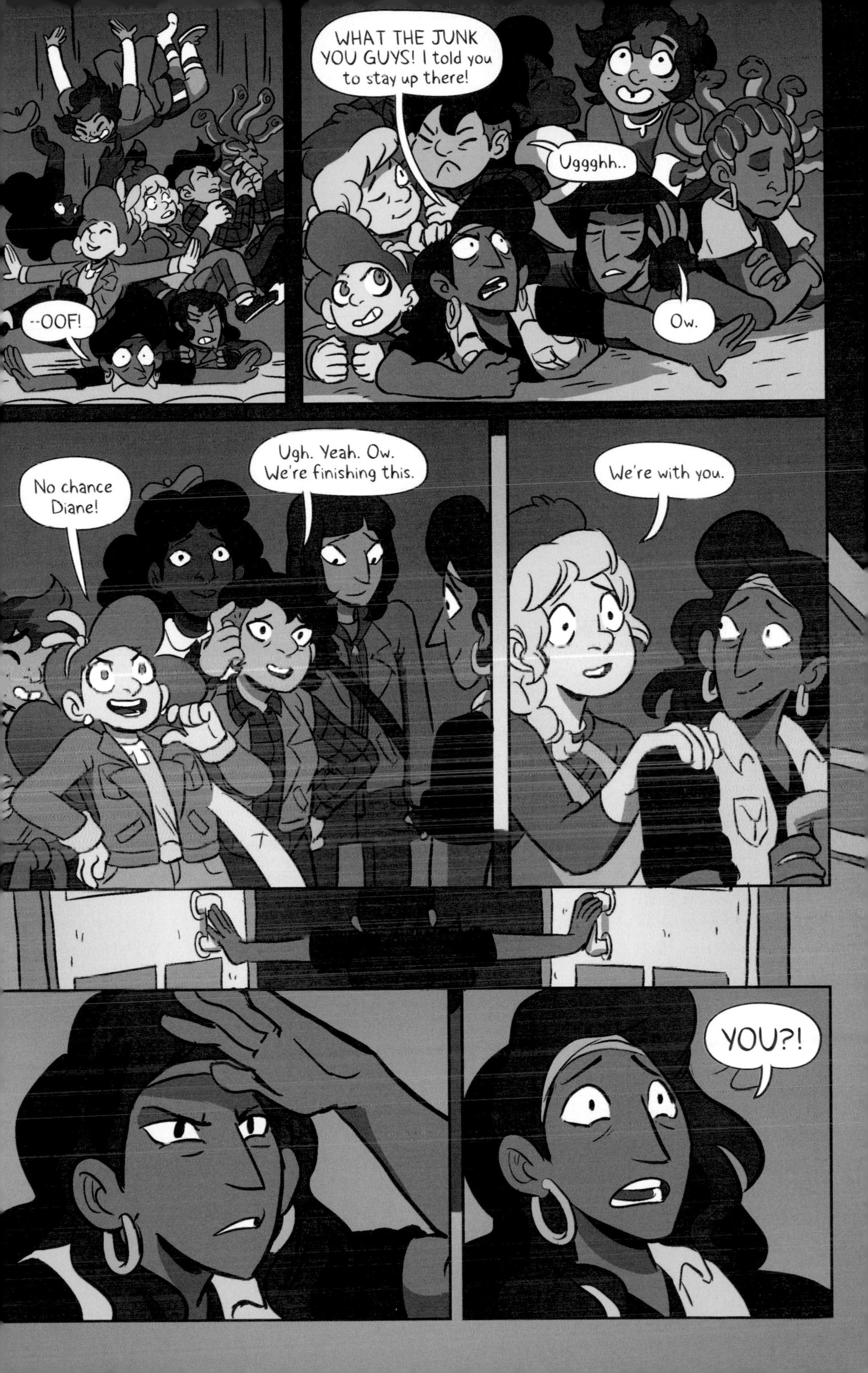
--OOF!
WHAT THE JUNK YOU GUYS! I told you to stay up there!
Uggghh..
Ow.
No chance Diane!
Ugh. Yeah. Ow. We're finishing this.
We're with you.
YOU?!

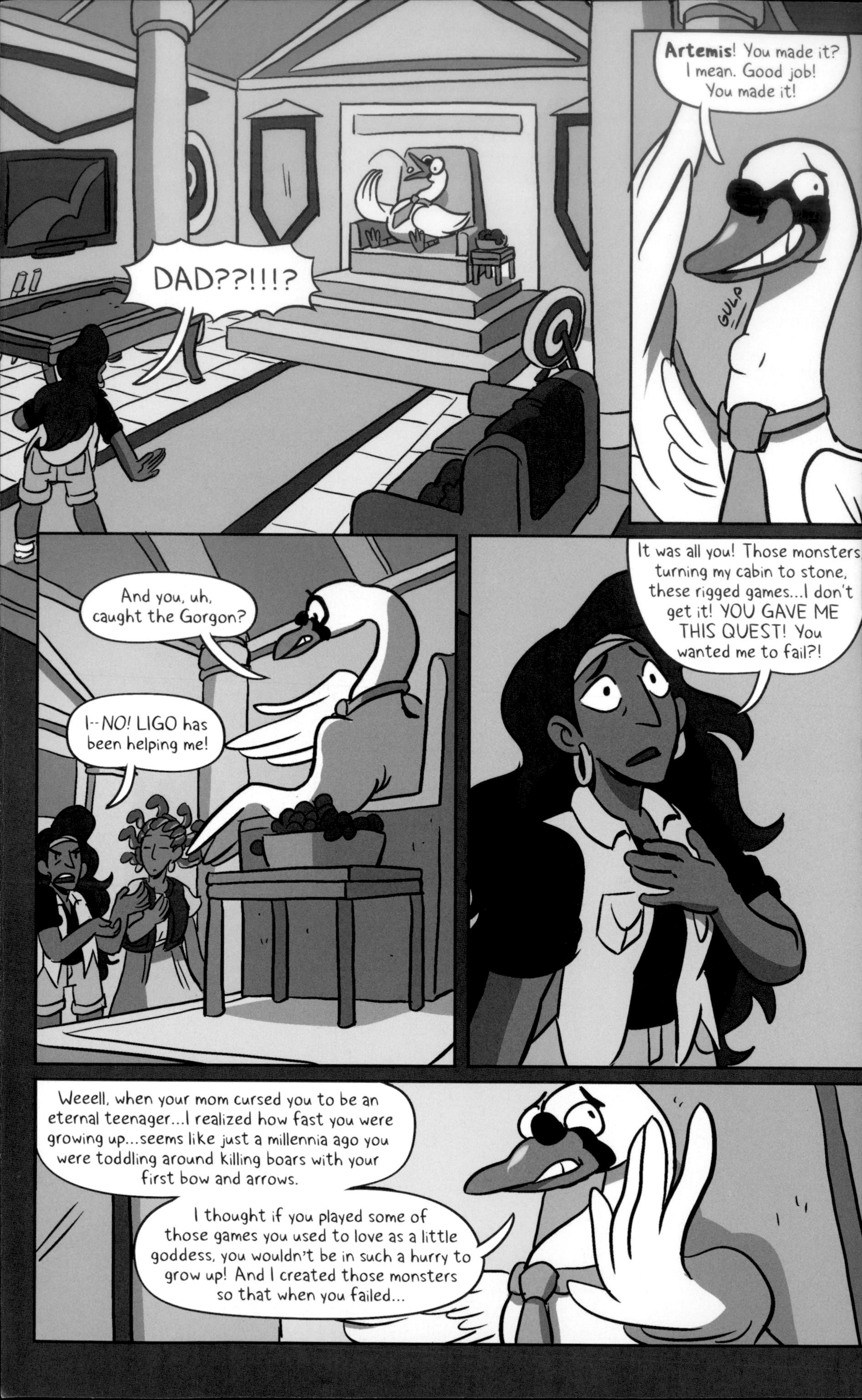
DAD??!!!?
Artemis! You made it? I mean. Good job! You made it!
GULP
And you, uh, caught the Gorgon?
I--NO! LIGO has been helping me!
It was all you! Those monsters turning my cabin to stone, these rigged games...I don't get it! YOU GAVE ME THIS QUEST! You wanted me to fail?!
Weeell, when your mom cursed you to be an eternal teenager...I realized how fast you were growing up...seems like just a millennia ago you were toddling around killing boars with your first bow and arrows.
I thought if you played some of those games you used to love as a little goddess, you wouldn't be in such a hurry to grow up! And I created those monsters so that when you failed...

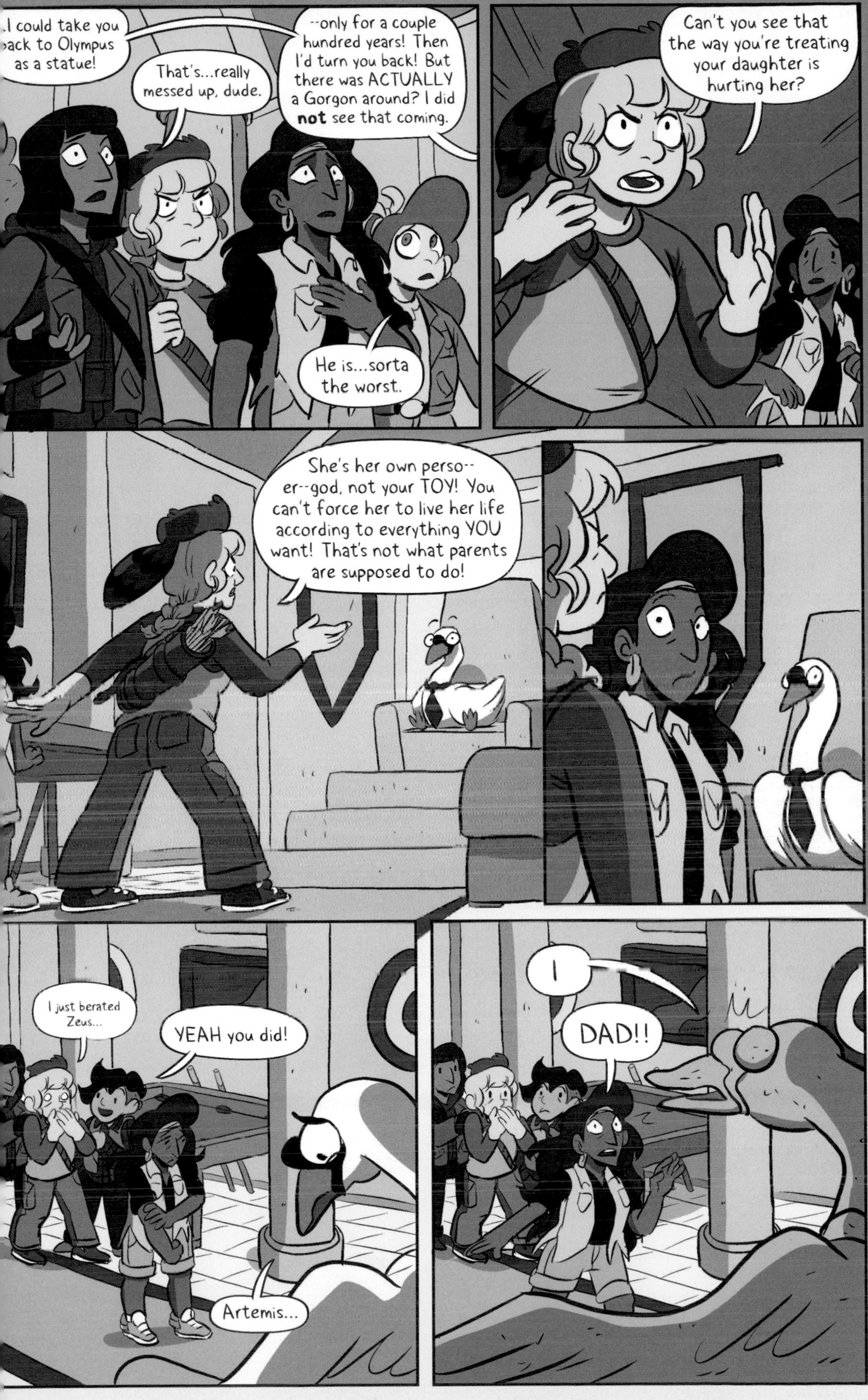
..I could take you back to Olympus as a statue!
That's...really messed up, dude.
--only for a couple hundred years! Then I'd turn you back! But there was ACTUALLY a Gorgon around? I did **not** see that coming.
He is...sorta the worst.
Can't you see that the way you're treating your daughter is hurting her?
She's her own perso-- er--god, not your TOY! You can't force her to live her life according to everything YOU want! That's not what parents are supposed to do!
I just berated Zeus...
YEAH you did!
Artemis...
I
DAD!!

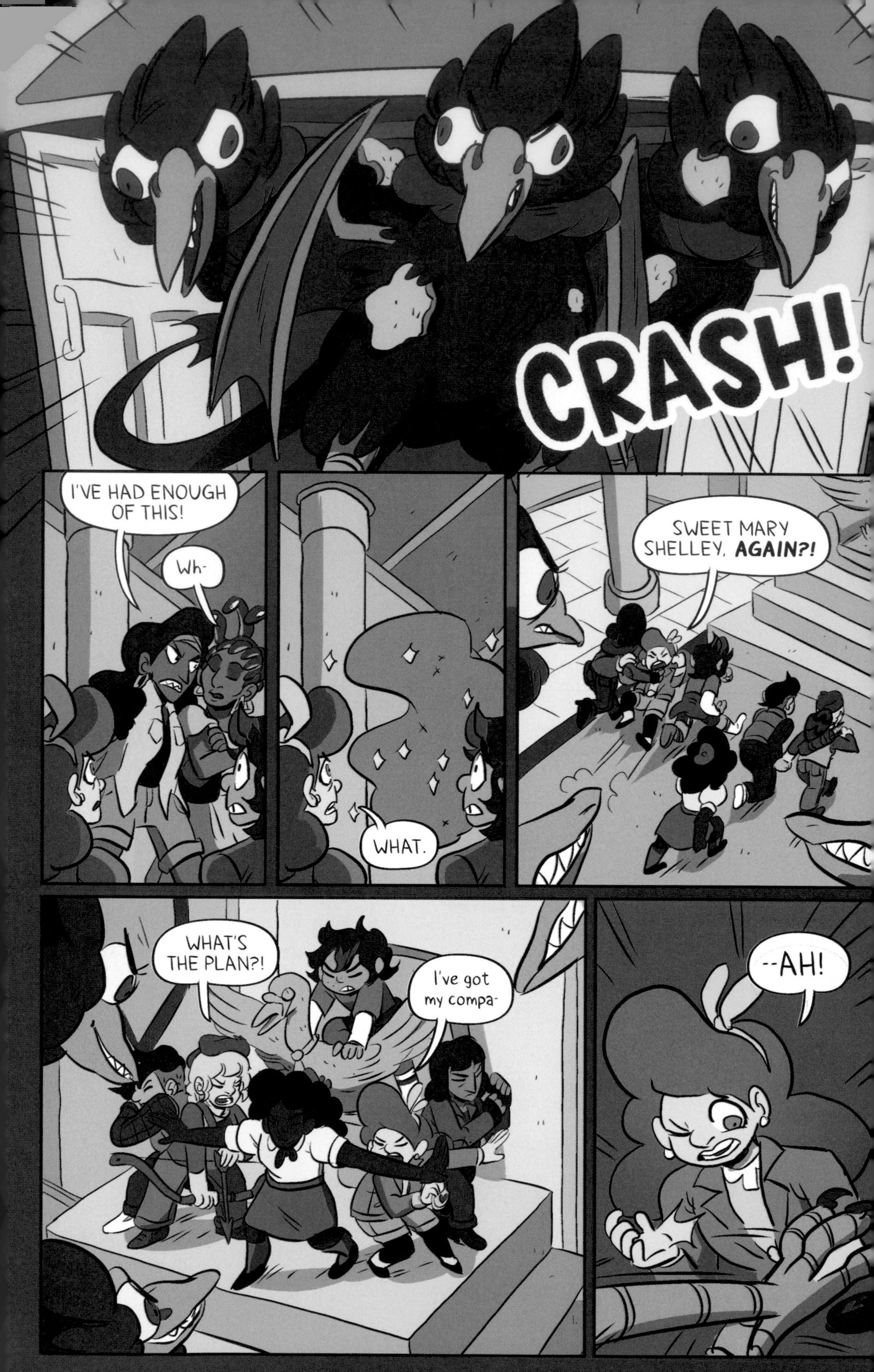
CRASH!
I'VE HAD ENOUGH OF THIS!
Wh-
WHAT.
SWEET MARY SHELLEY, **AGAIN?!**
WHAT'S THE PLAN?!
I've got my compa-
--AH!

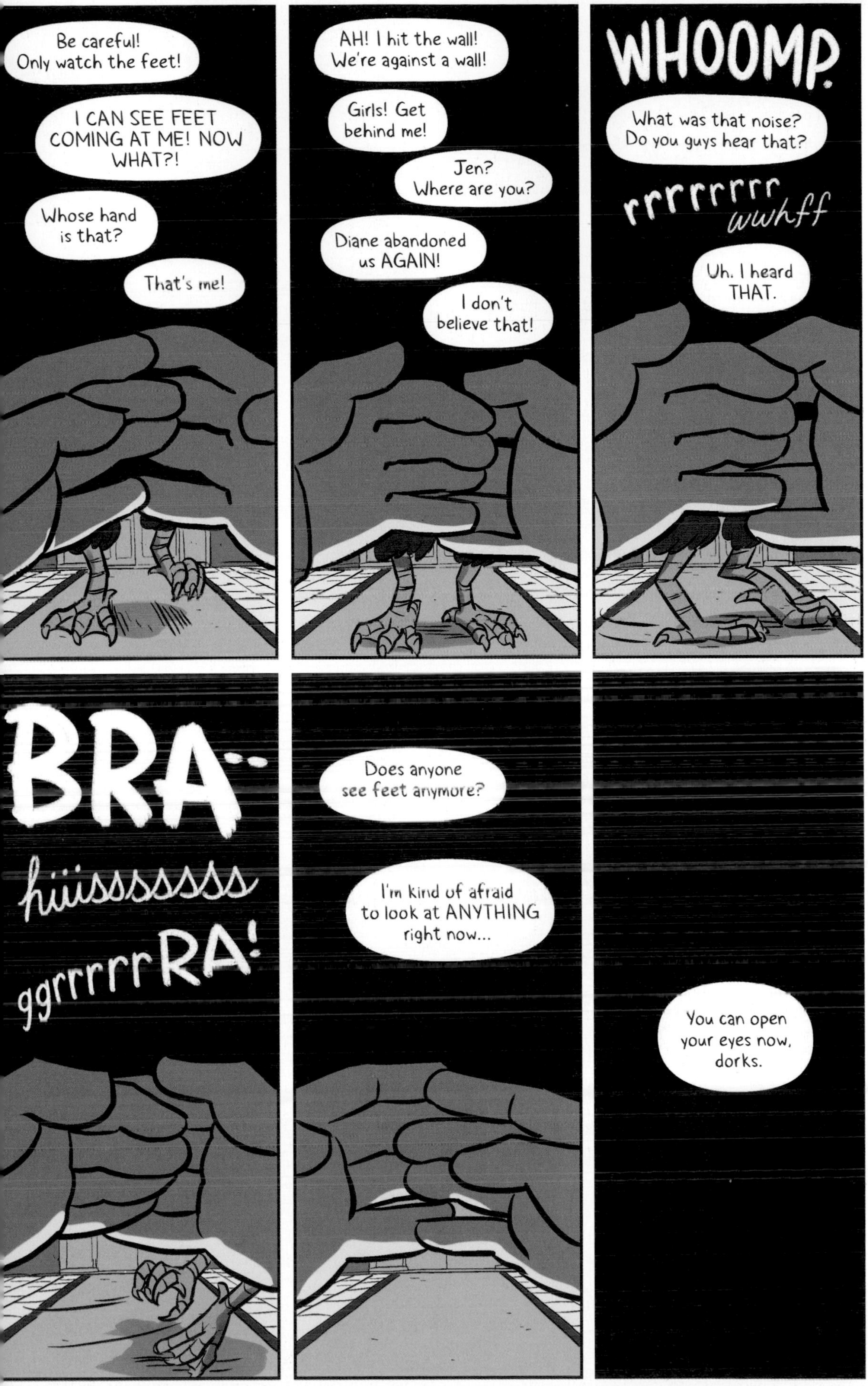
Be careful! Only watch the feet!
I CAN SEE FEET COMING AT ME! NOW WHAT?!
Whose hand is that?
That's me!
AH! I hit the wall! We're against a wall!
Girls! Get behind me!
Jen? Where are you?
Diane abandoned us AGAIN!
I don't believe that!
WHOOMP.
What was that noise? Do you guys hear that?
rrrrrrrr wwhff
Uh. I heard THAT.
BRA..
hiiisssssss
ggrrrrrRA!
Does anyone see feet anymore?
I'm kind of afraid to look at ANYTHING right now...
You can open your eyes now, dorks.

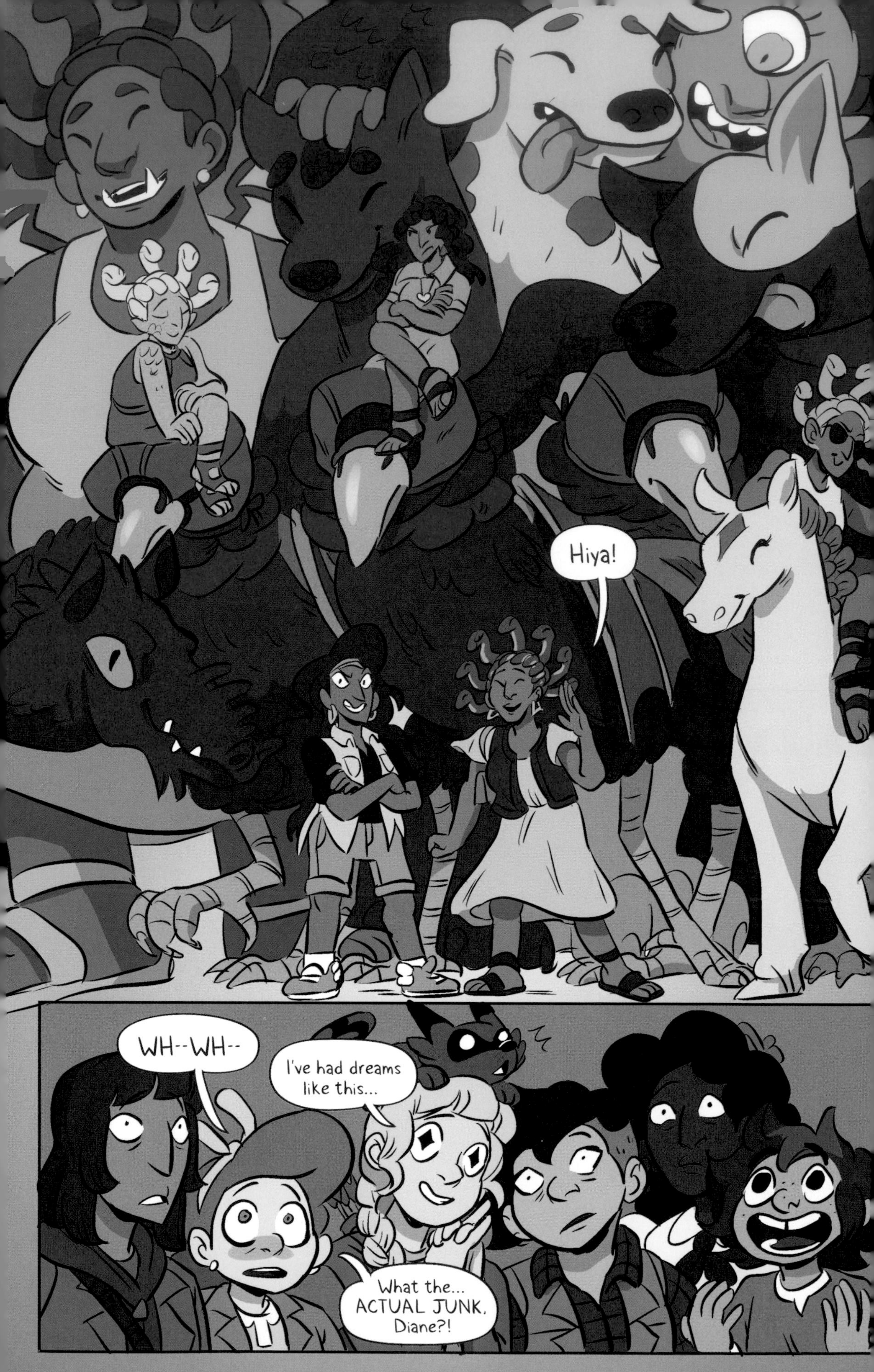
Hiya!
WH--WH--
I've had dreams like this...
What the... ACTUAL JUNK, Diane?!

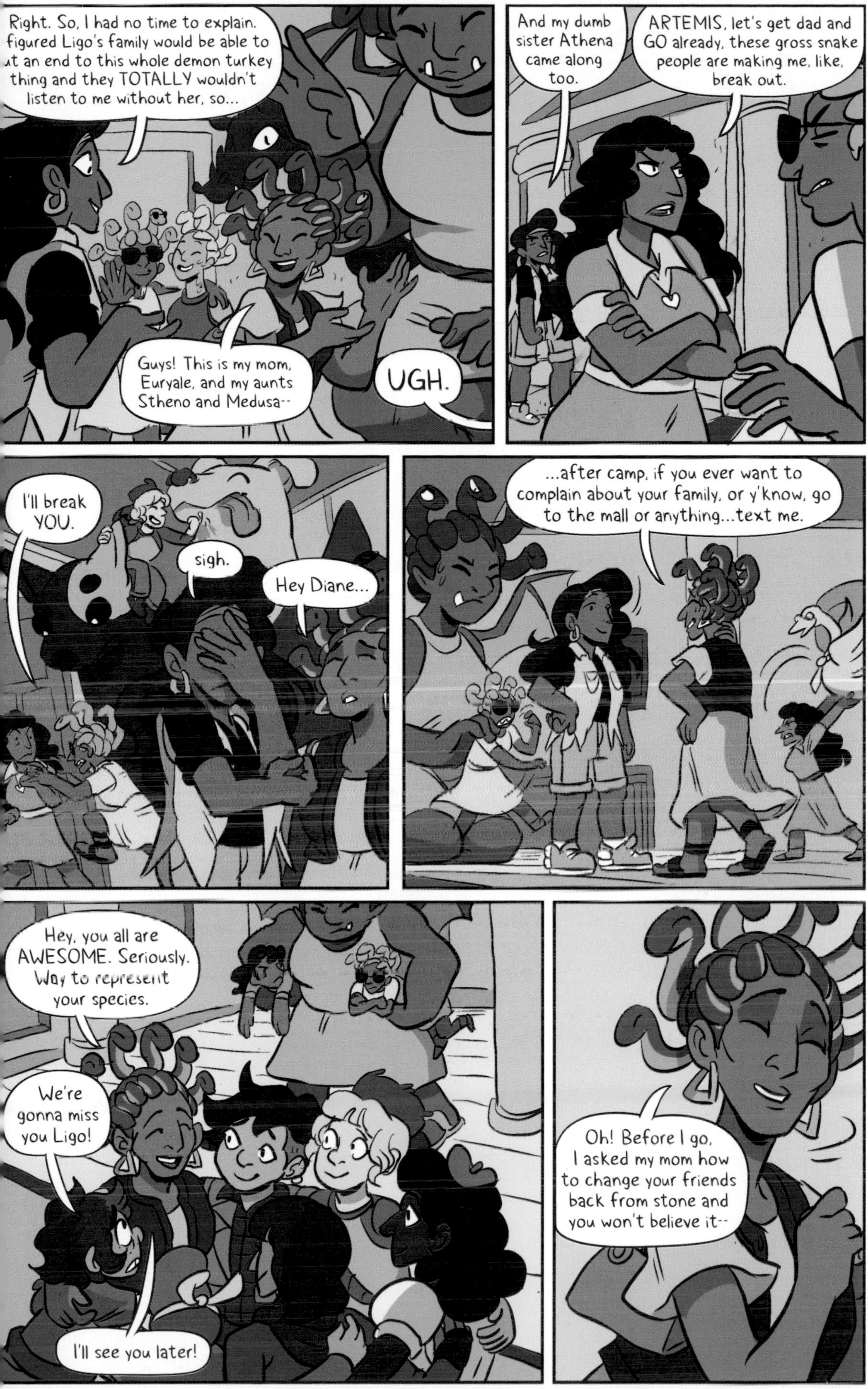

Right. So, I had no time to explain. figured Ligo's family would be able to ut an end to this whole demon turkey thing and they TOTALLY wouldn't listen to me without her, so...
Guys! This is my mom, Euryale, and my aunts Stheno and Medusa--
UGH.
And my dumb sister Athena came along too.
ARTEMIS, let's get dad and GO already, these gross snake people are making me, like, break out.
I'll break YOU.
sigh.
Hey Diane...
...after camp, if you ever want to complain about your family, or y'know, go to the mall or anything...text me.
Hey, you all are AWESOME. Seriously. Way to represent your species.
We're gonna miss you Ligo!
I'll see you later!
Oh! Before I go, I asked my mom how to change your friends back from stone and you won't believe it--

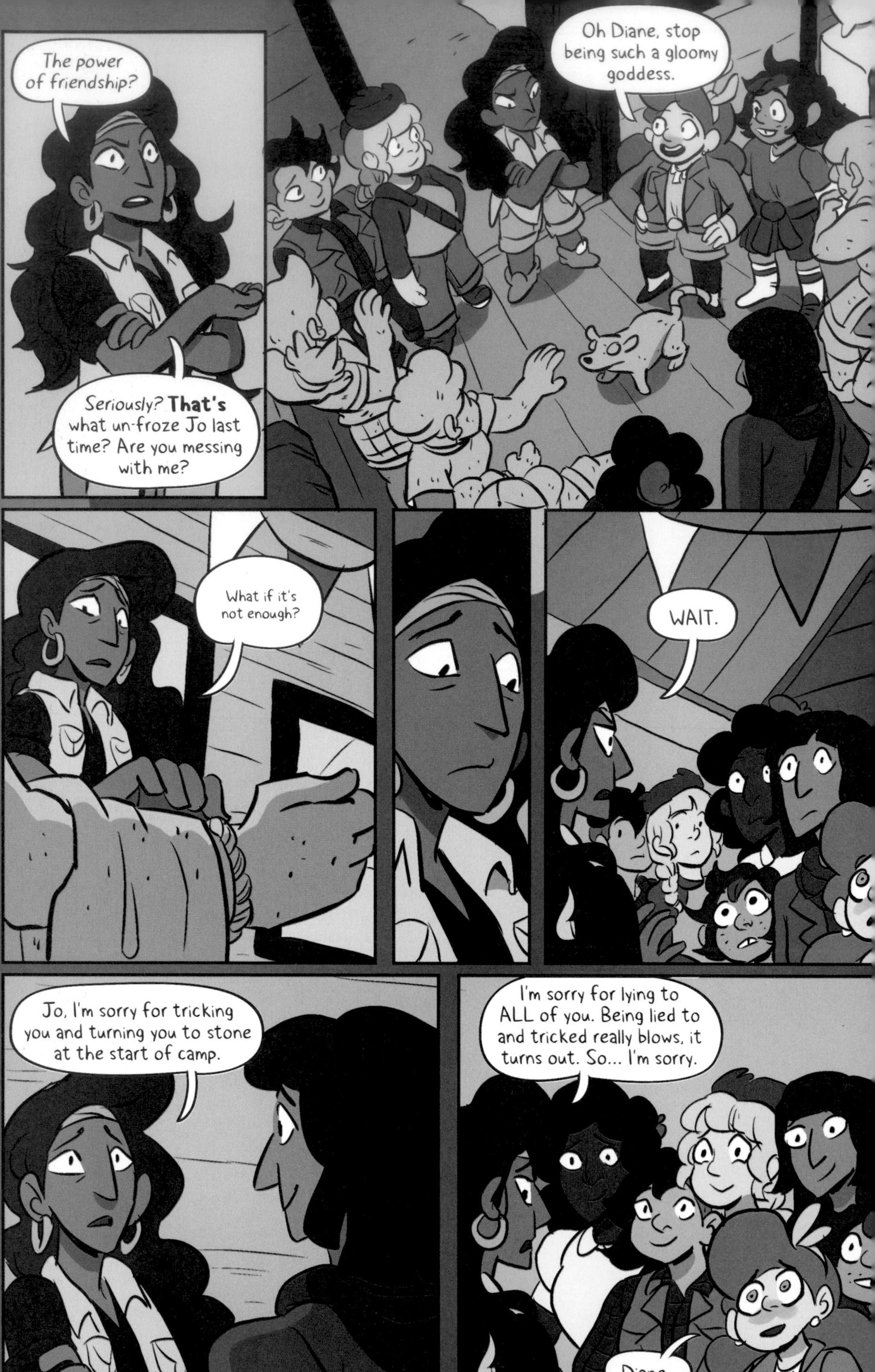
The power of friendship?
Oh Diane, stop being such a gloomy goddess.
Seriously? **That's** what un-froze Jo last time? Are you messing with me?
What if it's not enough?
WAIT.
Jo, I'm sorry for tricking you and turning you to stone at the start of camp.
I'm sorry for lying to ALL of you. Being lied to and tricked really blows, it turns out. So... I'm sorry.
Diane...

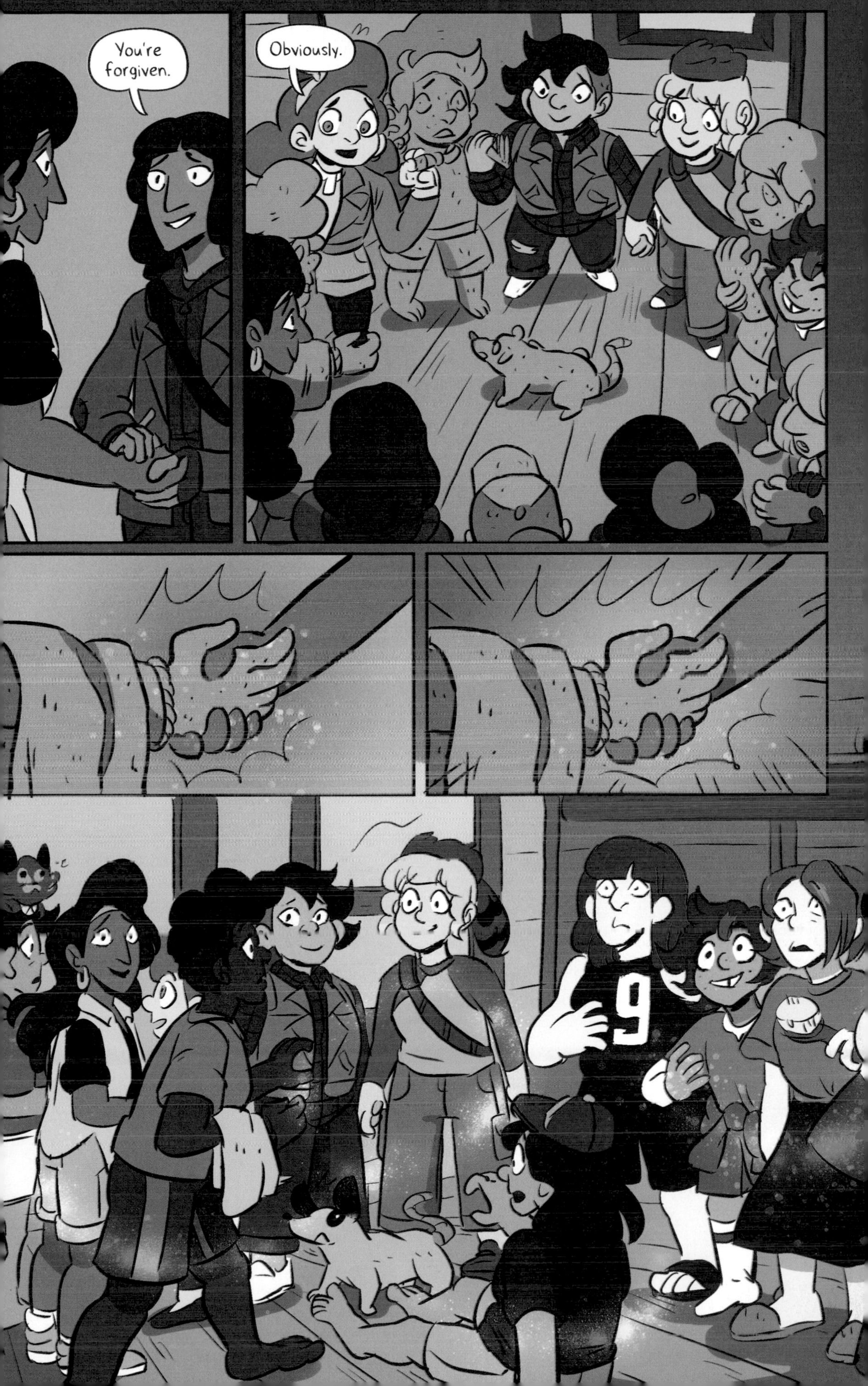
You're forgiven.
Obviously.

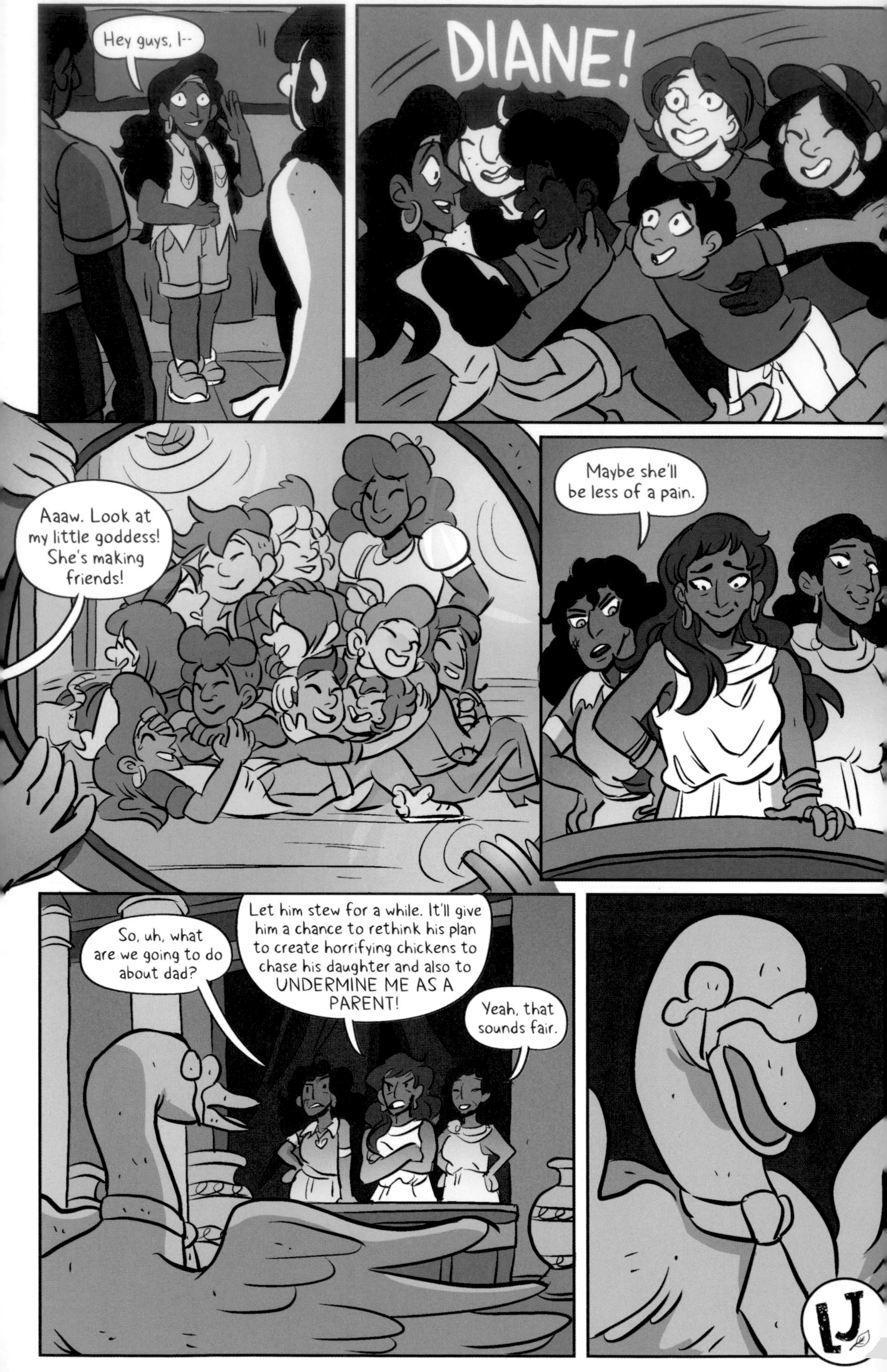
Hey guys, I--
DIANE!
Aaaw. Look at my little goddess! She's making friends!
Maybe she'll be less of a pain.
So, uh, what are we going to do about dad?
Let him stew for a while. It'll give him a chance to rethink his plan to create horrifying chickens to chase his daughter and also to UNDERMINE ME AS A PARENT!
Yeah, that sounds fair.

HIDE AND SEEK

DIANE NO!

DIANE YES!

will co...

The in...
It hel... ...should be worn at camp
appearan... ...events when Lumberjanes
dress fo... ...may also be worn at other
Further... ...ions. It should be worn as a
Lumber... ...the uniform dress with
to have ...rect shoes, and stocking or
part in ...
Thiskv... ...out grows her uniform or
Hardc... ...ng to ...ter Lumberjane.
have ... ...a she has
them ... ...her
...her

THE UNIFORM

The ...
yellow, short sl...
emb...
the w...
choose...
slacks, ...
made o...
out-of-do...
green bere...
the colla...
Shoes ma...
heels, rou...y ...ngs or
socks shou... ...ith the shoes or wi...
the uniform. Ne... ...es, bracelets, or other jewelry do ...
belong with a Lumberjane uniform.

HOW TO WEAR THE UNIFORM

To look well in a uniform demans first of ...
uniform be kept in good condition—clean ...
pressed. See that the skirt is the right length for your own
height and build, that the belt is adjusted to your waist,
that your shoes and stockings are in keeping with the
uniform, that you watch your posture and carry yourself
with dignity and grace. If the beret is removed indoors,
be sure that your hair is neat and kept in place with an
insonspicuous clip or ribbon. When you wear a
Lumberjane uniform you are identified as a member of
this organization and you should be doubly careful to
conduct yourself in a way that will show everyone that
courtesy and thoughtfullness are part of being a
Lumberjane. People are likely to judge a whole nation by
the selfishness of a few individuals, to criticize a whole
family because of the misconduct of one member, and to
feel unkindly toward and organization because of the

The unifor...
helps to cre...
in a group. ...
active life th...
another bond...
future, and pr...
in order to b...
Lumberjane pr...
Penniquiqul Thi... ...ore Lady
Types, but m... ...es will wish to have one. They
can either bu... ...e uniform, or make it themselves from
materials available at the trading post.

COVER GALLERY

Lumberjanes "Heart to Heart" Program Field

CUT LOOSE BADGE

"It's just one of the hair necessities"

The styling and coiffure of one's hair is something that we all must grapple with-- whether with combs and gel, or clips and elastics, or even bodkins and curlers. Whether it's long and strong, or short and pert, your hair can speak volumes about you. Hair can reflect one's culture as well as one's personality, and while you are away at camp, you have the freedom to do with and to your hair as you like.

Perhaps when you were a little child, your parents would insist on helping you with your hair-- teasing out tangles, fixing it up in braids and pigtails for school, telling the stylist what cut they thought would look most becoming on you-- but you are coming into the years of young adulthood now, and your hair will start to become more and more your own responsibility.

While you are here at camp, your hair can truly be yours, maybe for the first time in your young life. When to wash it, how to brush it, even how to cut it… these questions are yours to answer, and yours alone.

While most hair stylists recommend against cutting one's own hair, and while perhaps in your older years you'll look back on these days and shake your more conservatively-styled head at your youthful enthusiasm

and bold choices, we encourage you to use your hair as a tool of reinvention and self-discovery while you are here at camp, as part of earning the Cut Loose Badge. There is no better time or place to try new things.

So, grow your hair as long as you like. Practice three, and five, and seven stranded braids. Cut the back short and keep the front long and flowing, or go in the opposite direction and wear a mullet with pride. Meet a sister you never knew you had and cut your hair to match hers, or shave your head down to only a quarter inch of stubble, and fall asleep each night running your hands over the peach fuzz of your skull.

Encourage your curls to grow outward and upward, and ever more and more beautifully voluminous, or tuck them safely into intricate cornrows. Tie your hair up into a scarf, or wear it long and tumbling and brightly colored, or trim it as short as can be, and never look at a comb again all summer. Here, you have the freedom to do what you will with your hair. After all, it does grow back.

Issue Twenty-Nine
KAT LEYH

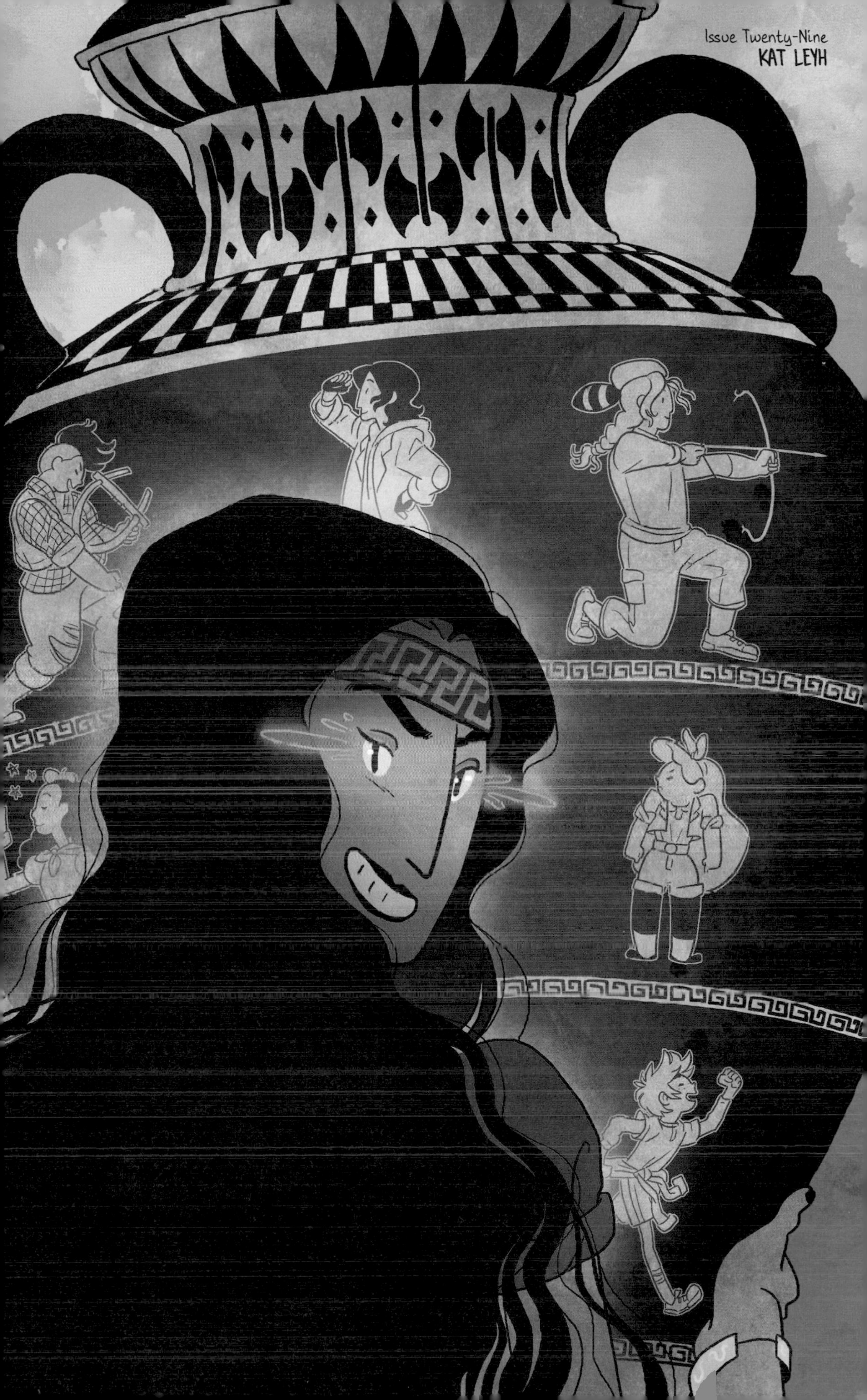

Issue Twenty-Nine Variant
RACHEL SMITH

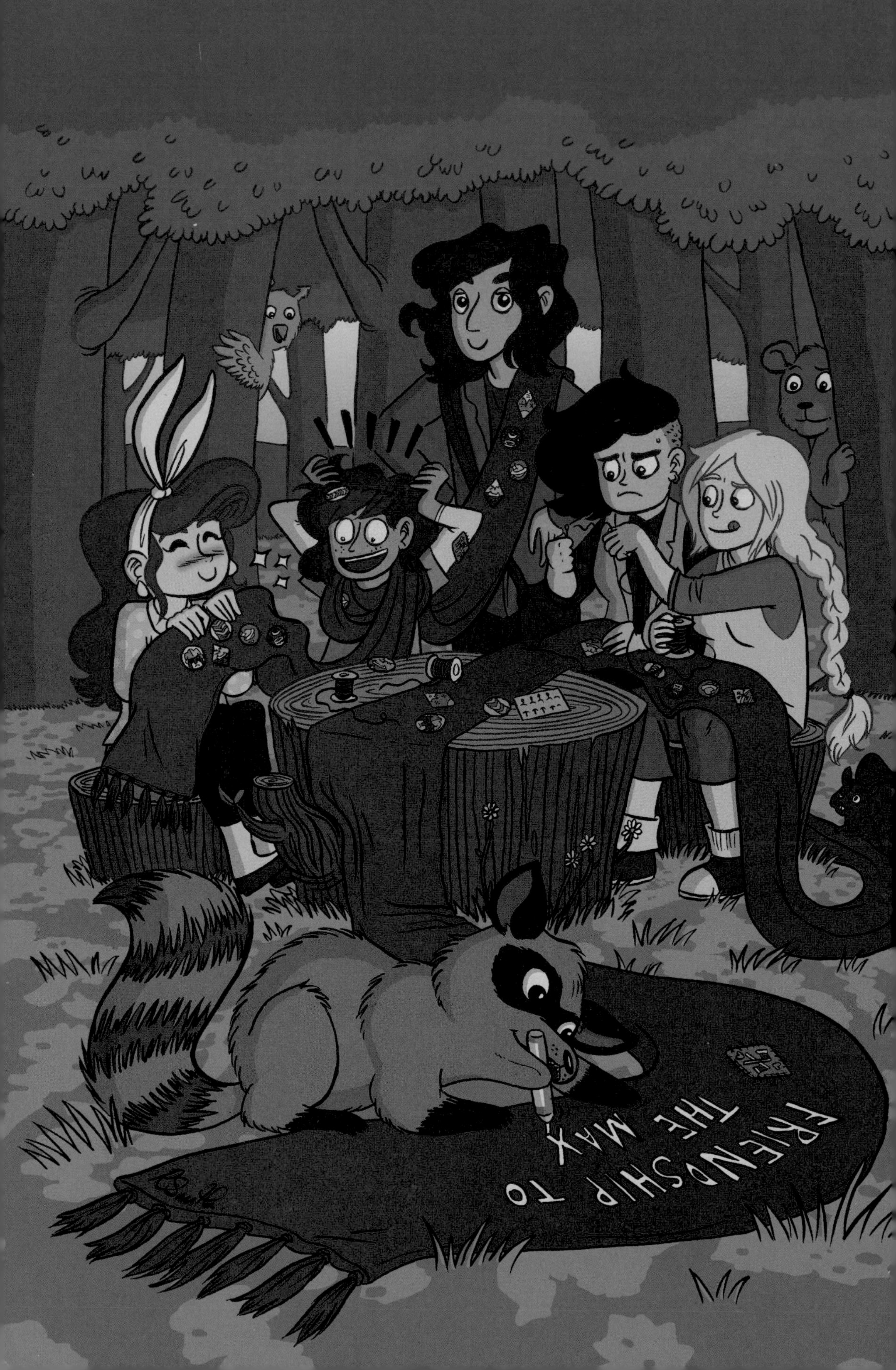
FRIENDSHIP TO
THE MAX

Issue Twenty-Nine
New York Comic Con Exclusive Cover
Natacha Bustos

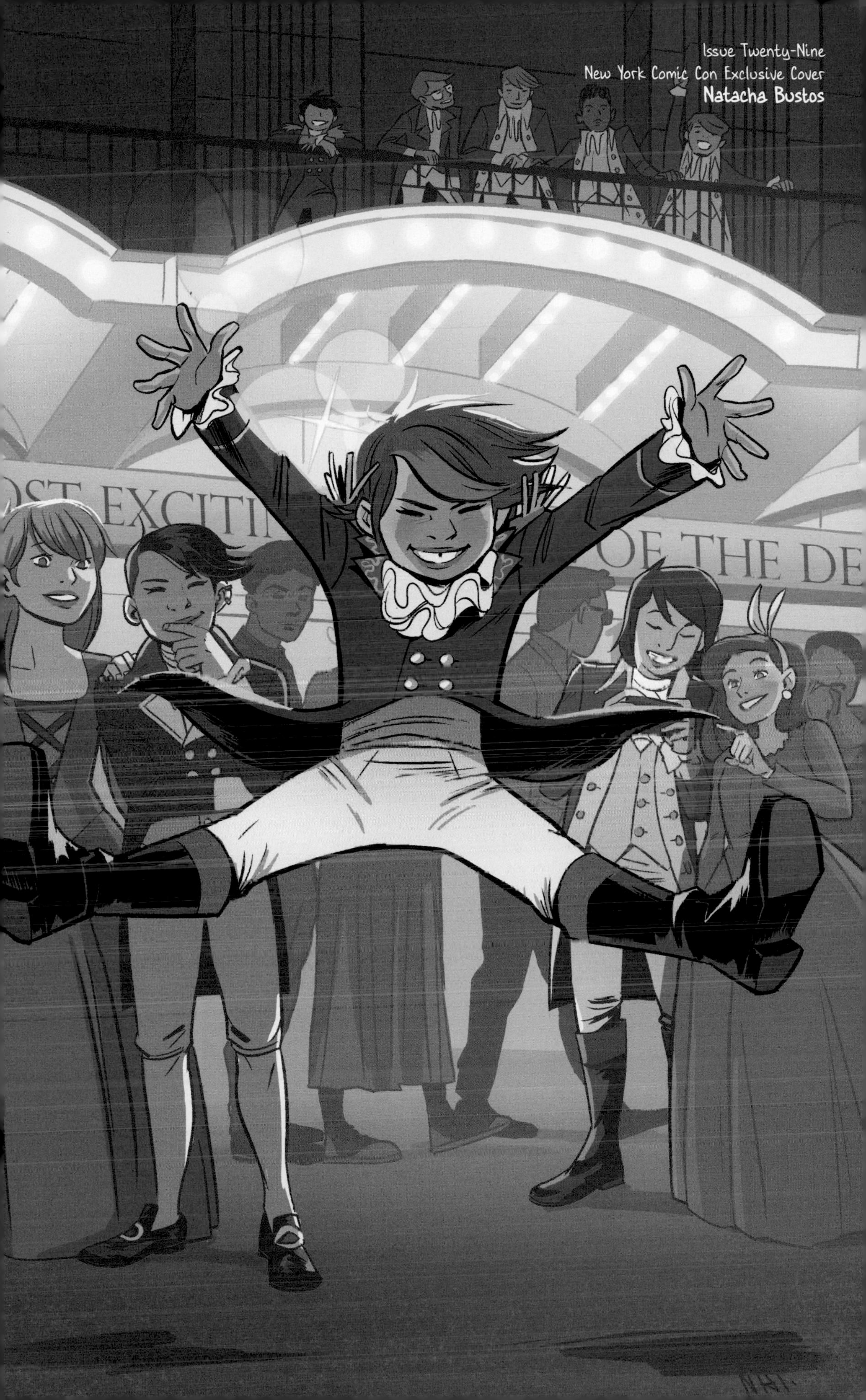
OST EXCITI
OF THE DE

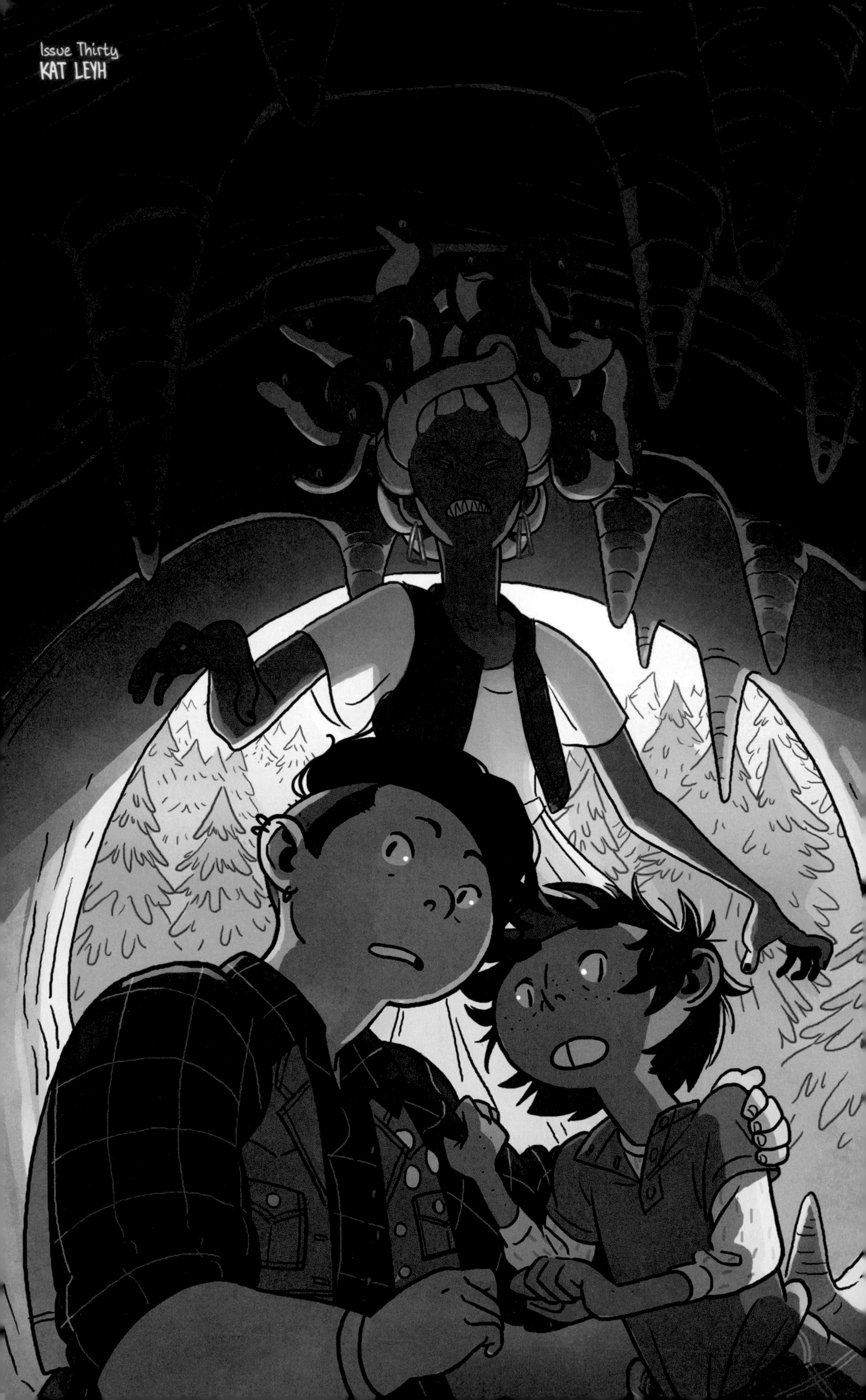
Issue Thirty
KAT LEYH

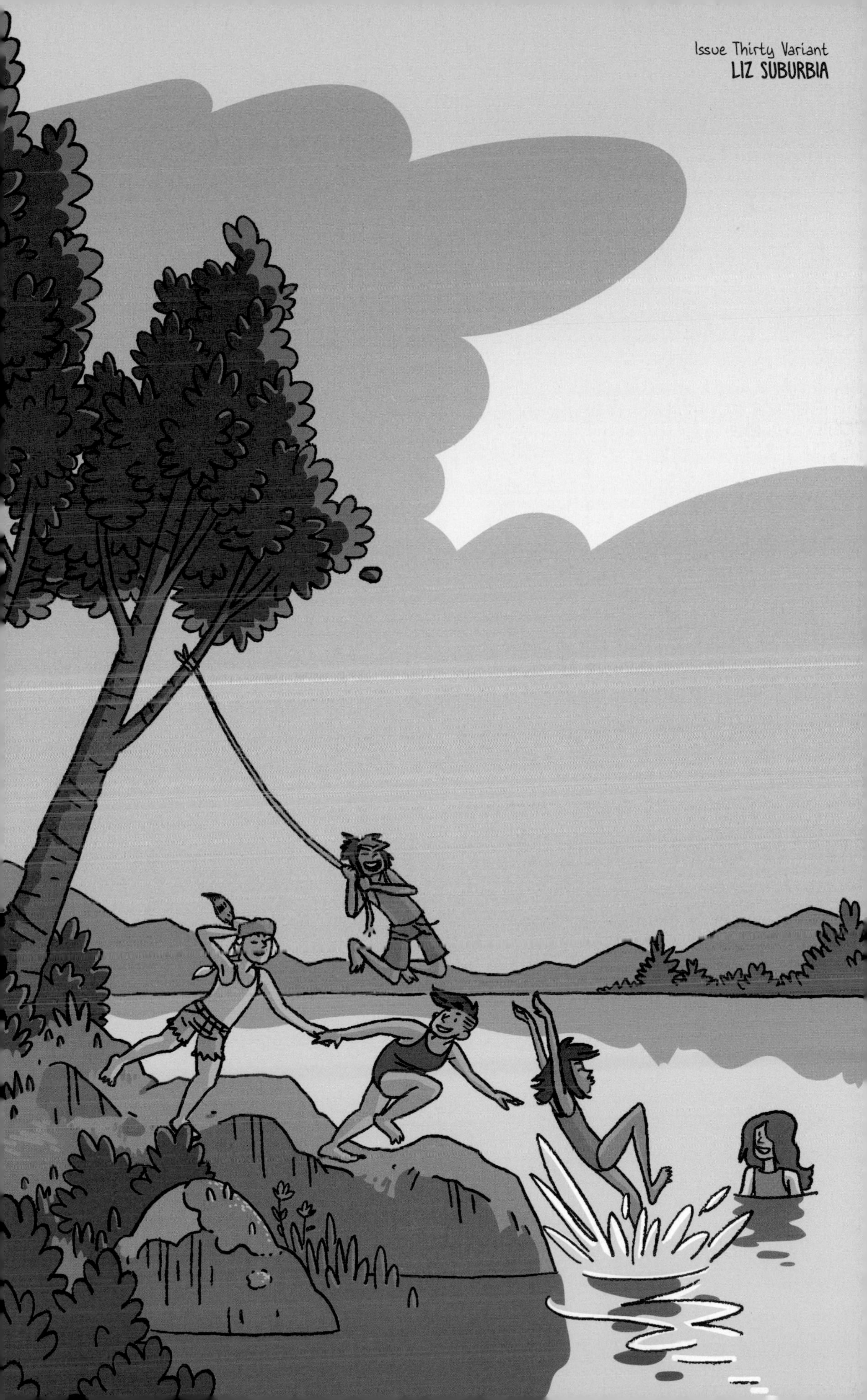

Issue Thirty Variant
LIZ SUBURBIA

Issue Thirty-One
KAT LEYH

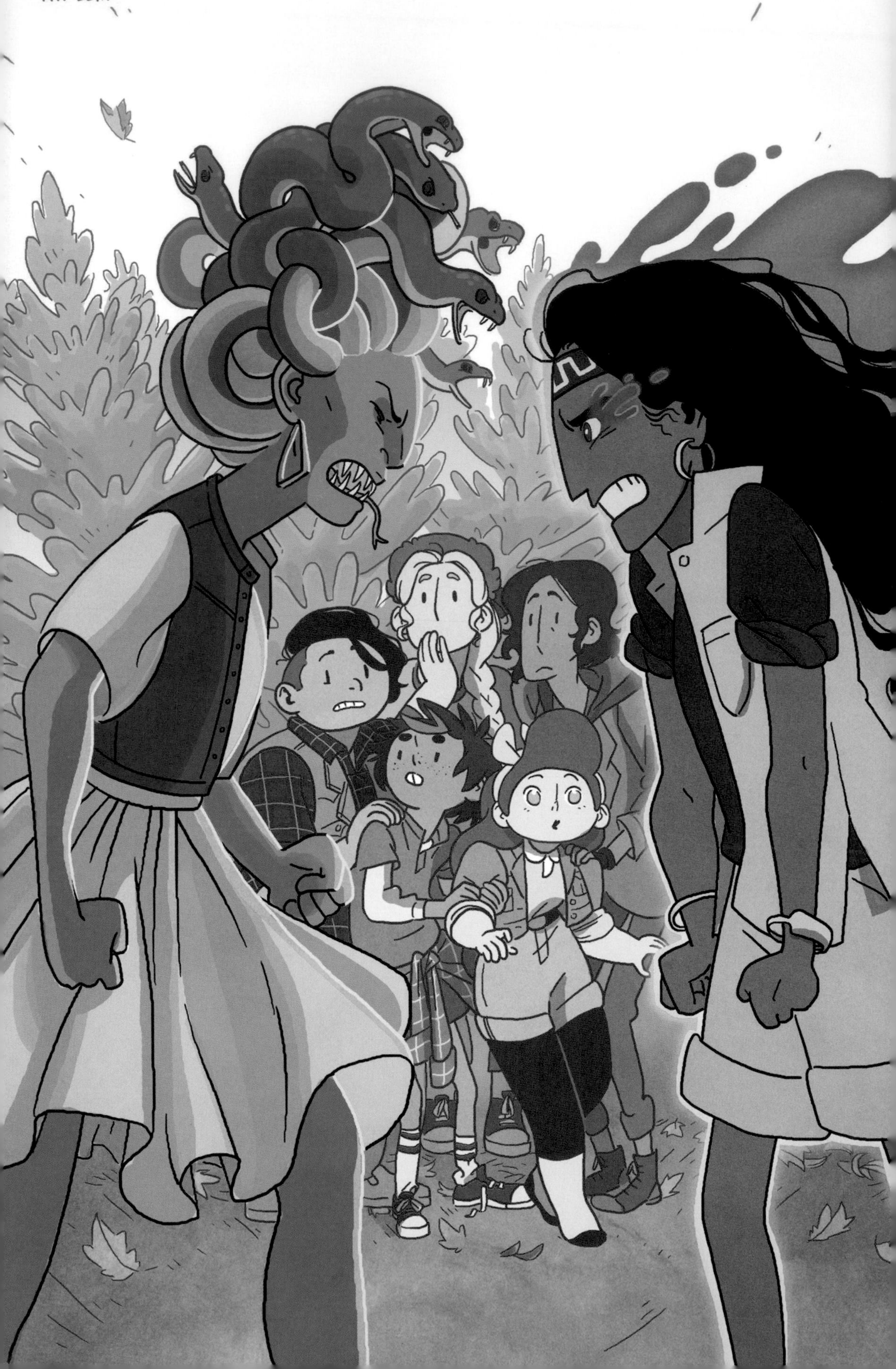

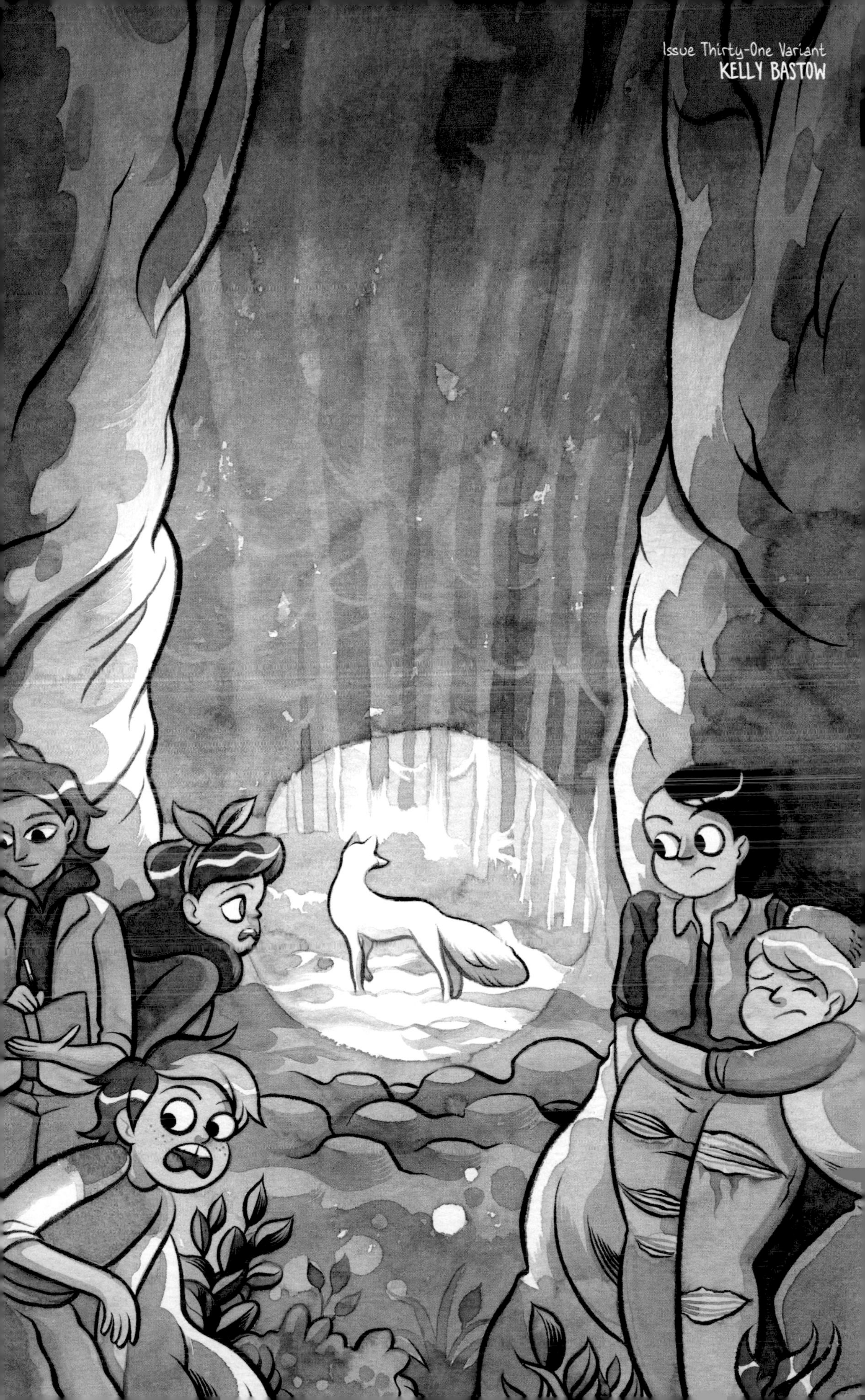

Issue Thirty-One Variant
KELLY BASTOW

Issue Thirty-Two
KAT LEYH

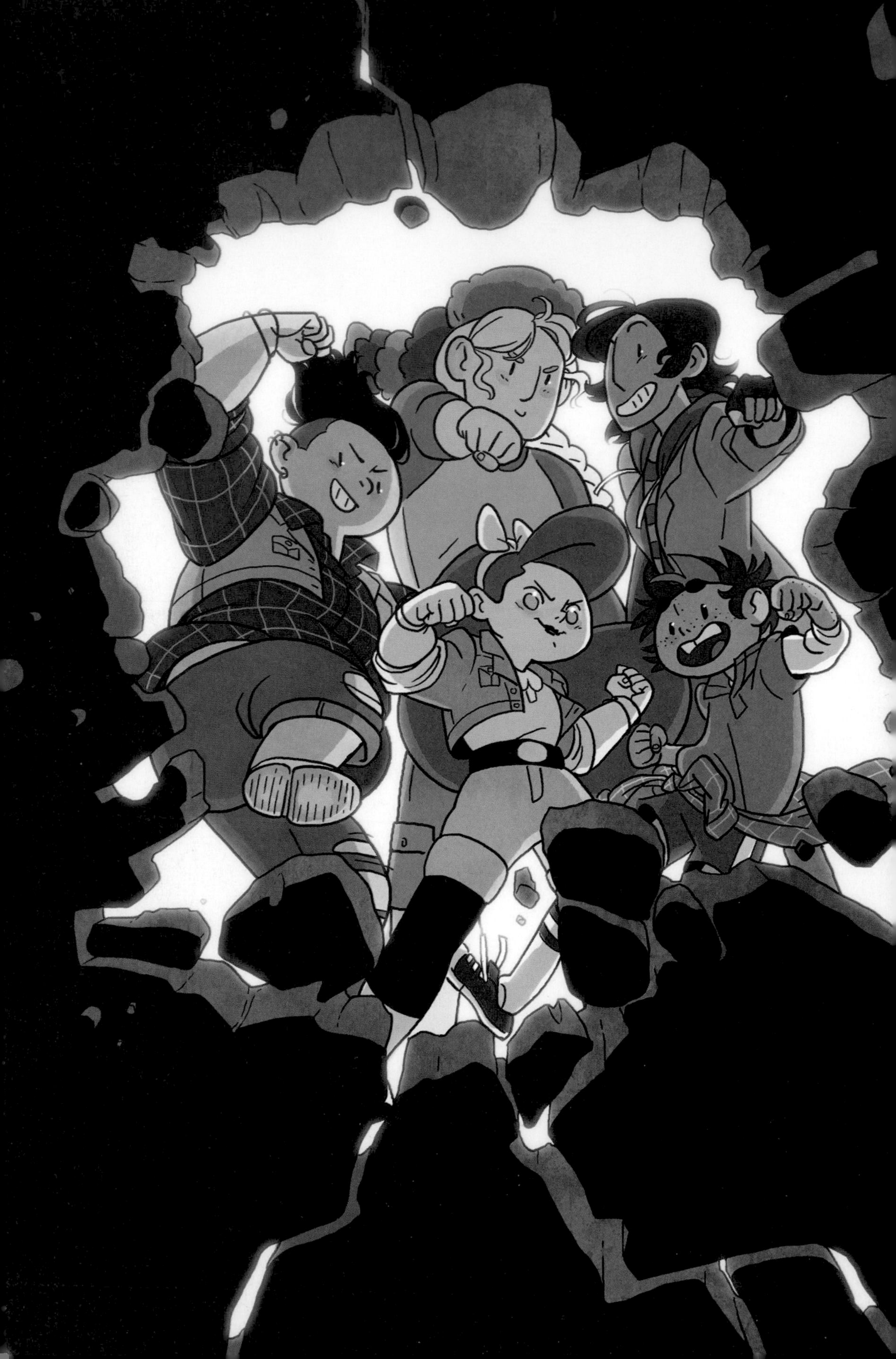

Issue Thirty-Two Variant
FEIFEI RUAN

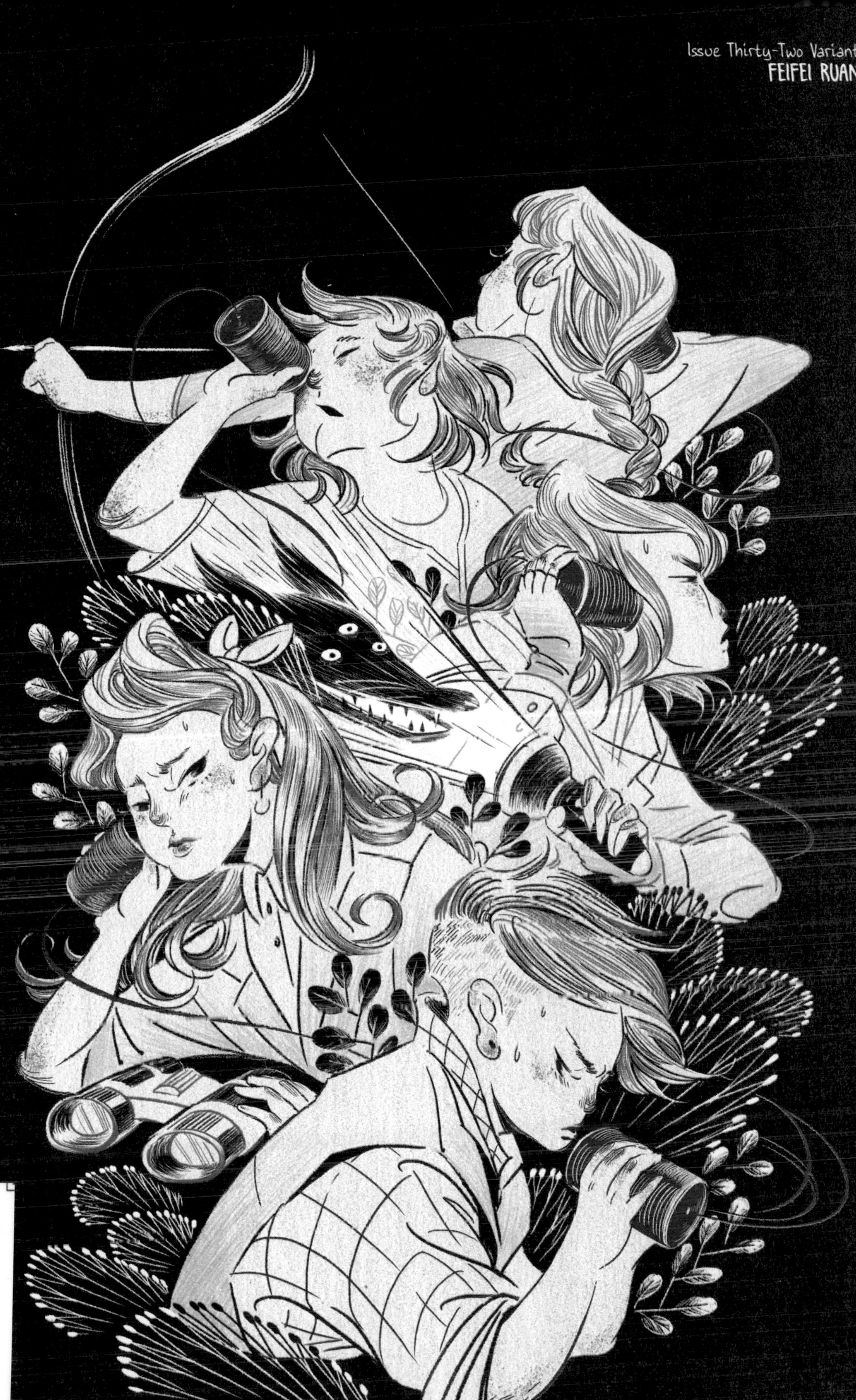

DISCOVER
ALL THE HITS

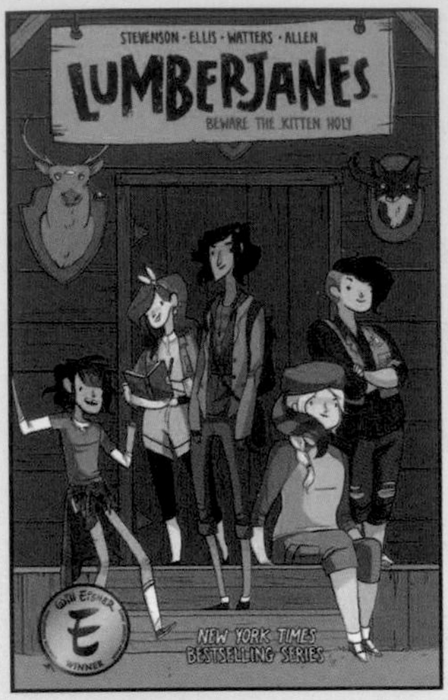
STEVENSON · ELLIS · WATTERS · ALLEN
LUMBERJANES
BEWARE THE KITTEN HOLY
NEW YORK TIMES BESTSELLING SERIES

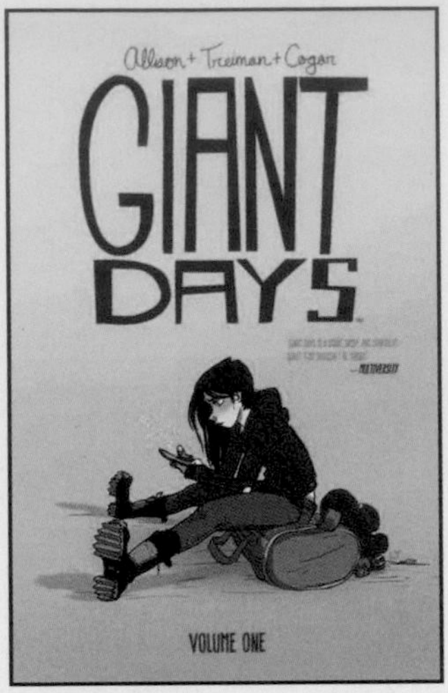
Allison + Treiman + Cogar
GIANT DAYS
VOLUME ONE

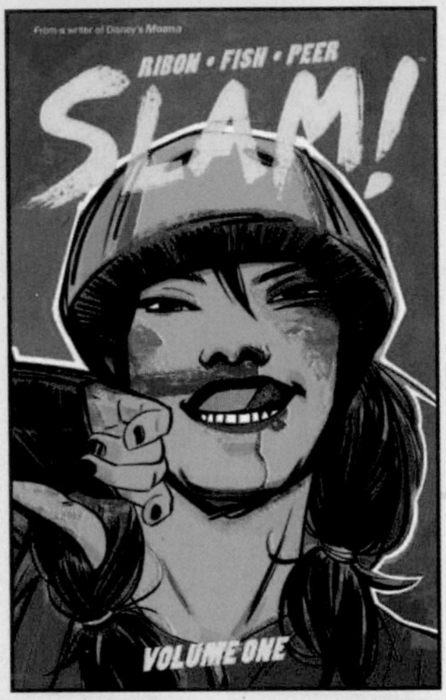
RIBON · FISH · PEER
SLAM!
VOLUME ONE

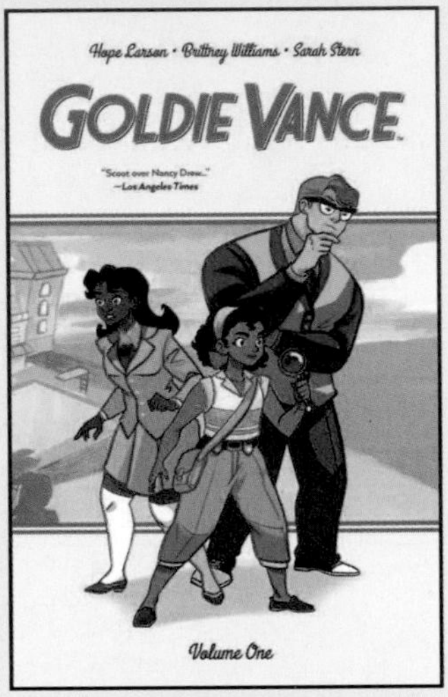
Hope Larson · Brittney Williams · Sarah Stern
GOLDIE VANCE
Volume One

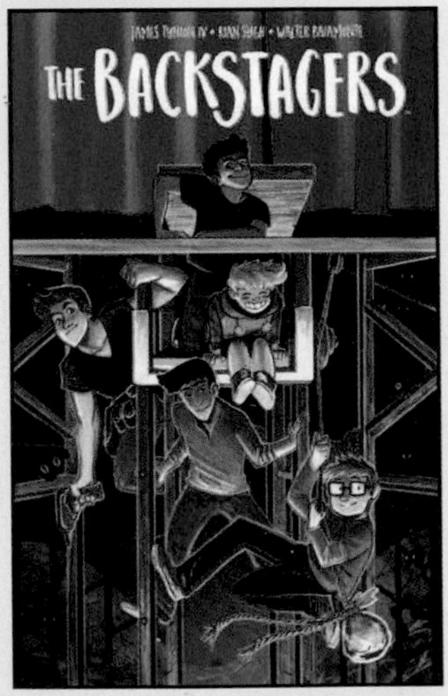
THE BACKSTAGERS

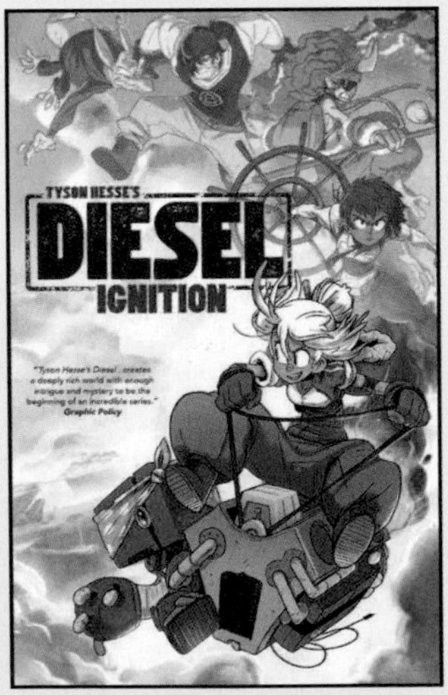
TYSON HESSE'S
DIESEL
IGNITION

Lumberjanes
Noelle Stevenson, Shannon Watters, Grace Ellis, Brooklyn Allen, and Others
Volume 1: Beware the Kitten Holy
ISBN: 978-1-60886-687-8 | $14.99 US
Volume 2: Friendship to the Max
ISBN: 978-1-60886-737-0 | $14.99 US
Volume 3: A Terrible Plan
ISBN: 978-1-60886-803-2 | $14.99 US
Volume 4: Out of Time
ISBN: 978-1-60886-860-5 | $14.99 US
Volume 5: Band Together
ISBN: 978-1-60886-919-0 | $14.99 US

Giant Days
John Allison, Lissa Treiman, Max Sarin
Volume 1
ISBN: 978-1-60886-789-9 | $9.99 US
Volume 2
ISBN: 978-1-60886-804-9 | $14.99 US
Volume 3
ISBN: 978-1-60886-851-3 | $14.99 US

Jonesy
Sam Humphries, Caitlin Rose Boyle
Volume 1
ISBN: 978-1-60886-883-4 | $9.99 US
Volume 2
ISBN: 978-1-60886-999-2 | $14.99 US

Slam!
Pamela Ribon, Veronica Fish, Brittany Peer
Volume 1
ISBN: 978-1-68415-004-5 | $14.99 US

Goldie Vance
Hope Larson, Brittney Williams
Volume 1
ISBN: 978-1-60886-898-8 | $9.99 US
Volume 2
ISBN: 978-1-60886-974-9 | $14.99 US

The Backstagers
James Tynion IV, Rian Sygh
Volume 1
ISBN: 978-1-60886-993-0 | $14.99 US

Tyson Hesse's Diesel: Ignition
Tyson Hesse
ISBN: 978-1-60886-907-7 | $14.99 US

Coady & The Creepies
Liz Prince, Amanda Kirk, Hannah Fisher
ISBN: 978-1-68415-029-8 | $14.99 US

BOOM! BOX™

AVAILABLE AT YOUR LOCAL COMICS SHOP AND BOOKSTORE
To find a comics shop in your area, call 1-888-266-4226
WWW.**BOOM-STUDIOS**.COM